The i-Spy Murders

A Sanford 3rd Age Club Mystery (#2)

David W Robinson

www.darkstroke.com

Discover us online:
www.darkstroke.com

Find us on instagram:
www.instagram.com/darkstrokebooks

Include **#darkstroke** in a photo of yourself
holding his book on Instagram and
something nice will happen.

About the Author

David Robinson is a Yorkshireman now living in Manchester. Driven by a huge, cynical sense of humour, he's been a writer for over thirty years having begun with magazine articles before moving on to novels and TV scripts.

He has little to do with his life other than write, as a consequence of which his output is prodigious. Thankfully most of it is never seen by the great reading public of the world.

He has worked closely with Crooked Cat Books since 2012, when The Filey Connection, the very first Sanford 3rd Age Club Mystery, was published.

Describing himself as the Doyen of Domestic Disasters he can be found blogging at **www.dwrob.com** and he appears frequently on video (written, produced and starring himself) dispensing his mocking humour at **www.youtube.com/user/Dwrob96/videos**

The STAC Mystery series:

The I-Spy Murders

A Sanford 3rd Age Club Mystery (#2)

Prologue

The younger woman opened her mouth to scream.

"Shut up," hissed the other. "Just shut it."

The youngster put a fist to her open mouth in an effort to suppress her cries.

Her elder chewed an anxious lip and pressed a hand to his neck again.

"Definitely dead."

The young girl burst into tears once more. The woman grabbed her by shoulder and shook her. "Listen, you silly little tart, this is no time to lose it."

"What… what are we gonna do? Call the cops?"

"If we do, we can both kiss goodbye to whatever careers we may have." The woman's mind ran into overdrive again, mapping out possible scenarios. "Come on. Give me a hand to dress him." She reached for the dead man's clothes.

Horror struck across the younger woman's delicate face. "I… I can't touch him."

"You didn't have a problem a few minutes ago, did you?" the elder said, dragging his shorts on over his ankles. "Now stop being childish and help me."

"What are we going to do?"

"I'll call Wellesley. He'll advise us."

***

Gasping with exertion, they dragged his body a final few yards and released him. The elder woman looked back towards her car. It was almost invisible from this point, only the faint glow of its rear lights showing through the forest.

The girl turned away, unable to look upon his dormant,

3

staring eyes. With an annoyed tut, the woman reached down and rolled him over so that his face lay buried in the mossy carpet of the forest floor.

"We're just going to leave him like that?" The youngster was still too shocked and horror-struck to allow the full implications of the night's events to sink in.

"There's not much danger of him being found at this time of year," the elder said. "The summer months, yes, but October or November? Not very likely. All the same we'd better cover him up." Shining her light around, she made for a mass of fallen twigs and branches. "Come on. We'll use these to cover him." She strode boldly across the small clearing and grabbed a branch. "Ouch! Bloody hell!"

The youngster picked her way through the darkness. "What's wrong?"

The other pointed to her right leg, where blood poured from a long cut just below the knee. "I've sticking plaster in the car," she said. "Let's deal with him first."

They spent the next twenty minutes dragging twigs and scooping up leaves to cover him.

When they were finished, the elder led the way back to the car. "Fifteen miles, now, and we're home free," she said.

Her younger companion sulked. "It's awful what we're doing. He deserves a decent burial."

"He was a pervert. He deserves what he got." Climbing into the car, the woman checked her injured leg. "Stopped bleeding," she said, examining the long, livid scar. "I'll get to A & E tomorrow and get a tetanus jab." She turned severe eyes on her companion. "Do you want to spend the rest of your life catering to pervies like him?"

A long silence followed. Eventually, the youngster shook her head.

The other started the car. "In that case, stop worrying about it. We've done the right thing. Now don't ever mention it again."

4

Chapter One

With the whine of a drill setting his teeth on edge, Joe Murray frowned and barked, "Say again. I didn't hear you for that noisy sod."

The driver stood before him, one of the Sanford Brewery dray men, grinned and raised his voice. "I said I'll have a full English, two rounds of toast and a tea."

Joe scribbled the order out and passed the note through the wall hatch to the kitchen.

While pouring the tea, Joe glanced sourly at a pair of workmen who were standing on table 13, to the right of the Lazy Luncheonette's dining area. One had a large hammer drill pressed to the wall, the other stood by with angle-iron brackets and wall bolts. The trigger pressed, the workman leaned on his drill and the high-speed bit whined once more, reaming its way into the solid brick behind the plaster and pine finish, showering dust out into the air.

"Can't you drill a bit quieter?" Joe shouted.

"What do you want me to do?" the workman called back. "Cover the bit with woolly earmuffs?"

"I need the earmuffs," Joe retorted. "And that bloody thing needs a silencer." He lowered his gaze to their heavy boots standing on newspaper which had been spread over the laminate top of table 13. "And you should have taken those pit boots off," he complained.

"You just get on with your job, Joe, and leave us to ours," said the senior man as he leaned on his drill again.

The dray man still waiting for service laughed. "What's it all in aid of, Joe?"

Pouring the tea, Joe clucked. "Brenda. She's on this I-Spy programme next week, isn't she? I offered to put a portable

5

on the wall but she and Sheila and Lee persuaded me to pay for one of those large TV screens instead." He waved at a large, cardboard box containing the set, currently resting against the seat back between tables 13 and 14. "We're gonna tune it to the I-Spy channel so you lot can eat your breakfast and gawp at Brenda making a fool of herself."

"I might come back a TV star," Brenda Jump shouted from the kitchen as the drill dug into the wall again.

"You might come back with your reputation in tatters, Brenda," called the dray man handing over a ten pound note in payment for his breakfast.

"Her reputation can't sink much lower," Joe commented, ringing up the sale and clawing change from the cash register.

"I heard that," Brenda shouted.

Sheila Riley hurried from the kitchen carrying orders. "She heard that. And have you arranged cover for next week? I'm not carrying the can for the delays if you haven't."

"It's done, it's done," Joe told her. He handed change to the drayman. "See. I own the bloody place and I'm just here to do as I'm told."

The driver wandered off to join his mates on the left hand side of the café, away from the drill, and Joe concentrated on his next customer.

Eight o'clock Friday morning and the Lazy Luncheonette was at its busiest. Outside, the hot summer continued, with no sign of an end to the heat wave which had engulfed the country for the past eight weeks. With the last of the brewery drivers queuing up for breakfast, and the factories across the road ready to start work, the combination of heat and never-ending queues caused Joe and his staff enough stress without the added irritation of two men hanging a TV on the wall, but the installers had insisted it had to be done now or not until Monday.

"Monday's no use," Joe had protested. "The programme starts running on Saturday and I need it working by then. Can't you do it at five in the afternoon, when the café's shut?"

They stuck to their guns and for once, Joe was beaten into submission.

"I just hope you're right about the extra custom it will bring in," he had said to Sheila and Brenda as the men arrived to begin work at seven in the morning.

Situated in the middle of Britannia Parade, a line of shops set slightly back from the busy dual carriageway of Doncaster Road, the Lazy Luncheonette had never suffered from a lack of trade. The industrial estate was directly opposite with all its factories and offices, Sanford Retail Park stood at the rear, and the café enjoyed the overspill from there. Sanford Brewery was less than a mile from the place, and its delivery drivers were regular callers, and since Doncaster Road was one of the busiest motorway feeders in the town, the café drew in a lot of passing traffic; everyone from truck drivers to company reps, council employees to white van man.

But the place did have those times when it was slack: the post-rush hour period, for example, the eye of the storm, as Joe described it, when the factories and truckers got on with their work, and the shoppers had not yet reached burnout in the retail mall.

Advertising Brenda as one of the I-Spy contestants would, the two women assured him, pull in more custom. Putting it on TV in the café would encourage those not in a hurry to stay longer and spend more money.

"I-Spy is big news, Joe," Brenda had told him. "Everyone will be watching."

"Wrong," he retorted. "I won't be watching for one. They did it before, didn't they? On the main channels. Not satellite. Cameras watching people twenty-four hours day and night. I tuned in once during the early hours of the morning and what did I get? Pictures of people sleeping? Sleeping!" his eyebrows had shot up. "It wasn't the most riveting TV I've ever watched."

"It was very popular, though," Sheila informed him. "I-Spy is slightly different. It only runs for one week every three months, and there are no evictions. It's hit top viewing figures every time it's run, and with Brenda in it, the viewing figures will go ballistic. You watch."

"Since you're making me put a telly in the café, I'll have no option but to watch, will I?"

The Lazy Luncheonette had stood in the centre of the parade since the end of World War Two. It had survived economic booms and busts of varying degrees. Through countless strikes, the demise of the pit and the foundry, and the rise of the service industries, the café had kept going, regularly re-inventing itself, changing first from Alf's Café to Joe's Joint, then Joe's Café, and finally the Lazy Luncheonette. And Joe knew it was due to his willingness to change with the times. Not him personally. No matter what changes the place underwent, he remained the same liverish grouch he had always been, but his business acumen was sufficient to carry this workman's diner through the best and worst of times, and when the idea was put to him, he saw the potential right away.

"There'll be a knock-on effect, too," he had said to the women, coincidentally, his two best friends as well as employees. "I can see the sign in the window for months, after. 'Brenda Jump, former I-Spy housemate, employee of the Lazy Luncheonette'."

Sheila tutted. "Brenda is a Housey not a housemate."

"A what?" Joe frowned. "A Housey? As in housey-housey? I haven't heard bingo called housey-housey since I was a kid."

"We're talking I-Spy, not bingo, Joe," Brenda clucked. "You know that roommates are called roomies, well the housemates on I-Spy are called Housies."

Having partly lost track of the conversation, Joe dragged it back to its start point. "It'll have a knock on effect, no matter what you're called. We could milk this for months."

"I'll be on for a pay rise, then, Joe," Brenda suggested.

"Let's not get carried away."

Before he could see any increase in profit, he had to pay out a large sum of money, and now he had to put up with the drilling.

To his relief, however, the whine of the drill bit suddenly ceased, and the workmen dismantled the equipment. Joe's joy was short lived. A minute or two later, they were back on table 13, working with large hammers, setting bolts for the TV support into the wall.

"This racket is giving me a headache," Sheila commented as she circumnavigated the queue on her way back to the kitchen.

"Yeah," Joe agreed, pouring tea for his next customers. "On a scale of one to ten, I rate it at minus five."

***

By the time Joe settled down for his break at 10:30, the TV, a 42" flatscreen, was up and running, and already the centre of attention with the staff and the few customers enjoying a mid-morning snack.

Joe seated himself at table 5, immediately in front of and to the left of the service counter, and opened the *Daily Express* at the cryptic crossword. Sheila was out delivering the morning's sandwich order to Ingleton Engineering, a mile or two from the café. Lee, Joe's nephew and the Lazy Luncheonette's head cook, was preparing lunches, and after Brenda served a middle-aged woman with tea and a toasted teacake, she poured herself a cup of tea and joined Joe, but promptly turned her head to watch the TV.

"Have you worked out what the point of this I-Spy programme is yet?" Joe asked without looking up from his crossword.

"It's reality TV, Joe," she explained for the umpteenth time. "You put eight people in a house, all of different ages and generations, and see how they get on twenty-four hours a day, for seven days. There are cameras all over the house... except for the lavatory and one other room."

"It's invasion of privacy TV, if you want my opinion," he responded. "And didn't that other one go on for weeks, and weeks, and weeks?"

9

"Yes. And at the end of every week, one of their housemates was evicted. I-Spy isn't as grand as that, but it's different because of the age gap of the Housies. At fifty-five, I'm the eldest, and I think the youngest is a girl of about twenty-three. We're from all walks of life, too. There's an actress amongst us." Brenda sipped her tea. "And an estate agent, and a nurse."

"And a woman who makes meat pies for truckers. You." Joe put down his pen. "No offence, Brenda, but I know what you're like with men. Do you suddenly want to become the star of the modern equivalent to a what-the-butler-saw machine?"

Brenda laughed throatily. "The Mata Hari of Middlewich? I shouldn't think so. Besides, there's none of that stuff allowed… well, there is, but there's a private room for it. It won't be going out on film."

"No, but the minute the millions of viewers see you heading for that room, they'll know what you're up to."

Lee appeared in the kitchen doorway, his hands white with flour. A former prop for the Sanford Bulls rugby league team, he was a huge, muscular young man, an excellent cook, having been trained by Joe and the local catering college, but notoriously clumsy. Even as he leaned against the door jamb. He dislodged a beaker and only just caught it before it shattered to the floor.

"Me and Auntie Sheila are looking forward to seeing Auntie Brenda on the telly next week," he chortled as he put the beaker back on the shelf.

"Break many more plates, lad, and I'll cut your TV rations off until the next millennium," Joe warned him. "Does your Cheryl know she's coming in all next week to cover for Brenda?"

"Yes, Uncle Joe," Lee replied. "She's looking forward to seeing Auntie Brenda on the telly an'all. She loves I-Spy, our Cheryl."

Joe shook his head. "And I thought your wife had more brains. Does she also know that you'll need her two mates, Pauline and Franny next Friday while we shoot off over to

10

Chester for Brenda's coming out party?"

"Yes, Uncle Joe," Lee reported. "We've got it all in hand."

"Good," Joe said. "And have you got today's lunches in hand?"

"In the ovens and cooking."

Irritated that he could find nothing more to pick Lee up on, Joe turned his attention back to Brenda. "And what the hell are you gonna do with the prize money if you win it?"

"Twenty-five thousand pounds, eh? If I win, Joe, I promise you one thing. I won't offer to buy you out." She drank her tea. "And it's D-Day, by the way, not the coming out party."

"D-Day?" Joe was appalled. "What the hell are you gonna do? Invade Wrexham?"

"Departure Day, Joe."

The trill of the doorbell prevented Brenda answering. Looking up, Joe's eyes fell on Captain Les Tanner.

"And talking of D-Day, look who it isn't," Joe said cheerfully.

Tanner stood over six feet tall. A slender man, maintaining the upright bearing which went with his rank, he had never seen military service other than with the Territorial Army Volunteers, but it was a role he took just as seriously as any full-time, professional soldier. An administrative manager with Sanford Borough Council during the week, a member of the Sanford 3rd Age Club from the earliest days, he was also one of Joe's fiercest critics.

Joe, Chair of STAC, delighted in their head to heads. It allowed him to deal with any irritation which had not found another channel, and he was secure in the knowledge that he was more popular than Tanner.

It was rare for Tanner to visit the Lazy Luncheonette. Old fashioned Lyons or ABC Tearooms were more the Captain's preference.

With a broad grin, Joe embellished his previous goad. "Les Tanner, honouring us with his presence. If you've come chasing last month's rates, they've been paid."

"I'm taking an occasional day, Murray," Tanner retorted, "and I was passing so I thought I might drop in and rub some salt in the wound."

Joe got to his feet, moved behind the counter and poured a beaker of tea for Tanner. Returning to the table, waving the Captain into the seat opposite, he asked, "Wound? What wound?"

"About the only thing you're good for, Murray. Making tea." He sipped from the beaker and grimaced. "And you're not very good at that." He dug into the inner pockets of his business suit and came out with an A4 sheet of paper. Dropping it on the table, he said, "I found that pinned to our notice board the other day, I suspect George Robson put it there. He's the only other council employee I can think of who's a member of the 3rd Age Club."

Brenda read it and cackled.

"What?" Joe growled. "Come on. Let us all in on the joke."

Still laughing, Brenda handed the sheet over, and Joe read it.

It was the last page of the monthly newsletter. Emailed to most members, Joe posted Xeroxed copies to those members who did not have access to a computer. This one was dated just a few days earlier.

The final words had been circled in red ink.

STAC is your club. Be prod of your member.

"Even without the prod, the member would pique my interest," Brenda laughed.

Tanner frowned his disapproval. Joe grunted. "It's a couple of typos, that's all. It should say be proud of your membership."

"It's what I've come to expect of you," the Captain said, taking another drink of tea. "Slipshod, haphazard, downright inefficient."

Joe appealed to Brenda. "He comes in here, gets a free beaker of tea and still has the brass nerve to criticise me when he works for the most inefficient organisation in town:

the council."

"I'm not responsible for the inefficiencies in the town hall," Tanner replied. "Only those in my department, and I come down hard on them. As for being outspoken, you're one of the worst, and at least my language is an improvement on yours." He turned his attention to Brenda. "Are you looking forward to your week of potential fame, dear?"

"Yes, thanks, Les."

"Don't approve of it, myself, but Sylvia and I will be there with the rest of the club to welcome you back next Saturday." His gimlet eye fell on Joe again. "Always assuming our chairman has managed to order the bus for Chester and not Chelmsford." He drank his tea.

"Miner's Arms, next Friday morning, eight o'clock," Joe told him. "You can find your way to the Miner's Arms, can you? Or would you like me to draw you a map?"

Les smiled. "Kind of you, Murray, but knowing you, it would probably show me the way to the Bull's Head." He beamed on Brenda again. "So, you're getting excited about the prospect?"

"And how," Brenda enthused. "A week away from the slave driver, here."

"I saw the application form," Joe chuckled. "It looks like someone from your department put it together, Les. They wanted to know everything, right down to the day she hangs her washing out."

"Really?" Tanner sounded as if he approved.

"Not really," Brenda replied. "Mind you, I'm cooking a special dinner for the Housies next Thursday, and they wanted a full list of ingredients and how I actually go about preparing and cooking it."

"Fire regulations." Tanner diagnosed.

"That's what I told her," Joe butted in. "Pains in the backside, all these petty rules."

"They're a necessity, Murray," Tanner argued. "They're designed to prevent people like you burning the place down and killing off your staff."

13

"Gar," Joe growled. "Over forty years I've worked in this place, and never had a fire yet. And Brenda isn't gonna burn the place to the ground, is she? Nanny state. That's what it is."

"Life saving, you mean." Tanner nodded smartly to them both and left.

"I think Les won that round on points," Brenda commented.

"I have to let him win now and again. So you were telling me what you're going to do with the prize money if you win."

"I don't know, Joe. Probably stick it in the bank for my old age. But the chances of me winning are pretty slim. It's a popularity contest, isn't it? Decided by a phone vote. Oh," she added as an afterthought, "You do remember you and Sheila are running me there tomorrow? Have you arranged cover for the café?"

Joe shook his head. "It's done. What time do you have to be there?"

"Eleven thirty."

"So if we leave about nine-ish we'll be in plenty of time. It's only two hours on the motorway…"

"No, Joe," Brenda interrupted. "We have to leave earlier. We've got to find the place. Let's leave at eight."

Joe fumed at the ceiling. "And she calls me a slave driver."

***

Marlene Caldbeck limped into the room, disregarding the angry stares of the other team members, and took her seat next to co-host Ryan Rivers.

In Scott Naughton's humble opinion, the pair were the worst possible combination for a show like I-Spy, and of the two, Marlene was the most difficult to work with. Carrying a prosthetic lower limb which had hampered her acting career, she had never been very good, relying a little too much on wiggling her bosom and backside at the cameras, but she had had the good fortune to land a role in a long-running soap, and the good sense to get out of it after five years, before the character, a self-serving bitch not unlike the real-life Marlene, became stale. At the age of 38, her head of dark hair swept majestically around her pear drop face, hiding any hint of cosmetic surgery, her behind had not yet spread, while the bosom was just as big, just as wiggly and just as camera greedy. With media clout behind her, she knew how to make the production crew jump to her every demand, and it was rumoured, although Naughton could not confirm it because that side of the business was outside his brief, that she had nailed the company to the wall for a ludicrously high salary on I-Spy.

Rivers, too, could be a pain. As a stand-up comic his observational improvisations had been good in his early days, but his singing voice had never been much better than a quality karaoke singer's, and eventually, as seemed to happen with many such comics, he had found himself sidelined onto comedy panel shows showing on satellite and cable TV. Now aged 31, a string of nationwide tours over the last five years, had seen him garner a reputation as a womaniser. He picked up and dropped women like some millionaire playboy, even though he was almost broke… allegedly. But he was still smartly turned out, and his ability to ad-lib, a natural consequence of his improv' act, made him the ideal candidate to front a show like I-Spy. As long as they could keep him away from the booze and the babes, and he didn't try to hit on the notoriously fickle Marlene.

Coming, as he did, from a military background, Naughton, the director on I-Spy, would have given anything to have the pair of them in uniform under his command.

Unlike other, similar programmes, I-Spy did not have a permanent home. Instead, the locations were different for each week-long series. Over the past four years, during which it had built up a dedicated following, it had travelled around the country as far afield as Fort William in northern Scotland and Exmoor in Devon. The programme had utilised old farm buildings, a closed down infant's school, even a defunct army base near Bedford, and now it had come to Gibraltar Hall, a manor house ten miles east of Chester.

The construction and technical team had moved into the hall a month previously and along with producer Helen Catterick, Naughton, whose job it would be to decide the shots for transmission, had little choice but to be there. It was boring work. Sat in the control room hour after hour, day after day, his trained eye concentrated on a bank of monitors, studying the feeds, working out whether camera 90 needed to be two feet to the left in order to counter early morning sunlight coming in through the windows, and whether camera 67 would be too intrusive set so high up in the women's dorm.

Tedious, but necessary work which had to be carried out before the start of every I-Spy week. And now that the arrival of the Housies was less than twenty-four hours away, it was time for the final meeting to ensure that, as far as possible, everything was tickety, if not boo.

Marlene arriving late (deliberately in Naughton's opinion) did nothing to help what was already a dour atmosphere.

"Now that we're all here," producer Helen Catterick began with a steely eye on Marlene, "let's see if we can make some progress." She shuffled her papers on the table. "We were talking about the contestants and the things we know in advance. Things we need to press in on, but particularly the things we need to avoid."

"If they have sensitive issues, why are they taking part?" Marlene asked.

"You've been in the public eye for the last, how long? Seven or eight years?" Naughton asked with unbridled malevolence. "Are there areas of your early life you'd rather not discuss?"

"I don't go on reality TV to air them," Marlene retorted.

"No. You just sue the Sunday papers when they air them," Naughton complained.

Marlene gave him a smile laced with acid. "You should

be careful, Scott, or I may be tempted to ask which of us is the more important to the show."

"No contest in my opinion," Naughton said. "If I had any say, I'd drop you in a second."

Marlene was about to bite back when Helen rapped her pen on the table. "Can we have a bit of order, please? The Housies are due in at noon tomorrow, and I'd like to get through this today." She rounded on Marlene. "We know about your ego, but this gig is going out on a tight budget... again. Don't run off with the idea that you're indispensable." She turned her fire on Naughton. "And you, stop working out your angst on the front team. We're all in this together."

Helen allowed a moment's silence to let the rising tempers cool. "Right. As I was saying, there are those issues in the background that we do not confront. Brenda Jump, for instance, is a widow. We do not ask her to go into details of her marriage and the death of her husband. Dylan Yorke's mother committed suicide when he was a child, so let's not get into that. You all have photographs of the Housies in front of you, and you know the drill. Familiarise yourself with them. I'll just run through them." Slipping on her reading glasses, Helen concentrated on her top sheet. "First, the women: Tanya Drake, a nurse, Brenda Jump, a waitress, Ursula Kenney an estate agent, Anne Willis, a receptionist. And now the men..." Helen trailed off, her eyes on Marlene. "Is there something wrong?"

"No, no," Marlene assured her. "I thought I recognised one of them, that's all. I was wrong."

"Fine time to tell us," Helen complained. "We were all shown photographs and asked whether we knew any of the Housies. That was weeks ago. Now is not the time to recognise someone."

"I said I was wrong," Marlene grumbled.

"Right. The men: Greg Innis, pub singer, Ben Oakley, former teacher and now a market trader, Marc Ulrich, an accountant, and Dylan Yorke, a mechanic. Let me ask you all, right now. Do any of you know any of these eight people?"

Silence prevailed. Helen reached down and scratched her leg. "Is everyone familiar with the procedure tomorrow?" She eyed her director. "Scott?"

"The Housies arrive no later than half past eleven in time for a pre-launch meeting at twelve noon. Caldbeck and Rivers will meet them informally before they shoot off to start the warm up…"

"Mr Rivers," if you don't mind," the comedian interrupted.

"And it's Ms Caldbeck."

"Why don't you two get together and disappear up your own egos?" Naughton retorted. After a pause, he went on to the rest of the room. "From there, Helen and Katy read the Housies the riot act, spelling out the dos and don'ts of I-Spy, and take them on a tour of the house while our two celebrities…" He laid sour eyes on the pair, "… I use the word in its loosest possible sense, keep the viewers entertained. After the tour, we hand them over, they'll be introduced one by one to their adoring fans by our emcees, and then enter the house."

Rubbing at her leg again, Helen dipped into her handbag and came out with a bottle of pills. "Painkillers," she explained in response to Naughton's interested stare. "Arthritis," she went on. "Don't worry, Scott, you'll get there in a few years." Cracking the cap on her water bottle, she swallowed a single pill. "Scott has just laid out the bare bones, which, I have to say, we should all be familiar with by now. Beyond their introduction to the viewers, the Housies are on their own. Now can we get back to their unmentionables?"

Chapter Two

Leaving Sanford just after eight o'clock on Saturday morning, they stopped at a motorway café at the junction of the M6 and M56 near Lymm, where Joe grumbled at the standards of food and service.

"You're always the same," Sheila told him. "If it's not the Lazy Luncheonette, they're not doing it right."

"I take a pride in my work is all," Joe countered.

"And so do these people," Sheila retorted.

Throughout the meal, Brenda kept an eye on the clock, worrying that they may have difficulty finding the I-Spy house.

"Will you quit fretting," Joe advised. "It's not even a quarter to ten, and we've less than twenty miles to the place."

"I like to be early, Joe. You know I do."

"It's a pity you're never early when we're opening up of a morning, then."

From Lymm, Joe cut onto the M56 and, following the prompts of his satnav, came off again almost immediately, taking the A49 to the south. After crossing the River Weaver, the noise of the car engine resounding from the iron trusses above and either side of them, Joe gloated, "Only another seven miles. We'll be there in no time."

Three miles further on, he turned right at a set of traffic lights, heading west on the A556 and almost immediately ground to a halt in a long queue of traffic.

"Maybe some kind of accident," he speculated. "Or roadworks." He leaned to his right in an attempt to peer round the car ahead. "No sign of any temporary lights, though."

"It'll be the sightseers heading for the public show area for I-Spy," Sheila suggested.

Her comment only increased Brenda's anxiety. "We're going to be late."

Joe glanced at the dashboard clock. "Relax. It's only five past ten. We've plenty of time…"

With the clock reading five minutes to eleven and Brenda in a state of near panic, a police officer waved them into a field on the right, where thousands of other vehicles were already parked, and hundreds more coming from east and west, waited to get in.

Indicating Brenda in the rear seat, Joe protested, "She's a contestant."

"Tell it to the parking stewards, mate," the officer replied and pointing again, urged Joe to get moving.

With an audible, "Tsk," Joe turned into the field and stopped again as a steward approached him.

Wearing a fluorescent, yellow vest, a cloth cap keeping the sun off his head, he held out his hand. "Fiver."

Joe frowned. "What?"

"You heard, mate. Five quid."

"A fiver? What for?"

"Parking charge."

"No, no, you don't understand," Joe said. "She's one of the contestants." Again he jerked a thumb at Brenda in the rear seat.

The steward was unmoved. "I don't care if she owns the TV company. If you're parking in this field, it's a fiver."

Joe scowled. "Didn't I see you in Parliament last week explaining why you're hiking the taxes on small businessmen?"

"Now listen, pal…"

Joe cut him off. "No, you listen, you dipstick. She, Mrs Brenda Jump, is one of the contestants in this farce."

"Then you should have gone to the contestants' entrance on Gibraltar Hall Lane. Now either pay up or clear off."

Joe slotted the car into gear. "Where is this Gibraltar Hall Lane?"

"Joe, for god's sake, just pay him the fiver," Brenda urged from the back seat. "I'm going to be late."

"Yes, but…"

"PAY HIM!" Brenda yelled.

Joe dug into his pocket and fished out five pounds. "I won't forget your face," he warned as he handed it over.

The steward took his money and pointed towards the far corner of the field. "If you drive over there, one of the lads will tell you where to park."

Joe looked over. It was at least five hundred yards away, and there was a queue of vehicles waiting to park. Bringing his gaze closer to them, Joe spotted gaps in the nearest lines of vehicles. "Why can't I park there?"

"Reserved," the steward said.

"You're expecting the Queen?"

"For crying out loud, Joe…"

"Disabled," said the steward.

"I'm disabled," Sheila said from the passenger seat.

The steward looked doubtful. "Well…"

"Honestly, she is," Joe promised.

"You have your parking badge with you?"

"Oh, yes," Joe lied.

"Well all right. Put it in one of those gaps, but don't forget to display your badge." Joe drove along, leaving the steward to negotiate with the next driver. Nosing the car into a gap between a people carrier and a 4x4, he killed the engine, and while his friends climbed out to retrieve Brenda's suitcase from the boot, he took a sheet of paper from his notebook, and began to draw on it.

"What the hell are you doing, Joe?" Brenda demanded.

"Showing my disabled badge," he said, and put the piece of notepaper on the windscreen.

Sheila studied it. He had drawn something that might have been a wheelchair as depicted by a 5-year-old child, and underneath it, he had written, 'disbled'.

"I wouldn't care but you've spelled disabled wrong," Sheila complained.

"Can we please get a move on?" Brenda demanded.

Joe locked up the car, and took the handle of her suitcase. "You got your letter with you, Brenda?" Sheila asked.

She patted her handbag as Joe retrieved her suitcase from the rear.

"Feeling nervous?" Sheila asked, and Brenda could only nod.

"You'll be all right," Joe assured her. "Just be yourself. You'll skewer the women with that warning eye of yours, and knock the guys out with your…"

"Careful Joe," Brenda warned finding her voice.

"I was going to say personality," Joe pleaded.

Most of the drivers and their passengers were making their way to the top corner of the field, from which direction they could hear loud music and, at intervals, equally loud cheering.

"That's where the live show is put on for the public," Sheila said.

"It's not likely to be where we want, then," Joe said, and led the way out on to the road where he spoke to one of the police officers on traffic duty. Returning to his companions, he said, "It's along here. Only a couple of hundred yards, Brenda."

She checked her watch. "Ten past eleven. Can we please get a move on?"

The hot, summer air hung even heavier with the tag of exhaust fumes from the queue of traffic. Joe led the way along the edge of the carriageway, grumbling at the noise, the fumes, the expense, while Brenda became more and more anxious with every step.

Police manned the junction at Gibraltar Hall Lane, where a temporary barrier had been erected.

"This lady is a contestant," Joe told the sergeant on duty, showing Brenda's letter of authorisation.

"You really should have made your way in by car, sir," the sergeant replied.

"Would you have charged me a fiver for parking?"

"No."

"In that case, you're right," Joe agreed. "Now, can we get

22

Mrs Jump into the house?"

"You and the other lady won't be allowed past the gates, sir, but go on through." The sergeant nodded to one of his constables and they lifted the barrier to let the trio past.

In contrast to the main road, the lane was heavily wooded, and it seemed to Joe that they had passed into another dimension the moment they crossed the checkpoint. The noise of the traffic had dissipated, the sounds from the entertainment field were muffled by the trees, and he could even hear the occasional call of wood pigeons.

A hundred yards ahead lay the entrance to the hall, and as they neared, so the sounds of civilisation returned: noisy generator vans, supplying power to a cabin sited by the gates. Security men, easily identified in their chocolate-coloured uniforms, prowled the gates, like hungry wolves ready to leap on any unsuspecting interloper.

Joe introduced Brenda to the nearest officer, and while she negotiated, he looked through the gates at the I-Spy house.

Having seen pictures of the hall when Brenda first applied, Joe knew that at the rear, there was a large, well-tended, south-facing garden, with more flower beds, fine lawns, and topiary in the shapes of birds, people and animals, but at the front, Gibraltar Hall did not live up to its grandiose name. A three-storey house of redbrick, four storeys if the obvious attics in the pitched roof were counted, but for its size, it could have come from any council estate in post-war England. Rows of paned windows gazed out from the bland front, and the door was a simple, black affair set into a broad frame.

The level expanse of the gravel forecourt was broken up by flowerbeds, and even they were bordered by concrete rather than brick or stone. On the outside, the place was surrounded by an eight-foot wall of faded brick, and the most ornate thing about Gibraltar Hall were the wrought iron gates, as tall as the wall, but decorated with some fancy coat of arms.

"Joe. Brenda's about to go in."

Sheila's reminder brought him back from his glum thoughts. "What. Oh, yeah." He moved forward, leaned into her and pecked Brenda on the cheek. "Good luck, and remember, knock 'em dead."

She gave them both a nervous smile. "Careful on the way back, you two. No funny business on the back seat of the car." She hugged Sheila, then Joe, and then disappeared into the reception cabin.

Once she had gone, Joe and Sheila made their way back to the main road, and the noise of traffic fighting its way into the car park.

"There's no rush to get back, Joe," Sheila suggested. "Shall we stay and watch Brenda introduced on the big screens at the live show? If we drive back, we'll miss it anyway."

Joe had been anxious to get back to the Lazy Luncheonette, but the sense of Sheila's words coupled with memories of the heavy traffic persuaded him otherwise. "Yeah, okay."

Turning into the car park, Joe found the steward who had caused him so much trouble, studying the note in the car window.

"Problem?" Joe asked.

"Oh, it's you, is it?" The steward scowled. "You told me you were disabled."

"Get your facts right. Mrs Riley told you she was disabled, I merely confirmed it."

"That," the steward said pointing at Joe's makeshift disabled badge, "is not valid, and you're gonna have to pay extra."

Joe shook his head and aimed a finger at the grass. "No markings to indicate disabled only parking," he declared.

"I told you about it," the steward retorted, giving vent to his sense of outrage.

"Insufficient. If you don't believe me, try talking to my friend, here." Joe gestured at Sheila. "Chief Inspector Sheila Riley of the Sanford traffic division. Now retired."

The steward gawped.

"Inadequate marking and no warning notices," Sheila tutted. "Under the Road Traffic Act of 2007, subsection 37, provision of parking places, and notification of parking restrictions, any attempt by you to impose a penalty could be seen as demanding money under false pretences, which carries a maximum fine of £2,000 and one year in prison."

The steward gawped. "Road Traffic Act?"

"Two thousand and seven," Joe said.

"Subsection 37," Sheila confirmed.

The steward coughed to hide his embarrassment. "I, er, well, in that case, I'll overlook it this once."

The steward wandered off. With a superior smile, Joe took Sheila's arm and they walked on. "Is there a Road Traffic Act of 2007?" he asked.

"Probably," Sheila replied as they joined the crowds funnelling into the upper field.

"And subsection 37?" Joe wanted to know.

"Probably," she repeated.

"But you don't know if it has anything to do with the notification of parking restrictions?"

"He bought it, Joe. Why won't you?"

Joe grinned savagely. "And you accuse me of confusing people."

Where access to Gibraltar Hall Lane had been confined to TV crew, authorised news teams, reporters and photographers, the upper field had no such restrictions. Vast crowds had descended on it and Joe and Sheila found themselves some distance from the arched, temporary stage, where a rock band sang and danced. Huge TV screens stood centre stage and either side, showing a digital countdown that now registered less than five minutes. There were food stalls and other traders selling souvenirs, all adding to the carnival atmosphere.

Beyond the stage was the woodland, and beyond the trees, Joe could just make out the high, pitched roof of Gibraltar Hall, and up above, a pair of helicopters flew in circles. The police, Joe guessed, and possibly media.

"I-Spy is certainly big news in this quarter," Sheila said.

"I wonder when it'll come to Sanford?" Joe said.

"Hmm?"

"Well, if they brought it to the Memorial Park, I could set up a hot dog stand." Joe nodded at the food traders lined up to one side of the field. "They're making a bloody fortune."

***

From the reception cabin, Brenda was led into the grounds, then around the side of the house to the rear, where she looked out over the large, lush garden and high retaining walls. Large screens had been erected down the centre of the garden. The Housies were not permitted any contact with anyone outside the house for the coming week, and this side of the screen was the production crew's entrance. The Housies' half of the garden was on the other side.

Before she could give too much thought to the prospect, a security officer ushered her in through the back door to a security station. Her luggage was searched, and then scanned, and her mobile phone taken for safe keeping. She was asked to sign to the effect that she carried no mobile telephones or any other communications device, such as a pager, that would permit her to contact anyone outside Gibraltar Hall, and then she was shown to a side room where her seven fellow Housies were already waiting, enjoying tea, coffee or juice, and chatting amongst themselves.

At the invitation of a young, dark-haired woman by the name of Katy Flitt, who introduced herself as the assistant director, Brenda helped herself to a much-needed cup of tea. Her nerves had settled a little now that she was actually in the house, but there was still that edginess, butterflies in the tummy, shaking hands, and a thirst that could only be conquered by tea.

A large whiteboard stood at the front of the room with eight names written on it. Brenda's was towards the bottom of the list, but its presence signalled that they were the names of the Housies.

Producer Helen Catterick joined them at midday and there followed a tedious forty minutes in which the pair laid down the house rules. Helen, particularly, spoke in drab monotones, and several times throughout the lecture Brenda had to suppress a yawn.

The debate sparked a little towards the end when the Housies were invited to ask questions.

"Just how much privacy do we get?" a blonde woman by the name of Ursula Kenney asked. Dressed in a tight mini-dress which showed more of the ample cleavage and strong legs than Brenda considered decent, she had already interrupted Helen on several occasions and it was clear from her various expressions, that the producer did not care for Ursula.

"A little," Helen replied. "In the bathroom, for instance."

"Excuse me," Brenda said, "but I thought I heard you say there are cameras in the bathrooms."

"There are, Brenda," Helen replied, "but they're carefully angled to show no more than your head and shoulders while you are taking a shower."

Dylan Yorke, one of the men, laughed. "So I can't show off me finest assets." He looked down between his muscular thighs.

Helen frowned. "Not in the bathroom, you can't, Dylan. If you wish to parade yourself in the bedroom, that is entirely your own affair." Addressing the whole group, she went on, "We're all adults, and it's in the nature of this kind of programme, that, er, shall we say, liaisons will form. There is one room in the house without cameras. It's on the landing between the two dormitories. Its official title is the Private Room. For those of you who have followed previous series, you'll know that the Housies christened it the Romping Room. If you wish to meet another Housey in private, then that is the place to do so, but please think of your fellow Housies. Make sure you lock the door while you're in there."

Her final words, delivered with a wincing smile, created a

ripple of naughty laughter through the room.

"And that brings me nicely to the subject of language," Helen went on. "Once again, we're all adults, but I would ask you to try to modulate your language for the sake of younger viewers."

"I thought you used a bleeper," Ursula Kenney challenged.

"We do. There's a 20-second delay between live action and broadcast that permits us to override unacceptable language, but if you come out with too much, it can create problems for the crew. So I ask again, please make an effort to moderate your language."

With the induction over, they were shown into and around the house. Brenda noticed instantly that their permitted areas of activity bore no resemblance to the actual size of the hall. The house was vast, but so many places remained off limits to them, and when she boiled it all down, they would see only the living room, the kitchen/dining room, the staircase, dormitories, with their en suite bathrooms, and (if they so wished) the Romping Room.

Brenda had already decided that she would have no need of the latter area. Amongst the members of the Sanford 3rd Age Club, she had a reputation as a merry widow which was largely fictitious and unjustified. Unlike her best friend, Sheila, she enjoyed the company of men, but that did not make her loose-legged.

Escorted to the exterior, Brenda got her first look at the Housies' side of the garden. It seemed to her to be no different from the crew side, with its share of flowerbeds and topiary, but there was no exit... unless she could vault the eight-foot retaining wall.

After the guided tour, they were led back to the reception room where each of them was fitted with a radio mike and power pack. The mikes were left disconnected for the time being.

Helen and Katy addressed them once more.

"Right, ladies and gentlemen, this is where it begins," Helen announced. "Before we go on, do any of you have any further questions?"

Silence greeted her.

"All right. In a few minutes, we'll cue your introduction to the watching public. You'll go through alphabetically by surname. As your name is called, my assistant will guide you through that door." She pointed to her left, the Housies' right. "There you'll meet Marlene and Ryan. There'll be a brief chat in front of the cameras, and after that, they will point you to *your* entrance into the house, and beyond that, it's I-Spy."

While Helen had a brief, whispered word with her assistant, Brenda glanced at the list of names on the whiteboard. It was in random order, with Ursula Kenney's name at the top and Dylan Yorke's at the bottom, but she quickly calculated that, alphabetically, she came third. A feeling of relief quelled some of her nervousness. At least she was not first. She would have the performances of Tanya Drake and Greg Ingham to guide her before she had to face the cameras.

Helen left. Her assistant, Katy, switched on the TV set. "Your names will be called one by one," she told them. "Tanya, you're first, I'm afraid, but that gives the rest of you an idea of what to expect."

"Could be worse," Tanya said. "They could have dragged us out in front of all those crowds in the public viewing area."

Her fellow Housies tittered, Brenda confined herself to a smile, but she had heard the slight trill in Tanya's voice. It gave her small comfort to know that her companions for the coming week were as nervous as her.

The TV screen came alive with a shot of Marlene Caldbeck and Ryan Rivers lounging on a large settee, chattering garrulously to the cameras. Katy turned up the volume.

"It's no sweat," Ursula Kenney said suddenly. "Try to remember not to look at the camera and just be yourself."

"You sound as if you know something about it," Brenda observed.

Ursula turned her baby blue eyes on Brenda, but they were no longer the eyes of a woman seeking friendship. Their stare was cold and calculating. In a second they had swept over Brenda's frame and assessed her.

"*I* am an actress," Ursula declared, with exaggerated emphasis on the personal pronoun.

Brenda pursed her lips. "That should give you an edge on the rest of us, then."

At the front, Katy paid attention to her headphones for a moment, then smiled at them. "Right Housies, we are go. Tanya. Do your stuff."

They watched Tanya make her way to the far door and disappear through it. Attention swung to the TV where Ryan Rivers beamed into the camera. "Let's welcome the first of our Housies... Tanya Drake."

While Rivers and Marlene greeted Tanya, Ursula scowled again at Brenda. "I don't need any advantage to beat you. Any of you."

***

Brenda put the woman's arrogance down to nerves, and did not rise to it. Fifteen minutes later, when Katy called her name, she completely forgot about Ursula.

Her legs trembled and for a moment she felt like her knees would give way. She opened the door, took a deep breath, and stepped through.

When the door closed behind her, she found herself off stage, several yards to the right of the presenters. A studio assistant stopped her from going further while Marlene Caldbeck spoke to camera.

"That's Greg Ingham. Sure to be a great success on this week's I-Spy." Marlene beamed at her partner. "Okay, Ryan, your turn."

The former stand-up comedian fixed a smile on his face. "Our next lady describes herself as a fun loving third ager from West Yorkshire, with the accent on fun-loving. So let's welcome our third Housey... Brenda Jump."

Brenda recalled the days when Rivers did a stand up act. Back then he would have had no hesitation in picking up on her surname and its sexual connotations. Surely he would not be so crass here?

While he had been speaking, the floor assistant had reached under Brenda's blouse to plug her radio mike into its power pack. Now the woman nodded Brenda forward. With her legs turning to jelly, Brenda strode across the floor and took Rivers' hands so he could lean in and peck her on the cheek, filling her nostrils with the scent of heavy aftershave.

Marlene greeted her the same way and directed Brenda to the armchair at the far end of the settee. Brenda noticed that when the actress sat, she crossed her shapely legs, baring a dangerous amount of thigh. Brenda decided not to do the same and, instead, sat forward, leaning on her right arm, keeping both feet primly on the floor.

"How are you, Brenda?" Rivers asked.

"Nervous," she admitted. Sheila and Joe (and Ursula Kenney) had told her to be herself.

"Absolutely nothing to be nervous about," Marlene promised her.

Brenda wondered if she could detect a hint of insincerity in the way the words were delivered. It would match the steel in the actress' eyes.

"So tell us a little bit more about yourself," Rivers invited.

"Well, Ryan, Marlene, I'm fif... in my fifties. I come from a lovely little town in West Yorkshire called Sanford, where I work as an assistant cook and waitress at a cafeteria. I used to be a bank clerk, but I lost my husband six years ago, and I felt I needed a fresh challenge, and cooking and serving meals to all those lorry drivers seemed just perfect to me."

"What's the name of the café, Brenda?" Marlene asked.

Brenda blushed. "Oh, I don't think I should mention it."

"Go on," Rivers urged. "Give the place a plug. We can always send a bill to the owners." He laughed.

Brenda, too, smiled, but it had less to do with Rivers' joke as the thought of how Joe would react if he received a bill for advertising.

Controlling the urge to laugh out loud, she said, "It's the Lazy Luncheonette on Doncaster Road, Sanford."

"What is it you think you can bring to I-Spy?" Marlene asked.

Brenda struggled to recall what she had written on her original application. "Maturity," she said, "but not the stuffy kind of maturity you see in so many people. I've lived a long time, Marlene, and if life is a game of two halves, I must be into the second half, and you learn, you know. You learn how to be happy, how to take as much enjoyment as possible out of every day, and how to pass that enjoyment on to others."

"And you're hoping to pass some of that approach onto your fellow Housies?"

It seemed to Brenda an idiotic question. Hadn't she just said so? Aloud, she said, "I hope so, yes. And I hope they can teach me, too. I have a friend who used to be a secretary in a large school, and she's always telling me that she learned so much from the pupils."

"Now, Brenda," Rivers said, "you're one of the Housies who's volunteered to prepare a special meal. Are you giving any secrets away about what it might be?"

Brenda smiled coyly. "Not yet, Ryan. Not until Thursday night."

He grinned at her. "I'll bet they can hardly wait." Gazing into the camera, he went on, "There you go, all you truckers," Rivers said to the camera. "The next time you're Sanford way, stop by the Lazy Luncheonette and try a plate of Brenda's *spécialité de la maison*... Egg and chips. Brenda, thanks very much. Time for you to go..." he paused, waiting for a signal from the audio engineers to tell him the echo was turned on. When he spoke, his voice boomed around the set. "... into the I-Spy house."

He and Marlene applauded, Brenda stood and made her way to the rear of the studio where another assistant waited to guide her through the rear door.

With the feeling that her moment of singular glory had been a somewhat muted affair, she found herself somewhere at the rear of the house. More crew waited for her. One handed over her suitcase, and ran through the rules for the last time.

"Are you happy to go into the house, Brenda?" The woman asked eventually.

Brenda nodded. The woman pressed the four digit lock on the door behind her. "Turn to your right, go up the stairs and you'll find the ladies dorm, just along the first landing on the left. Live transmission begins at three, and all Housies must be in the living room by five minutes to. Good luck."

Brenda stepped through and the door closed and locked behind her. She turned to look at the door. There was no means of opening it from this side.

Chapter Three

Brenda's biggest problem was getting her suitcase up the steep flight of stairs to the first floor landing. She had to stop twice to get her breath back while mentally cursing herself for her stupidity of packing excess clothing.

"You've enough here for a Caribbean cruise, you daft old bat," she muttered to the empty staircase.

After much puffing and panting, pulling and tugging, she finally made the landing and hauled the case along on its castors.

She guessed that the corridor ran the entire length of the house. Lit only every five yards or so, and then by low-wattage lamps, it was narrow, windowless and gloomy. There were a number of doors, the first of which, as promised, bore a 'ladies' sign with a line drawing of a bed beneath it. Before entering, Brenda left her suitcase and wandered further along the corridor. On her right, the next two doors, one on either side, were locked, the third bore a plaque which read, *Private Room*. Continuing along the corridor, she found three more locked doors and finally, the men's dormitory. There was, she noted, only the one staircase, only the three rooms they could access.

She retraced her steps, collected her suitcase and stepped into the ladies' dorm, to find Tanya Drake had commandeered the bed nearest the door and was busy unpacking into what looked like a cheap, self-assembly wardrobe.

Although the room was large, the four beds, each with a small cabinet, and wardrobes had taken up so much space, that it felt uncomfortably cramped. Above each bed was a shelf and Tanya had already set up a couple of books and her toilet bag on hers. A narrow door in the far corner, led to the bathroom where there were two showers and separate toilets.

"At least we can have some privacy," Brenda commented, "but there are no windows."

"Not allowed," Tanya said. She giggled. "They're frightened we may be signalling to our secret lovers in the woods outside." She offered her hand. "We were not properly introduced. Tanya Drake. I'm a nurse. From Derby."

Brenda shook her hand. "Brenda Jump, a waitress from Sanford." She noticed Tanya's puzzlement. "West Yorkshire. Not far from Leeds."

"Ah. What brings you on this gig, Brenda? Apart from the twenty-five grand, that is."

"It's a bit of fun, isn't it?" Brenda took the bed opposite and slightly further into the room. Throwing her suitcase onto the mattress with a grunt, she turned the combination lock and threw open the lid. "And we all need a bit of fun in our lives. What kind of nursing do you do?"

"General," Tanya replied. "I want to go into midwifery, but I'm not long out of my training. I want some experience on the wards under my belt, first."

Brenda was puzzled. "I-Spy won't harm your prospects?"

"Oh no. I cleared it with my bosses, first." Tanya sat on the edge of her bed. "I'm not really, er, flighty. You know. I don't make a habit of…" she trailed off and blushed.

Brenda smiled and, for the first time since she had entered the place, began to feel at ease. "Bed hopping? Getting drunk? Chasing the boys? Showing off?"

Tanya smiled bleakly. "Boys don't really have the kind of equipment that interests me."

"Pity," Brenda observed. "I've always found them such good fun." At once she realised how awful it sounded. "Forgive me, Tanya. I wasn't having a go at you or your lifestyle. It just, sort of, slipped out."

The younger woman shrugged. "No prob. I'm used to that sort of comment, and others say it and mean it. You like

35

waitressing?"

It was a sledgehammer way of changing the subject and Brenda was glad of it. "No. I hate waitressing, especially serving bone idle truck drivers." She grinned. "But I work with some very special friends, and they make it a joy to turn out every morning. Besides, I wasn't always a waitress. I was a senior teller in a bank for years. Before my husband died."

Tanya did not have time to be shocked before the door burst open and Ursula Kenney walked in.

"Why the bloody hell don't they have someone to help with our luggage?" she demanded.

"You could have waited downstairs and asked one of the men when they came through," Brenda suggested.

Ursula glowered. "When I need your opinion I'll ask for it." She gazed around the room. "So this is it? I have to doss in this dump? And all for a lousy twenty-five grand?"

Brenda felt her gorge rising. "Are you usually this offensive, or have you been practising?"

Ursula glared again. "Don't try riding me, old woman. You'll find you're no match for me."

Brenda suppressed the urge to strike out at her. "Let's get one or two things straight, shall we, Ursula. I guess I'm old enough to be your mother, so I expect you to show me some respect. If you don't I may just be tempted to behave like your mother, put you over my knee, and tan your backside."

Ursula opened her mouth to speak, but Brenda carried on before she could utter a word.

"I've known you less than two hours and already I find you behaving like a spoiled little brat. What's worse, you're making some primary, erroneous assumptions. You are equating my age with weakness and senility. Many a better woman than you has tried it and come unstuck." She injected some real venom into her voice. "Start with me, chicken, and I'll knock your silly bloody head into the wall so hard, you won't wake up until Christmas." She allowed a moment for her threat to sink in. "Now, we all have to live together for the coming week, so I suggest we start by trying to be civil with each other."

Ursula's malevolent feature did not shift. "We're competitors, old woman, and I see no reason to be nice to someone who wants to rob me of what's rightfully mine."

**

Climbing the hill to Junction 22 on the M62, Joe soothed Sheila's worries.

"It's only two o'clock. They don't start the live broadcast until three, and we've only thirty miles to go. We're in plenty of time."

"That's what you said to Brenda when we got to Warrington," Sheila retorted, "and she only just made it."

"And you're beginning to sound like Brenda when we got to Warrington," Joe replied.

They had kept up the conversation in the entertainment field until Brenda finally left the screen to enter the house, at which point, they made their way back to Joe's car.

"If I get a bill from the TV company for Brenda's free plug, there'll be hell to pay," Joe had warned as he climbed behind the wheel.

Sheila had found Rivers' comment amusing. "I don't think he meant it, Joe. He was just being… well… comic."

"I've seen these so-called comics before. They're usually wearing hats marked Tax Inspector."

Once back on the road home, Sheila had begun to press for him to get to Sanford before the live broadcasts began at three. For Joe, it wasn't a problem, but in deference to her, he put his foot down. They met little in the way of traffic, but Joe's suggestion that they stop for a cup of tea met with a stern rebuke from his companion.

In stark contrast to the outbound journey, Joe's prediction proved accurate. With no significant delays, even in the busy areas around Leeds and Bradford, he pulled up outside Sheila's bungalow at 2:40.

"Why not come in, have a cup of tea and we can watch it together, Joe?" Sheila invited.

Joe hedged. "I was thinking of getting back to the café, before Lee and Cheryl close up."

"Oh don't be so mean-spirited," Sheila rebuked him. "Your nephew and his wife know how to cash up and they'll give you a full run down when you go to their house for lunch on Sunday. Come on. Have a cup of tea and watch Brenda's TV debut."

He grudgingly agreed and followed her up the path, past a pair of dwarf conifers and well-tended flowerbeds, to the side door, where Sheila let them in, hurrying ahead of Joe to silence the intruder alarm.

Joe had visited the place many times, but he could never quite get over the impression that it was more of a shrine than a home; a memorial dedicated to Sheila's late husband Peter. Display cabinets were filled with photographs of the couple, and many of Peter alone; his graduation through the Open University, his promotion to Inspector, looking immaculate on his wedding day, and impeccably dressed on his 50th birthday, only a matter of a few months before the two heart attacks which killed him.

Sheila did have other photographs about the house; their two children, Peter Jnr, and Aaron, both graduates, both married, and long moved from Sanford, now enjoying better lives.

And the house, unlike his apartment above the Lazy Luncheonette, was spotless, the furnishings in pristine condition. The walnut dining table gleamed in the afternoon sun, every china ornament around the room sparkled, and he half expected to see a twinkle come from the dust-free TV screen. Sheila was nothing if not house proud.

Joe was at his ease with the two women, but he felt less comfortable when he was with only one of them. Their tripartite friendship had endured 50 years on and off, but it had done so because it was platonic. There had been a brief moment during their teens when he fancied Sheila, and there had been a slightly longer period when he had dated Brenda, but it never came to anything, and by unspoken agreement, they were quite happy with that situation. And yet, whenever he was alone with one of the women, he found himself wondering whether he should make a pass at her.

He never did. It would be the fastest way to compromise both their friendship and working relationship. All the same, he sometimes wondered…

"Do you think Brenda's made a mistake going on this nonsense?" he asked as Sheila returned with a tea tray.

"I think if Brenda has made a mistake, she won't spend long regretting it, Joe." Sheila poured tea into a rose china cup and saucer, and passed it to him. "Help yourself to milk and sugar."

Joe, more at home with a beaker, spooned a small amount of sugar in, added a little milk and stirred vigorously. "Not the kind of thing you or me would do, though, is it?"

Settling into a recliner with a cup and saucer, Sheila leaned back and aimed the remote control at her flat screen TV, turning up the volume. "Brenda has always been more gregarious than either of us."

Joe sipped his tea as the I-Spy opening credits began to run. "Gregarious? That's a new name for it."

She chuckled. "You know what I mean. I've always been reserved, preferring my privacy. You never sought fame and fortune. Fortune, yes, but you prefer to do it quietly in the background, via the Lazy Luncheonette. Brenda… well Brenda has always believed in enjoying herself. That was true even when Colin was alive." She glanced quickly at his severe features. "Are you worried about her, Joe?"

"Worried? No." The opening shot was of all eight Housies seated around the bizarre furniture in the living room. Biting into a Hovis digestive, Joe waved at the screen. "She's more than a match for any of them. I just wouldn't like to see her make a fool of herself. That's all."

"If she does, it won't be the first time, but I don't think it's likely. There's a complete ban on alcohol. Brenda doesn't often get drunk, but when she does, that's when she's likely to show herself up. No alcohol, no antics."

They honed their attention on the TV.

"Good afternoon, Housies. I am the Master Spy."

Brenda had heard the disembodied voice known as Master Spy many times on TV. It was the only communication with the outside world permitted to Housies. A soft, persuasive voice of indeterminate gender, everyone who had watched the programme knew it.

What she (and presumably her fellow Housies) had not realised was that inside the I-Spy house, the voice came from everywhere at once. Something to do with the way the audio was set up, no doubt, but it was disconcerting nonetheless.

They had been congregated in the living room since 2:30, ready for the three p.m. launch. In the 75 or so minutes she had officially been a Housey, Brenda had met and chatted with the fourth woman, Anne Willis, a receptionist from a car hire company in Middlesbrough, and talked to two of the men, Greg Ingham, a pub singer and street entertainer from Bristol and Dylan Yorke a mechanic from North London. She had nodded greetings to the other two men, Ben someone or other and Marc Ulrich, both of whom sounded as if they hailed from the Midlands.

The conversations came about quite naturally as a result of three large TV screens dotted around the living room, showing various scenes from about the house.

"I noticed you took particular care on setting that little photograph up, Greg," Brenda said when they had introduced themselves.

As she spoke, she nodded at the centre screen, where Ben Oakley was busy emptying his suitcase and beyond him on the far, left hand bed, Marc Ulrich was hanging up a drab, dark blue, old fashioned dressing gown.

Like the women's dorm, the men each had a shelf. Greg, the first in the men's dorm, had chosen the bed on the right, furthest from the door, and his shelf, instead of standing above the bed, was angled into the corner of the room. He had set up his shaving brush, soap and razor, the head encased in a shiny, plastic sheath, and alongside them was a selection of paperbacks, in the centre of which was a small, framed photograph.

"My wife and two sons," he explained to Brenda. "I set them there because the missus will be following the programme this week, and every time the camera is in the men's dorm, she'll see the photograph, and know that I'm thinking about her."

"Aw, that's nice," Brenda simpered as Dylan joined them.

"Good thinking," Dylan said. "I put a picture of my mum on my shelf." He pointed to his bed, closest the door on the right. Lowering his hand, he offered the open palm to Brenda. "Dylan Yorke."

"Brenda Jump." Brenda shook the hand, noticing that it buried her tiny fingers. "And your mum will be watching, will she Dylan?"

His toothy smile vanished. "No. She's dead."

Brenda blushed. "Oh, I'm sorry. That was tactless."

He shrugged but his smile did not return. "Been dead, like, twenty years, now. Happened when I was a nipper, but I still miss her."

Brenda told them she was a widow and there followed a brief, over-animated conversation on the subject of deceased family, before Dylan meandered off to talk with Ursula.

"Bit of a cow, that one," Greg commented.

Brenda picked up Ursula's fluttering eyes and generous smile while she talked with Dylan. "She's making no bones about what she has for sale, either."

Greg laughed and Brenda smiled.

Since their confrontation in the dormitory, Brenda had been careful to avoid the woman. She had not come this far to be drawn into arguments with a 40-year old who, on the face of it, was little short of an arrogant and ignorant tart.

Congregating in the living room, waiting for the Master Spy to announce him (or her) self, Brenda found her mind meandering around mental images of her friends and family back in Sanford, wondering what they would be doing at this hour on a Saturday afternoon. Shopping, cricket, even football if the new season had begun. Sheila, she was certain, would have urged Joe to get a move on so she could be home to watch the programme launch and if she had not persuaded Joe to stay and watch with her, he would be back at the Lazy Luncheonette counting the day's takings.

Tonight they would meet in the Miner's Arms for the regular, unofficial Sanford 3rd Age Club get-together, and they would insist the landlord tune the TV to I-Spy to watch their friend and companion at...

At what?

For the first time since she applied to take part in the programme, Brenda began to question her motives. It had seemed liked a fun idea. Something different. But here she was ensconced in a sealed-off environment with seven strangers, no television, no pub, no drink even, and she did not know what she was supposed to be doing.

Master Spy seemed to read her mind.

"Most of you will be wondering what you're supposed to be doing. Act naturally, is the only advice I can give. Do whatever it is you do best."

***

In the control room, Scott Naughton's eyes darted around the half dozen monitors carrying images from the living room, and he periodically barked orders to his assistants when he wanted to shift the view.

"Look at her," Helen Catterick said, pointing at the main view currently feeding to the live transmission.

Irritated by the interruption, Naughton followed Helen's pointing finger to the right of the screen where Ursula Kenney had insinuated herself on the second sofa, between Dylan Yorke and Ben Oakley.

"Unusual," he agreed, and the barked, "Switch to 12."

Sat alongside him, Katy carried out the instruction and the view on the main monitor switched to pick up the four men and Ursula crammed onto the three-seater sofa.

"She's making her bed," Helen went on. "How long does it usually take before we have a gender mix? Five or six hours at least. She's been in the house less than two hours and already she's chasing studs."

"Go to 10," Naughton ordered as the Master Spy made small talk with the Housies. There were several actresses on call for the role of Master Spy, and when on duty, the individual was enclosed in a sound booth two rooms away.

The view switched again, taking in the three women on the other sofa.

Naughton allowed the shot to run while Master Spy spoke with Anne Willis.

"Go back to 12. Master Spy, pick up on Ursula sitting with the men."

He listened into Master Spy's comment.

"I wonder, Ursula, why you're sitting with the men. Do you always prefer male company?"

Ursula's response was accompanied with a large grin. "Isn't that what life's about? Men and women getting together?"

"Tart," Helen grumbled.

Naughton chuckled. "I dunno. I thought she had a point."

"I'll take side bets on who's first to the Romping Room this week," Katy laughed. "Heavy betting on little miss loose legs."

"Jealous?" Naughton asked. "And switch back to 8."

"Jealous? Of these losers?" Katy laughed again. "Action on 12," she said. "Dylan is stroking her thigh."

"Go to 12," Naughton ordered and studied the view. "At least his hand is where we can see it."

"They are not losers, Katy," Helen assured her. "They are simply gregarious people, eager to make something of themselves."

"Go to 13," Naughton ordered. "Ben has his arm around Ursula's back."

"Ursula is keen to make something of Dylan," Katy observed. "A mattress sandwich, I reckon."

Naughton laughed. "Maybe she could go for Dylan and

Ben at the same time and turn it into an MFM mattress sandwich... Go back to 8."

"Don't be disgusting," Helen admonished him.

"We never know what goes on in the Romping Room, Helen."

Katy laughed lasciviously. "We could get the techs to set up a pinhead camera when they throw fresh linen in through the hatch."

"Put the result up on YouTube?" Naughton grinned.

"YouTube would ban it in less than a minute," Katy observed, "but I know plenty of other sites where it would stay forever."

"Will you two kindly concentrate on your jobs, and stop this twittering," Helen rebuked them.

"Twitter is no good, Helen," Naughton told her. "It's text only." He laughed at her grimace, switched his attention back to the main feed, and checked the clock. "Cut to 10, and Master Spy start bringing the opening session to a close. Let's leave them to show the world their sad little lives."

The voice of Master Spy filled the control room. "That's all for the moment, Housies. Don't forget to get your chores scheduled. I'll be back later to see how you're getting on."

Chapter Four

"There's nowhere to sit," one of the dray men complained.

"Tell some of your pals to hutch up a bit," Joe replied, and pushed a beaker of tea across the counter. Passing the order though the hatch into the kitchen, he said, "Full English and tea, call it six fifty for cash." He took a ten pound note, rang it up, handed over change and watched as the unhappy dray man headed for table 13 beneath the wall-mounted TV.

"You coulda put a telly on the other side," the driver complained.

"This is a café, not a bloody drive in movie. And you lot should be out delivering beer by this time. I've had your boss on the phone complaining about the time you spend here."

"He's not complaining about all the extra beer we're selling to the pubs while Brenda's on I-Spy," one dray man retorted.

Ignoring him, Joe glowered at the next customer. "What do you want?"

"I suppose a tenner out of the till is a non-starter?"

It was Wednesday and although the promised filling of seats had materialised, the extra income had not matched it, for the simple reason that people were spending more time in the café, but spending the same money at the till.

Without one of the mainstays of the business – Brenda – Joe's irritation had hit new heights. He carped constantly at Sheila, Lee, and Lee's wife, Cheryl, who was deputising for Brenda. They took it in their stride and as always the café muddled through from day to day, with the staff determined to pass as much time watching TV as the customers, causing

Joe's anger to reach even greater peaks.

"I'll be glad when it's Friday and you lot take Uncle Joe to Chester," Cheryl had said to Sheila on Tuesday afternoon. And she made sure Joe was within earshot when she said it.

He, too, had been captivated by the antics of Brenda and her fellow Housies. While publicly decrying the programme as inane and purposely intrusive, he nevertheless found his attention straying to the screen during slack periods and, upstairs, in his private apartment, he had his smaller TV permanently tuned to the station.

Four full days into the week, it was obvious that Ursula Kenney was going all out to make a major mark on I-Spy, and he felt sorry for the other three female Housies, Brenda included. Whatever they did, wherever they were, Ursula was not far behind, determined to wrest the limelight from them.

The men were all over Ursula, and when he tabulated the number and types of visit to the Romping Room, Joe guessed why.

Anne Willis and Tanya Drake had gone there alone, Tanya twice. Brenda had never even ventured into the place. Of the men, Greg, Ben and Marc had each gone there alone, and they had also visited when Ursula was known to be there. Dylan, on the other hand had not gone there alone, but he had been in there four times with Ursula.

Their performance in going to the Romping Room amused Joe. It was usually late at night, when everyone else was asleep. One or other of them would make their way out of the dorm, along the landing into the room, eyes everywhere, checking ahead and behind in case they were observed. The other would soon follow suit and follow the same, furtive procedure.

"Why are you bothering?" Joe said to the TV screen. "There are cameras watching your every move… except the obvious ones."

Ursula's effect on the men was especially puzzling in the case of Greg. He was married with a family. During one session in the men's dorm, he had reached across to his bedside shelf and held up a photograph of a blonde woman and two fair-haired children, declaring, "Those are my precious angels. All three of them."

Not to be outdone, Dylan had then held up a photograph of his deceased mother similarly close to the camera, saying, "And this is my mum. With the angels."

Disregarding Dylan's obvious obsession with his mother, Joe had wondered about Greg's actions. If he was so captivated with his wife and kids, what the hell was he doing in the Romping Room with Ursula?

A few of the Housies had declared in advance their intention to make special meals for their fellows. Indeed Brenda had told him in advance that she had ordered the ingredients for a meat and potato pie, which she would prepare on Thursday night. Hadn't he seen the application form and spoken with Les Tanner about it the day before Brenda went to Chester?

Joe watched these culinary efforts with cynical interest, denouncing a vegetarian lasagne as tasteless Mediterranean tripe, and a beef goulash as a glorified pan of Scouse.

Uncharacteristically, it was the genial Lee, whose training as a chef Joe had financed, who took him to task on the issue the morning after the broadcast. "It didn't look nowt like Scouse, Uncle Joe."

"All right," Joe argued, "so it looked like a glorified Lancashire hotpot. Trust me, boy, Brenda will win in the cookery stakes. You can't beat one of her homemade meat and taters."

Joe's sympathy and support lay with Brenda, as did most of the town's judging by the coverage she was getting in the *Sanford Gazette,* but he noticed that she was not her usual garrulous, jovial self.

"I told you she'd be all right without drink, and she has been," Sheila told him when he confided in her after the Wednesday morning rush had died off. "But you are right. She's a fish out of water, and I have to wonder if she's not regretting going in for it."

"It looks to me like she'd love to have a real go at that

Ursula. And it would probably do her good. Get it off her chest." Joe waved at the café. "It's how she deals with everything here."

"But she's not here, Joe. Like I said, she's out of her natural environment and it's making her retreat into her shell a little. I'm sure she'll be fine when she comes back to us on Saturday."

"I hope so. The last thing I need is Brenda brooding on a bad week."

Sheila giggled. "Oh dear, what are we going to do with you, Joe? How do you cope when Brenda and I go away on holiday together?"

"The same way I cope when you're here. I manage the staff. And talking of holidays, you're going away soon, aren't you? Maybe that will help Brenda get over this fiasco." This time he waved at the TV screen where Brenda and accountant Marc Ulrich, sat out in the gardens, were debating the glorious summer weather.

"That's not until the first week in October," Sheila replied. "Another six weeks. Can you handle a depressed Brenda for the next month and a half?"

Joe shook his head. "I'll give George Robson a call. He'll cheer her up."

She laughed again. "She and George haven't been 'an item' for months now. You'll have to do better than that, boss."

***

Joe and Sheila were only partly right about Brenda's state of mind. She did wish she had never entered, and she was homesick, missing her friends, and there were so many aspects to I-Spy she had been unaware of before coming onto the show: the wearing of a radio-mike, for instance, and the constant need to replace the battery pack.

Even though it had been explained in the induction as necessary to ensure that their audio delivery would be properly picked up, Brenda (and one or two others if they were to be believed) had complained about it. At varying times during the day or evening, Master Spy would call each of the Housies to the video room for a one to one, and the replacement battery pack was waiting there for them (Brenda did not know how they got there, but assumed there must be an access panel as there was for bed linen and other 'necessities' in the dorms.

However, Master Spy, monitored telemetry from the packs and there was occasional need to change them during the day, if and when the battery alarm signalled low power. At such times, the Housies were expected to drop whatever they were doing to attend to the matter.

They were merely niggles. Brenda's major problem was anger, directed exclusively at Ursula Kenney.

When talking to the men, Ursula had unashamedly sucked up to them within hours of entering the house, but when dealing with her three female fellow Housies, she was never less than catty, often spiteful, clearly vindictive, and the confrontational approach which had manifested in the induction interview room on Saturday, was played out to the full before the cameras.

Everything about her annoyed Brenda. She complained that the cameras did not pan low enough to let her show her figure when she was in the shower, she whined when having to carry out her share of the daily chores, and even taking pills at bedtime was carried out with a showy, theatrical air.

"I need them for my pain," she had said on the first night. "I suffer terrible pain day and night and these are the only relief I get."

But she had never spelled out what the pain was or how it had come about.

The daily video interview with Master Spy provided an inadequate channel for the frustration. There were monitors all over the ground floor of the hall, where Housies could watch the same transmission as the viewing audience, but the one-to-one with Master Spy was the exception. None of the other Housies saw or heard the exchange, and it granted each of them the opportunity to be candid about their compatriots. A firm believer in never speaking ill of anyone she did not know well, Brenda lowered that strict standard when it came to discussing Ursula's antics.

"In a post-apocalyptic society, Ursula is the kind of woman who would be burned at the stake for her bitchiness," she said in one such interview. "And quite frankly, I'd be happy to light the bonfire."

Master Spy's response was typically unemotional. "Is this envy, Brenda? Is it because you fear that Ursula's popularity is higher than yours?"

"Not envy," Brenda replied. "Anger. She is manipulative with the men, scathing and autocratic with the women. If it goes on, I cannot guarantee to hold my tongue."

"The I-Spy house is a free environment, Brenda. You are at liberty to say what you feel, so long as you are not overtly abusive."

"What's she if not abusive?" Brenda demanded. "And she's not quiet about it, either."

"Your popularity has remained stable so far, Brenda. Are you afraid that if you were to try putting Ursula in her place, that popularity may nose dive?"

"Nothing of the kind. I'm so far gone I really don't care what the viewers think of me anymore. I'm simply concerned with not making a total fool of myself by letting that bloody woman get to me."

"We will watch developments with interest, Brenda. Thank you for your video thoughts."

Brenda was not the only one entertaining angry thoughts about Ursula. Tanya and Anne had both confessed their fury with the woman, and so too had the men.

Greg Ingham, a former street entertainer and pub singer, had told her, "Ursula is such a slut. She's screwing Dylan for all he's worth, and still coming onto me and the other two men. She lured me into the Romping Room once, and then did nothing but talk about her."

"I'm surprised you went for it, Greg," Brenda commented. "Especially as you're married."

He had laughed easily. "If she'd dropped her knickers

and said, 'come on, do your worst', I'd have turned her down. I went there because she said she wanted to talk to me, in private." He had laughed a second time. "Talk to me? Talk to me about her, more like."

Brenda had had no serious conversation with the carefree Dylan (although she did privately wonder if his freewheeling, good-humoured approach was a front generated by association with his Christian name) but both Marc Ulrich and Ben Oakley had admitted their dissatisfaction with Ursula's outrageous behaviour.

Marc, an accountant from Coventry, a man with an almost obsessive interest in the gardens at Gibraltar Hall, had admitted to Brenda that he had "visited the Romping Room with Ursula," but it was not something he was particularly proud of, and he wished he hadn't done it. Even though, like Greg, he had insisted nothing happened, Ursula had taken to referring to "big men" in his presence. "Men who know how to make it big."

Marc confessed he could not decide whether Ursula was referring to his physical attributes or his lack of ambition. At the age of 34, he was one amongst a team of accountants working for a large practice, and even to Brenda, it appeared that he was in no hurry to branch out alone, or even pursue a full partnership with his present employers. He preferred the 'safe' option of a regular salary.

If Brenda was the Mother of the House, then Ben Oakley was the Father. Aged 52, a widowed market trader from Birmingham, he was so close to Brenda in terms of age and outlook, that for a brief moment she even considered a meeting in the Romping Room when he suggested it. She changed her mind after he let slip the news that Ursula had lured him, too and, like Marc, Ursula had made him pay for the pleasure (of her company and chat only, Ben had insisted) often referring to the way "younger men have more going for them."

During the four full days they had been resident in the I-Spy house, Ursula had managed to alienate just about everyone other than Dylan. She had turned what should have been an enjoyable, knockabout week, into a trial by innuendo and insult, and Brenda found herself counting the hours to D-Day. Any thoughts of what she might do with the £25,000 prize (which she had never considered much of a possibility anyway) were pushed to the back of her mind in the simple desire to be out, home and with good, honest folk she knew and could trust.

Her Wednesday evening one to one with Master Spy took her mind from some of it, when the disembodied voice asked, "Have you received all the ingredients for your Thursday evening dinner, Brenda?"

"Yes thank you."

"You're under no obligation to do so, but would you like to tell Master Spy what the meal will be?"

"I gave this a lot of consideration before I came into the house," Brenda admitted. "I enjoyed Anne's apple pie, Marc's vegetarian lasagne and Dylan's beef goulash, but I come from a mining area in the north of England, where traditionally hard working men and women needed solid, nourishing food which wasn't hard to prepare and came within their limited budgets, so I've chosen to make a meat and potato pie."

"It sounds delicious, but does it come within the remit of nourishing, inexpensive and relatively simple to prepare?" Master Spy asked.

Brenda wondered about the actor behind the voice, how old (s)he was and whether (s)he had ever even heard of such plain food.

"Yes," she replied at length. "In fact, when I was a child, it would be considered something of a treat, usually enjoyed on a weekend when money was too tight to buy a roast. And I have my own way of doing it, and I like to spread a light dusting of flour on the crust after it's done."

She felt a thrill of good humour run through her when she said it, her mind's eye focussing on an image of Joe applauding her. She almost laughed aloud when that mental vision changed to one of Joe screaming at her for her habit of dusting the finished pie with flour.

"You're wasting flour," he would shout. "This is a meat and tater, not a bloody summer fruit pie, and the lorry drivers don't care whether it has a pretty dusting of snow on it or not."

Master Spy's voice brought her back to the reality of the cramped video room. "Alcohol is banned in the house, Brenda, but what wine would you serve with this meal?"

Brenda could not help herself this time she laughed aloud. "Bottled beer," she said. "Brown ale, light ale, milk stout, maybe even a bottle of Guinness."

"You're not a lover of wine?" Master Spy asked.

"I love a glass of wine, but you have to consider this meal in context. In a mining town such as Sanford, during the fifties and sixties, wine would not have been on the weekly shopping list."

She came out of the video room feeling a little brighter, having educated Master Spy (whom she saw as a young, cultured actor whose life had been a constant round of cocktail parties) on the finer points of colliery life in the mid-20th century. The news that her popularity had risen a point or two helped.

***

Watching Brenda's performance in the video room as it fed to the network, Scott Naughton shook his head. "Where the hell do we get these actresses to play Master Spy?"

Alongside him, Katy followed Brenda's progress back to the living room and a potential confrontation with Ursula. "Try 8. Looks like there's a row brewing up."

"Cut to 8," Naughton ordered.

"What do you mean about our Master Spy actresses?" Katy inquired.

"Brenda is how old? Fifty-five? She comes from a working class area in the north of England. What would they know about wines back then?"

Katy shrugged. "Search me. I know nothing about wines, now."

"So why did Master Spy ask the question?" Naughton grumbled. "It's time we got some people on this show who've lived a little." With an eye on the main feed, he said into his microphone, "Master Spy, get ready to intervene if this turns nasty."

"Lived like you, you mean?" Katy asked. "Shot a few baddies in the Falklands?"

"It was Bosnia, not the Falklands," Naughton snapped, "and I didn't shoot up a few baddies, as you put it. We were part of the UN peace-keeping mission." He narrowed his eyes on the screen once more. "Go to 12. This is hotting up."

***

"Good long session in there. Pouring your heart out, were you, Granny?"

Coming from anyone but Ursula, the remark would have been teasing, jocular, but with the addition of the ridiculous title and uttered by the shapely blonde, it finally got to Brenda.

"Can I ask what your problem is, Ursula?"

The baby blue eyes stared innocently into one of the cameras (and Naughton ordered a quick switch to 13). "I don't have a problem, Brenda."

Cheeks colouring, her gorge rising, Brenda rounded on her. "Aside from the pole sticking out of your backside." Her voice became a hiss. "In my job, I meet plenty of objectionable men and women. People who have no patience to wait their turn, people who are never satisfied no matter what you do for them. But I have never come across anyone as arrogant, spiteful and vindictive as you. I don't know where you went wrong in life, lady, but someone should have put you over their knee and tanned your arse until it was raw."

***

In the control room, Helen blanched. "Should we bleep

that out?"

"What? Arse?" Katy demanded. "That's nothing."

"I still think we should bleep it out."

***

Back in the living room, the argument quickly became more heated.

"At least I'm not trying to live my fifteen minutes of fame before I snuff it," Ursula shouted.

"No? You could have fooled me," Brenda snapped.

In the background, Ben could be heard muttering "hear, hear," and Ursula turned her fury on him.

"And what is it with you? A pair of crumblies sticking together, or are you hoping to get her knickers off?"

Dylan laughed, Ben blushed.

"Hey cool it, gals," Dylan suggested. "We don't wanna be coming to blows."

"And you can shut it, too, you gormless sod," Brenda snapped. "You've been jumping her since we got here."

"Hey, Granny, this is a free country and it ain't like I forced her."

"And less of the granny," Brenda retorted. She turned her fire on Ursula once more. "You're little better than a whore, tarting yourself for the cameras."

"You can't speak to me like that," Ursula screamed. "I'm under the doctor."

"That doesn't surprise me," Brenda growled. "You've been under all the men in this house at one time or another."

Tanya cackled, Anne Willis applauded (back in Sanford, half the town, including Joe and his crew, cheered Brenda on) and the men tried to look away.

The voice of Master Spy filled the room. "Ladies, this argument is getting personal. May I suggest you back off and chill out a little?"

Brenda glowered into the nearest camera. "And you can bugger off, too, you half-wit."

She turned on her heels and marched out of the room.

In the control room, Naughton breathed a loud sigh of relief. "Thank god for that. For a minute I thought they'd come to blows."

"It would have been an interesting scenario," Katy commented. "The old mare against the young viper. My money would be on Ursula."

Naughton snorted. "You think? I've met women like Brenda many times. She may be getting on a bit, but never bet against experience. She would have made mincemeat of that little tramp."

From her seat, Helen shook her head. "Can she speak like that to Master Spy?"

Naughton shrugged. "I don't see why not. The rules say that the Housies are obliged to respond to Master Spy. They don't say anything about telling her to bugger off, or calling her a half-wit." He removed his head set, and leaned back in his seat, allowing Katy to take over direction. "Besides, I don't know who we have on as Master Spy today, but she is a half-wit. And quite frankly, Helen, Brenda had a point. Ursula has been winding everyone up since day one. Everyone except Dylan, and she's been *getting* him up."

"It's what I-Spy is about," Helen pointed out. "Showing the Housies, warts and all, to the public."

"Then we shouldn't complain when one of them snaps."

"Hey up," Katy interrupted. "Look at Brenda."

They watched the monitor where Brenda appeared on the upper landing and marched past the ladies' dorm.

"What's she up to?" Naughton asked, slipping on his headset. "Go to 58 and track her."

Katy smiled. "She's going to the Romping Room."

"Stick with that feed. See if anyone follows her."

***

"You're charging me for the room?" Joe's disbelief was several decibels higher than normal.

Mick Chadwick, licensee of the Miner's Arms, nodded. "It's not my fault your members aren't interested in your disco."

"Yes it is," Joe argued. "You put up that TV for them to follow Brenda." He gestured across the room at the flatscreen TV hung on the wall.

"And you're playing that crappy music you all listen to," Mick responded, "but they're all more interested in Brenda than dancing, and that's not my fault. Besides, you put a telly up in your café for Brenda's I-Spy week."

"Yes, but I don't charge people to come in and watch. They buy food."

"And they buy ale here, but I still can't make them dance to your rubbish. I'm sorry, Joe, as far as I'm concerned, you're renting the room, the same as you always do."

Joe left the bar and rejoined Sheila at their table on the podium where his disco music poured from the laptop computer and through the room's speakers.

Ever since the formation of the Sanford 3rd Age Club, Wednesday evenings had seen the Miner's Arms host the weekly disco, with Joe as DJ, Sheila and Brenda his assistants. It was well-supported, and Mick's takings were guaranteed to be higher than any other weekday evening, as a consequence of which, he charged Joe only a nominal fee for the hire of the room and the sound set up.

Joe played music exclusively from the fifties, sixties and early seventies, the kind of music most of the club members had grown up with, and under normal circumstances, while Kathy Kirby blared *Secret Love* from the speakers, the dance floor would be packed.

Interest in Brenda's progress at a peak, everyone sat down, filling the tables around the dance floor, all eyes on the TV set where their favourite lady was tearing into Ursula, Dylan and Master Spy with a vengeance.

"Usually, I don't mind," Joe complained to Sheila, "but no one's taking a blind bit of notice of the music this week."

"They will," Sheila promised. "As soon as I-Spy's focus switches from Brenda to one of the other Housies."

"Gerra load of this," George Robson guffawed loudly. "Brenda off to the Romping Room. What's the betting Ben or Greg turns up in a minute?"

Sheila tutted her disapproval. "Idiot," she said to Joe.

"Yea, George is an idiot, but not as big a fool as that Ursula for taking Brenda on." Joe sipped his lager. "You don't think Brenda has something on with one of the men?"

"Jealous?" Sipping daintily at a gin and tonic, Sheila gave him a teasing glance. "Of course not. She may be a little free and easy, but she's not a tart." She put her glass down. "You don't know her as well as I do, Joe. She's not as rude or abrupt as you, but she can be very outspoken and when she loses her temper as she has with that Ursula Kenney, she needs to get out of everyone's way and cool off. That's why she's going to the Romping Room. It's the only place in that appalling house where they're guaranteed absolute privacy, and right now, she needs to be on her own, away from everyone, so she can cool down. You see if I'm not right."

A cheer went up from the floor. Checking the TV, Joe saw Ben Oakley making his way along the landing towards the Romping Room.

"Gerrin there, Ben," George Robson urged, and a ripple of laughter ran through the audience.

The crowd watched, their attention riveted, while Ben knocked on the Romping Room door. "Brenda," they heard him say. "Are you all right, Brenda?"

Her reply was muffled, as if she had removed her radio mike, but subtitles appeared at the bottom of the screen. "Go away, and leave me alone."

Sheila nodded her satisfaction. "See. I told you so."

***

Locking the door of the Romping Room and switching the 'engaged' light on, Brenda threw herself on the freshly made bed and stared up, concentrating her gaze on the ceiling light, breathing deeply until she could feel the virulent anger subsiding and her true self coming to the fore.

The process was underway when Ben knocked on the door, succeeding only in disturbing her concentration and irritating her again. She wanted to ask, "Where the hell were you when I needed you downstairs?" She refrained. Another argument would harm no one but her.

With him gone, calm overtook her once more, and as she came down from her raging high, she gradually began to take in her surroundings.

The crew had been quite particular when describing the place as the Private Room, stressing that it was not a 'Romping Room' as everyone called it. But the description, like so many other aspects of I-Spy, did not match the reality. The video room was more in keeping with Brenda's idea of a private room. In here there was nothing but the bed, a few hangers on the wall where Housies could hang their clothing, and the ubiquitous hatch which, so legend had it, was where the backroom staff left fresh bed linen for users.

It may not be known officially as the Romping Room, but the overall ambience was of exactly that. A room where men and women could do little but get together on the king sized divan bed. A room where they could romp.

The thought only ignited her anger once more. Not for the first time, she considered taking part in I-Spy to be a mistake of the highest magnitude. She and her fellow Housies had ceased to be human beings; Joe had said they were animals and he was right. They had become exhibits in a zoo, with their pluses, minuses, highs and lows, foibles and frailties on display to the media and the millions following the programme.

Chapter Five

By three o'clock Thursday afternoon, Brenda felt slightly better.

Ambling around the gardens, enjoying the sun, talking with Anne Willis, she candidly admitted her relief that they had less than forty-eight hours of the nightmare to endure.

"I shall be glad to get back to my life and friends," she said. "Don't you feel the same?"

"It depends on what you call a life," Anne replied. "Where I come from unemployment is rocketing and car rentals are down. We're never quite sure if we'll be in business from one month to another." She sighed. "That twenty-five thousand would have been useful, but I reckon the serious betting is on Ursula."

They reached the high, waney lap screens which cut this part of the garden off from the crew's access, and turned back towards the topiary exhibits.

"Don't they have the same statues on the other side of the screens?" Anne asked.

"Can't remember," Brenda said, chewing her lip. In truth, overnight events were still playing on her mind and she was not interested in the garden landscaping. "Yesterday didn't help matters. I had to see Master Spy early today because I'm cooking dinner, and according to him or her, my popularity took a bit of a dip, probably because of the argument. I just wonder if that's a polite way of hinting that Ursula picked up a few sympathy votes."

Anne laughed. "What we need is someone to come along and bump Ursula off. Give the rest of us a fighting chance."

"Now, now," Brenda said, frowning her disapproval. "For all that I don't like her, we can't blame her for the way she behaves. It's par for the course these days, isn't it? Any and every celebrity, no matter how small, behaves like they own the world, and we shouldn't wish any harm on her." She, too, laughed. "You couldn't kill her anyway. My boss, Joe Murray would be on the case in no time."

Alarm spread across Anne's face. "Your boss? Are you with the police, or something?"

Brenda chuckled. "The law? Not likely. Joe's too short for the police. No, he owns the café where I work, and he's an old, old friend. He's also the best amateur detective in the country. He's helped the police solve loads of crimes, including a few murders." Brenda's smile faded to wistful. "He's a very clever man, and trust me, nothing gets past Joe." They walked on. "He's one of those I'm so looking forward to seeing at the weekend," Brenda went on as they skirted the ballerina-shaped bush. "Dear friends; lots of them, and they're all coming to Chester for D-Day."

Anne laughed. "A reception committee?" Her smile faded, too, but not all the way. "You're lucky. My old man's coming down with the kids, but that's about it."

Brenda's eyebrows shot up. "You're married? I never realised. I'm sorry."

"Nay bother. I don't think I've mentioned it to anyone. Been wed twelve years now. Three kids, too. It'll be nice to see 'em again, but I was hoping I might have seen them with a bit more money in me pocket."

"How does your husband feel about you leaving them for a week to live with three other women and four men?"

Anne shrugged as they turned for the house. "He doesn't mind as long as I'm not up to... you know... anything. And I wouldn't, would I? Not on telly. Anyway, he's outta work, so he has nothing better to do than sit round the house looking after the kids."

Brenda felt bewildered by the confession. "All I can say is if my Colin were still here and I'd suggested it, he'd have gone right up the wall."

"Ballistic, you mean? Why?"

"Because when I got married, back in the 1970s, it wasn't

the done thing." Brenda's features became glum. "Mind you, when I got married, there was nothing like I-Spy on telly. We had this documentary thing called *The Family*, but that was a genuine, fly-on-the-wall series, not a deliberately false set up like this."

They reached the rear patio where Tanya sat talking with Greg and Ben. Brenda greeted them with a smile, Anne with a wave.

"We were just saying we're looking forward to your meal tonight, Brenda," Greg reported. "Not going to give us a hint what you're doing?"

Brenda and Anne joined them. "All I will say, Greg, is you enjoyed Anne's apple pie on Monday, and Dylan's goulash on Tuesday, so you should love this." She looked around. "And talking of Dylan, where is he? And where are Marc and Her Ladyship?"

"Dylan is with Ursula, somewhere," Ben said.

"No prizes for guessing where." Greg laughed and the rest joined in.

"Don't know about Marc," Tanya said. "Haven't seen him since lunchtime."

"Maybe Ursula is into threesomes," Greg suggested with a saucy gleam in his eye.

"Don't get me started," Brenda warned, and she, too, smiled to show she was only joking.

She took a lounger and leaned back, gazing up into the sky. An airliner circled, on approach to Liverpool John Lennon Airport, and lower down, was a media helicopter.

"Don't look now," she said, "but we're all on candid camera."

As one they looked up and waved at the press.

"That'll be all over the tabloids tomorrow," Ben declared. "Warring Housies call a truce to sunbathe."

Marc came out of the house and joined them, his face edged with worry. "Hi, guys. Has anyone seen, er, the cord from my dressing gown?"

Brenda turned her face away in an effort to hide her smile. Marc had proved a notorious fusspot, and reticent to the point of near silence in speaking out. Old for his years, he had arrived in the living room most mornings still wearing striped pyjamas and a faded, dark blue dressing gown, its cord tied tightly around his midriff.

"Not me," Ben said.

"Haven't seen it," Greg replied. "You could ask Dylan, but I think he's busy right now, with the bitch queen."

Marc grimaced. "Yes. I heard them when I passed the, er, Romping Room."

"That bed must be built like the ones we have at the hospital," Tanya said. "Or maybe they're secretly working for the company that makes them."

"Bed testers not so anonymous." Greg laughed and again everyone joined in.

Even Marc managed a smile before saying, "Oh, they're not… you know. They were talking when I passed. Sounded a bit, excited, too. The both of them."

"Maybe they were just building up to it," Greg suggested, and everyone laughed again.

Brenda checked her watch. "Half past three," she declared. Time I was getting things together for dinner."

***

With the wall clock registering four in the afternoon, Joe closed the door on the last of the day's customers, locked up and turned the sign to 'closed'.

As always, the moment the Lazy Luncheonette ceased trading for the day, most of his irritation left him, and he joined Sheila and Cheryl near the counter for a final beaker of tea. Once they left, he would take the day's takings up to his apartment, bring the books up to date, and then switch off totally.

On the wall above table 13, the TV played out the I-Spy drama, showing Brenda working in the kitchen, a bag of plain flour at her elbow, rolling out her pastry for the evening meal. Her forearms were bared, covered in the flour and she worked with a strength belying her feminine frame.

"She was always the best with a rolling pin," Sheila commented.

"And I suppose there's many a man who can vouch for it," Joe quipped. "You know what you're doing for tomorrow and over the weekend, Cheryl?"

"What?" Cheryl dragged her eyes from the TV. "Oh. Yes. Stop worrying, Uncle Joe. Me and Lee have run the place before for you, and we've never bankrupted you yet. We know exactly what to do."

"Good girl," Joe approved. "Remember, one of these days, all this will be yours."

Cheryl gazed glumly round the café. "I'm so thrilled."

Sheila laughed, Cheryl grinned and Joe rolled a cigarette. "Bloody kids. You're just trying to wind me up so I'll have a heart attack and you can get your hands on the place sooner." He drank more tea. "I'll be here first thing in the morning, but I have to leave at half past seven to get everyone on the bus at the Miner's Arms. You've arranged for your two pals to come in? Pauline and Franny?"

Cheryl nodded. "They'll be here. And you want me to pay them out of the takings?"

"Back pocket earnings," Joe grumbled. "If the tax man ever rumbles it, we're all in the sh... sugar." He turned his attention on Sheila. "Did we circulate the members who are on the trip? Only everyone was too interested in Brenda last night."

"I emailed them all first thing this morning, Joe, and those I couldn't email, I phoned. Everything is in hand. So stop worrying."

"I'm not worrying. I'm just being organised." He nodded at the TV. "Which is more than those clowns are."

Sheila frowned. "How do you mean?"

"Look at the space Brenda has to work in. I noticed the other night when that Anne woman was making the apple pie. One tiny worktop and she had to prepare the fruit and the pastry in the same area. Too much cleaning down between jobs."

Sheila, too, studied the cramped area where Brenda was

working on her pastry. "I see what you mean. I have more space in my kitchen, and that's not particularly large."

"It's for the hatches," Cheryl said, and they both looked at her for further explanation. "See, the Housies are not allowed to bring anything in with them, other than a few personal items. But they need stuff as they go through the week. Brenda needed the diced steak, the flour and potatoes. The backroom bods have to get all that to her, so the house is riddled with hatches where they can pass stuff through. And behind the hatches there's, like, massive spaces, nearly the size of the rooms, where the crew operate. I should think it's taken something off the kitchen."

"You seem to know an awful lot about it, Cheryl," Sheila observed.

Cheryl laughed. "It's one of my favourite programmes. Our Lee bought me the I-Spy Annual last Christmas and there's loadsa pages in it, telling you how it all works behind the scene."

"The I-Spy Annual?" Joe asked. When Cheryl nodded, he shook his head sadly. "I think I'll stick with the *Beano*."

***

Camera 27 blinked and blacked out for the third time in four hours.

"Stock feed on twenty-seven." Naughton barked. "Ten seconds ago." With an irritated sigh, he asked, "What the hell is going on with that camera?"

"Been like it all week." Katy said. "We've replaced it three times, now. One of the techs reckoned it must be something to do with the heat coming from the ovens."

"Never been a problem at any other location," Naughton pointed as the stock feed showed on 27 and the blanked screen moved to a fresh monitor.

It consisted of footage taken in the kitchen during the month when Gibraltar Hall was being prepared for the series. Such footage had been taken from all cameras to be used in the event of a breakdown.

"Maybe we had more space to work in other locations," Helen speculated. "Or maybe they were better ventilated. I'd have to check on that. Cut to the wider shot, Scott. Greg is poking his nose in and I think Brenda is about to give him a piece of her mind."

"Cue 13," Naughton called, "and go."

The view on the main monitor switched to a wide angle of Brenda approaching Greg who was checking the canisters on the worktop by the ovens.

"These cameras are designed to work in a range of temperatures, Helen," Naughton said. "Maybe the problem is with the wiring."

"With less than forty-eight hours to go, I'm not sending a team in to rewire 27," Helen declared. "We'll have to muddle through as best we can.

"Cut to 12," Naughton ordered. "No argument between Brenda and Greg."

***

In the kitchen corner of the living room, Brenda had caught Greg checking through the various shakers on the worktop.

"What are you nosying at?" she demanded as he replaced the lid on her flour shaker.

"I'm looking for sugar," he pleaded and held up a cup and saucer. "For my coffee."

Brenda moved the flour shaker to the rear of the worktop and slid the sugar across to him. "You're the second one. Dylan was looking for it earlier. Now clear off."

"Thanks," he grinned and shook some into his coffee.

While he stirred, he checked the ovens. "Smells delicious, Brenda. Some kinda pie, but what's in it?"

Brenda grinned. "I was going to do *Ursula au vin*, but I couldn't find a van to run her over with."

Greg laughed. Keeping his voice low, he said, "You're just as evil as her, but you're more fun."

"Fun is my middle name."

Working late into the evening on the Sanford 3rd Age Club monthly newsletter, Joe found his attention constantly distracted by events in the I-Spy house.

Brenda's meat and potato pie had gone down well with the Housies. All except Dylan who, despite his earlier appetite, had gone off his feed by the time they sat down to eat.

He was full of apologies, naturally. "Sorry, Brenda. Been nibbling between meals. Excellent, though."

The only other comment had come, predictably, from Ursula, who had cleared her plate before saying, "God knows what this'll do to my figure."

Joe was mad as hell at her. He recognised it as another attempt to have a go at Brenda. "It's not a real gripe," he said to Sheila on the phone. "She gobbled that pie down like she hadn't eaten for a month."

Brenda, however, was wiser than Joe. Unlike Wednesday, she refused to rise to Ursula's sly dig. Instead, she said, "It won't do you any harm to put a few pounds on, Ursula. It'll turn you into a man's woman."

For a moment it looked as if Ursula would rise to the bait, but she did not. Instead, she opened her mouth in a gaping yawn. "Tired. Early night for me, I think."

That did not happen either. After dinner, the Housies retired outside to enjoy the last of the evening sun, where they began to chat, and inevitably, the talk soon turned to reminiscences of their collective experience over the last few days. To Joe's relief, and no doubt Brenda's, the spat of the previous evening was not mentioned. Even Ursula took part in the debate with minimal animosity.

With one eye on them, Joe found his concentration on the club newsletter and a potential Murder Mystery Weekend in Lincoln later in the year, at best distracted, at worst waning.

At 11:15, he gave it up and switched off the computer. He had to be up early the following morning anyway ("When don't I?" he grumbled to himself) and his enthusiasm for the newsletter had been taken over by the promise of a weekend in Chester, D-Day at the I-Spy house and the programme itself. But now that everyone had gone off to bed at Gibraltar Hall, there was nothing of to keep him up.

He picked up the TV remote and was about to switch off when the view, which had been swapping between the men's dorm and the ladies, suddenly switched back to the latter, where Ursula was sitting up on the edge of the bed.

She took a cautious glance around at her companions, all of whom appeared to be sleeping, then slid her feet into carpet slippers and quietly left the room.

With a cigarette to finish, Joe put the remote down, and watched. It was not, in his opinion, the most riveting spectacle on TV, and if Brenda were not taking part, he would not have tuned in at all, but like so many viewers (according to the newspapers) this vexatious woman had attracted and fixed his attention.

Unlike so many of the viewers (again according to the newspapers) Joe did not believe her actions were real.

Several psychologists and sociologists, all of them way better qualified than he, had commented on her behaviour, putting forward many theories for her antics, but in Joe's humble opinion, they had missed the obvious. She had trained as an actress and that meant she was well capable of faking anything she wanted. It did occur to him that he was biased in favour of Brenda and he could well be wrong, but he had expressed the opinion so many times in the last week, he'd left no one in doubt as to where he stood.

The view switched to the upper landing as Ursula emerged onto the landing, looked both ways and then turned to her left. Joe wondered how the camera switch worked. It was his understanding that there were no technicians or backroom boys on after ten in the evening.

"Movement sensors," he said to himself. "It's the only way."

Ursula carried on along the corridor, weaving from side to side, and once put out a hand to steady herself, leaving Joe to assume she was drunk; an idea which gave him hope for Brenda. Alcohol was against the I-Spy rules. Halfway along the landing, Ursula stopped. Again she looked left and right and then entered the Romping Room.

"Dirtbag," Joe grumbled.

He watched for a few minutes longer. The view switched back to the men's dorm, then the women's as one or other Housey moved in their beds, but no one got up. Eventually Joe shut down the TV, and following the Housies' lead, went to bed.

***

Ursula yawned and checked her watch again. Where the hell was he? His note had said half past eleven and it was almost midnight.

Her thin nightwear already removed, she felt warm enough in the temperature controlled environment, but even naked, she felt the weight of fatigue pressing in on her. She really didn't feel like it but he'd been her only true ally this week. It was the least she could do to reward him for his loyalty.

The paradox was not lost on her. His loyalty had been secured by sex and now she would grant him her body again to ensure that same loyalty.

"Well, girl, what's your body for if not to get what you want?"

The thought brought back memories of twenty years ago and another night with another man. To this day she still felt the full revulsion at some of the things she had done. And for what? Oh, he had kept his side of the bargain, but the promise of stardom had never quite materialised. She also remembered her fear when the police interviewed her after he had died. As if she had anything to do with it.

He got what he deserved, she thought to herself, *but I never did.*

In order to suppress the distressing recollections, she forced more memories to the fore. If that hadn't happened she wouldn't be here, now, standing on the threshold of a renewed career in the spotlight. Victor's death, ignominious and shaming though it may have been for his reputation, had nonetheless brought her to this point.

Where the hell was this idiot? Why wasn't he here? She checked the time again and read only a few minutes further on from the last time she had looked.

She would give him another twenty minutes. After that, he could sod off. With less than 48 hours to go in this hell hole, she would have no more need for him anyway.

Fantasies of her new rich and famous lifestyle invaded her mind, and while she indulged them her eyelids began to droop and she nodded off to sleep.

***

"Where is Ursula?" Naughton grumbled. "Don't tell me she's in the Romping Room again."

On the main feed, seven of the eight Housies were settling down to breakfast in the dining area of the living room. Some of them had complained verbally about headaches, Brenda, Naughton noticed, had taken two paracetamol, and without exception they appeared to be drinking a lot of water.

"Is there some kind of bug running through the house?" he had asked before his comment on Ursula.

"Dunno about a bug," Katy said, "but if Ursula is in the Romping Room, she's on her own. The rest of them are here." She waved a hand vaguely at the main monitor.

"Master Spy," Naughton ordered, "ask the Housies for a volunteer to drag Ursula out of the Romping Room. Preferably one of the women, preferably not Brenda and not Tanya."

"You're not leaving me a lot of choice, are you?" Master Spy's voice came back over the private channel.

"Brenda might throttle her and Tanya might try to seduce her," Naughton retorted.

"That's appalling," Katy protested. "Tanya might be batting for the other side, but it's not been an issue with anyone all week."

"Playing it safe," Naughton assured her. "We don't want another battle like the one we had the other night."

Master Spy's voice burst through the main feed. "Anne, may we ask you to go to the Romping Room and check on Ursula, please?"

"No problem," Anne replied and excusing herself, left the breakfast table.

Greg also excused himself to visit the toilet. "Told you I wasn't too good last night, didn't I?"

In the control room, Naughton groaned. "I knew it. A stomach bug. Get onto services. I wanna know about that meat we gave Brenda for her pie yesterday."

Katy picked up the telephone.

"And get Helen in here," Naughton ordered as his assistant began to speak into the receiver. "Tell her it's hit the fan big time." He jabbed his microphone button. "Master Spy, ask the Housies if everyone is feeling yuk."

Almost immediately Master Spy's voice overrode the muted conversation of the Housies. "May I ask, are you all feeling unwell this morning?"

A general chorus of assent came from the occupants of the living room as Helen entered the control centre and studied the monitors.

"What's the problem, Scott?" she asked.

"Dunno for sure, but the best odds are on a tummy bug."

"Damn, no. Not this close to the end. Serious?"

"I told you it looks like a tummy bug," Naughton grumbled as the Housies reported their symptoms to Master Spy. "You now know as much as I do."

Helen pointed to camera 58 and Anne making her way along the upper landing. "What is she doing there?"

"Ursula is in the Romping Room. We sent Anne to get her."

"But if she's at it with…"

"She's alone," Naughton interrupted. "Switch to 58 and follow Anne for the moment."

The main monitor came up with the view and Naughton

concentrated his attention on the side monitors where the Housies were amplifying their complaints.

Anne knocked on the door. "Ursula. Are you in there, Ursula?"

"Idiot," Katy griped. "Of course she's in there. Nowhere else she can be."

Anne knocked again.

"Master Spy, deal with it," Katy ordered.

"Knock one more time, Anne," Master Spy's voice came over, "and if there's no response, enter the room. Ursula may have fallen asleep."

Anne did as she was told. After knocking again, she timidly opened the door and stepped into the Romping Room, saying, "Ursula. It's me. Anne."

There was a moment of silence, then an ear-splitting shriek filled the upper landing. Anne raced out of the room and stared into the camera, her face white, a mask of pure horror.

"Ursula. She's dead."

Chapter Six

"Kill that feed," Helen barked.

"Kill fifty-seven and fifty-eight," Naughton ordered. "Run stock feeds from 201 and 202." His eye fell on the side monitors where the Housies had heard Anne's scream and were making for the exit to the stairs. "Master Spy, get the Housies to stay put and order Anne back down the stairs."

"Kill live transmission," Helen barked.

"What? On the strength of Anne's say so?" Katy demanded.

"Just do it. Run stock feeds. And get a tech up to the Romping Room service hatch," Naughton ordered. "Tell them to check on Ursula and radio direct to us on channel 3." He picked up a handheld radio, switched it on and tuned it to the appropriate channel.

Katy leapt to obey.

A near riot was breaking out in the living room, and Master Spy floundered in a futile attempt to hold it off.

"What the bloody hell is going on?" Ben shouted, his face unnervingly close to a camera.

"That scream sounded like Anne," Greg said. "Has Ursula attacked her?"

As live transmission gave way to stock footage, Naughton overrode the flustered Master Spy. "This is Scott Naughton from the control room," he barked through the communication channel. "There's been an incident upstairs." He glanced at the live feed from the landing where Anne was on her knees sobbing. Concentrating on the living room again, where the Housies had all paused to listen to him, he went on, "Tanya, you're a nurse. Brenda,

73

you're possibly the calmest right now. Get yourselves upstairs to the landing and help Anne. Bring her downstairs. Guys, I'll have to ask you to stay put until we work out what's going on."

The Housies watched the two women scurry to follow Naughton's orders.

"Anne, Brenda and Tanya aren't in any danger, are they?" Ben asked. "Only it sounded like someone has been attacked."

"No. No danger. Anne is safe. You have my word on that." Naughton killed the channel and opened his link to Master Spy. "Keep the guys occupied," he said.

Almost immediately the hand radio beeped for attention. Helen picked it up. "Control."

"Security here, ma'am, at the service hatch behind the Romping Room. Lady is telling it like it is. Ursula is hanging from one of the coat hooks. Just looking at her, I'd guess she's been dead some time."

"Thank you. Seal that hatch off. No one goes near it." Helen put down the radio and addressed her crew. "Kill all transmission, get me a video line to the TV station and someone call the police."

On screen 58, Naughton saw Tanya helping Anne to her feet while Brenda edged her way into the Romping Room. "Brenda, no," he barked and, recalling he had shut down his communication channel, opened it again and repeated, "Brenda, don't go in there."

"Scott –" Brenda began but the director cut her off.

"Ursula is dead," he blurted out. "No one can go into that room until the police have examined it. We don't know what evidence you may disturb. Now please. Just shut the door and come back downstairs."

Brenda looked into the room as if she were about to disobey, but then reached for the door, closed it, and turned back to help Tanya with the distraught Anne.

Helen was already speaking to the TV station headquarters in London.

"Has this been confirmed?" the suited executive at the

other end of the link demanded.

"Visual confirmation only, sir," Helen replied with due deference to his superior status. "We've called the police and we really cannot carry on with the broadcast until we have clearance from them."

"We'll need something to fill the screens," the executive replied. "All right, Helen. We'll handle the matter from our end, but you'd better speak to your head office, too."

"I'll be on the line to them in a few minutes, but I thought you should be first to know, sir, since your channel is carrying the programme."

Naughton turned away, a scowl registering his disinterest in corporate politics. "Open me a line to the Housies," he ordered Katy.

He watched Brenda and Tanya help the still-distressed Anne into the living room.

"All right, people," he said, "Get yourselves sat down and you'd better prepare yourselves for a shock." He watched as they provided Anne with a cup of tea, then announced, "We cannot positively confirm it right now, but we believe Ursula is dead." He paused a moment to let the news sink into the stunned faces. "From the description security have given us, it looks as if she took her own life. For the time being, we are off air, and we have no choice but to restrict your movements until the police arrive and tell us what we can and cannot do, and where we can and can't go. Stick to the living room. I know it's awkward with you all being unwell and only the one toilet down there, but please stay there until the cops are through with their initial inquiries."

Marc appeared worried. "Will the, er, the police want to, you know, speak to us? I mean, if she killed herself, what can we, sort of, tell them?"

Brenda, hugging Anne, spoke up before Naughton could say anything. "Doesn't matter how she died. They'll want statements from each of us."

Her assuredness irritated the director. "You sound pretty certain of that, Brenda."

"I am. I've been involved in this kind of thing before."
Brenda appeared instantly aware of the focus of attention on
her, and hurried to clarify her meaning. "I don't mean I've
been accused or interrogated, you idiots."

"Then what do you mean?" Naughton asked.

Brenda sighed. "I was telling Anne yesterday, I have this
friend. He's also my boss. Joe Murray. He may be a simple
cook and small businessman, but don't let that fool you.
He's the best detective this side of a bloodhound. He's on
his way to Chester, today. It was a prior arrangement. He
and some of my friends are coming out to meet me for D-
Day. When Joe gets to know about this, he'll check it out,
and believe me, if he suspects anything he'll persuade the
police to let him investigate. And when Joe Murray gets his
teeth into it, the police will question us all seven ways from
Sunday."

"How will he get to know?" Tanya asked.

"The police will give a statement to the press." Brenda
checked her watch. "It's five to nine. Joe will have been on
the coach from Sanford for the last fifty-five minutes, and
they'll get it on the bus's radio. He'll be knocking on the
door here before lunch."

***

Brenda's analysis was almost right, but Joe would not
learn about events at Gibraltar Hall via the radio.

Clipboard in hand, he saw the last of the club members
onto the coach at 7:50, and then climbed aboard himself.
Sheila and Brenda liked to sit together, and usually, Joe
would take the jump seat by the door, but in Brenda's
absence, he sat with Sheila on the front, nearside seat.

Ahead of him, Keith Lowry, the driver always appointed
to STAC outings, stood fiddling with a TV receiver fixed
behind his seat and above the centre of the aisle where
everyone but he would be able to see it.

"It's a brand new bus, Joe," he reported. "The boss
bought it for long haul, continental tours so the passengers

would have something to watch while they're going through Europe."

"And he hasn't got any continental tours on right now?"

Keith grinned. "A three-day trip to Disneyland, Paris. But that's not until after Christmas."

"You're telling me that this telly will pick up English channels while it's in Europe?" Joe's tones spelled out his disbelief.

"Do you still have to shovel coal into the boiler on your TV?" Keith demanded, aiming the remote that controlled the TV set. "We're talking satellite, man. On the move. These buses have had it for years."

In no mood for lectures on modern TV, mobile or otherwise, Joe asked, "So why has the old man given it to us? If he expects me to pay more, he can whistle for it."

Keith laughed again as he found the channel he was seeking. He handed the remote to Joe who tucked it in the pocket of his gilet. "There you go, you miserable old bugger. You can be in charge of the telly between counting your coppers. And, no, he isn't charging you more. He figured it would be a bit of goodwill. He said you'd want to watch Brenda while we were on the way to Chester."

Keith took his seat, closed the door, shutting out the heat of another fine, summer's day and, with the clock approaching five minutes to eight, they pulled off the car park of the Miner's Arms into the morning traffic jam on Doncaster Road.

"How long?" Joe asked when they dropped onto the M62 ten minutes later.

"At this time of day a good two hours," Keith reported. He waved at the traffic climbing the hill to the junction with M1 outside Leeds. "It'll be like this all the way over the Pennines, and then we have to get round Manchester. That's another half an hour. Once we get past Manchester Airport, it'll be what? Forty minutes. We'll be there for ten."

"Time's not a problem, Joe," Sheila said, digging into her bag and coming out with a glossy visitor's guide to Chester. "We've nothing formal planned for today, so it's only a case

77

of checking into the hotel and then everyone can do their own thing."

"You know me," Joe responded. "I like value for money and we're booked into the hotel for ten a.m. Getting there on time means we get the most out of the weekend, and even if we're ten minutes late, I feel like I've been cheated." He nodded to the PA mike above Sheila's head and she passed it to him. Switching it on, he tapped the head to ensure it was working before speaking into it. "All right, good morning everyone. Can I just spell out what's ahead for the weekend? Keith tells me we should be in Chester on time, for about ten o'clock. Once you've checked into the Victoria Hotel, the day is yours to do as you wish. Tomorrow, we have the big coming out parade for Brenda and we're going down to Gibraltar Hall to welcome her. Then there's a party in the hotel tomorrow night. I'll be running the disco, as usual. On Sunday you can do as you please, but the Victoria do a very nice, three course lunch. I'll be running another disco from half past eight Sunday evening. For Monday, we've come to an arrangement with the hotel. You need to be out of your room by ten in the morning, but they'll store your luggage until Keith comes for us at four in the afternoon. Remember, none of this is compulsory, but it's all included in the amount you paid, so it's up to you whether you take part or not. That's all I have to say for now. I'll leave you to watch Brenda in the I-Spy house."

He switched the mike off, handed it to Sheila who hung it back up, and Joe dipped into his rucksack for a paperback copy of *From Russia with Love*.

"James Bond?" Sheila asked, her eyebrows rising.

Joe grinned. "Well, Brenda's been ruled by Master Spy all week."

While Joe lost himself in the machinations of SMERSH operatives Kronsteen and Klebb, his concentration only occasionally disturbed by laughter or comments from his fellow passengers, the coach stuttered its way through the heavy traffic between Leeds and Bradford and into the heavier stuff making for Manchester, when angry interjections from Keith also began to disturb his reading.

Forty-five minutes later, they were cruising down the hill towards Rochdale, Joe's head filled with the potted biography of Donovan 'Red' Grant when a general chorus of complaints reached his ear and Sheila nudged him.

"What?" He demanded. "I'm trying to read."

Sheila pointed up to the TV set. "It's gone off."

Joe fumed. "Hey, Keith, this telly's on the blink."

"So what do you want me to do, man? Wave a magic wand?" Keith grumbled. "Have you seen the traffic? Friday bloody morning and Manchester is its usual hell and I've more to think about than the bleeding TV reception."

Joe fished the remote control from his pocket, and aimed it at the TV. As he was about to press the button, the face of a station announcer filled the screen.

"We're sorry about this interruption to the transmission from the I-Spy house. We understand that there is some kind of problem at their end. We're working to resolve the matter. In the meantime, here's a cartoon."

She disappeared and *Tom and Jerry* appeared on screen.

Joe put the remote back in his gilet and returned to his reading.

Keith continued to struggle with the traffic, which showed no inclination to thin out, even after he left the M62 at junction 18 and joined the M60 (East) following the signs for Manchester Airport. The drone of the engine, combined with the hum of conversation were enough to send Joe into a stupor where the words of Ian Fleming began to make no sense, and as the coach passed the Junction for Oldham and Central Manchester, he gave up and put the book away.

"I'll get some shuteye instead," he said to Sheila, and leaned back in his seat.

A further twenty minutes went by and they were passing the airport when she nudged him again. "Joe. Quick. The news."

Startled into full awareness, he looked up at the TV screen. The cartoons had gone, and now they were looking on the grim face of a reporter standing outside the I-Spy house where they had said goodbye to Brenda the previous Saturday.

"I-Spy ceased transmission just before nine a.m.," the reporter declared. "A few minutes ago, we were given a statement by on site producer, Helen Catterick to the effect that Housey, Ursula Kenney was found dead in the Private Room at eight fifty-five. All the signs are that she took her own life."

***

Detective Chief Inspector Frank Hoad grimaced at the sight of Ursula's body being carefully let down from the clothing hook from which she had been hanging. The mortuary attendants lowered her into a body bag and sealed it up, then looked at him for approval.

"All right," Hoad said. "Take her away."

At the age of 43, Hoad had been in the police force over 20 years, and had seen death violent and otherwise, too many times for it to have an effect upon him. "This is different, Azi," he said.

Detective Sergeant Azizur Rahman adjusted his thick glasses. "Different, sir?"

"We've been watching her all week," Hoad pointed out. "She's been there on the TV, alive, causing ructions in this bloody place, and now..." He sucked in his breath. "All right, lad. Let's talk to these people."

With Rahman leading, they followed the mortuary attendants from the Romping Room and along the landing, past the men's dorm to the access door at the far end, which had now been unlocked, so the police could get to the Romping Room without meeting the Housies.

In contrast to Rahman's younger, leaner, more athletic frame, Hoad was a stocky, powerfully built man. Not made for pursuing villains, he was nevertheless quite at home confronting them. He had made his way slowly, methodically through the ranks, and if his approach had changed with promotion, it had more to do with age than any lack of willingness to physically tackle criminals.

Rahman, on the other hand, had only recently been promoted to CID. Aged only 28, he held the Queen's Police Medal after taking action to resolve a hostage situation during an armed robbery. His action had almost cost him his sight, and there had been many debates about the role he could fulfil after he returned to duty. Eventually, the Police Federation had secured a posting to Chester CID on his behalf and, Hoad had to admit, the younger man was an asset, even if he did miss certain things thanks to his defective sight.

At the top of the back staircase, they waited, allowing the mortuary attendants to manhandle Ursula's body down the stairs.

"You been following this drivel, Azi?" Hoad asked.

Rahman chuckled. "Only by compulsion, sir. My wife and daughters have, but it's not really my thing."

"Me neither but I have a couple of teenagers at home, and they've been glued to the TV all week." The chief inspector frowned. "Rum do, this. She's been acting like a complete bitch all week, and now she's decided to top herself. Why?"

"Maybe that's why she's been behaving like a complete bitch all week, sir."

"Yes. Maybe. All right, lad, we need to talk to the backroom crew here, and then the other lags." He held up an evidence bag containing the long, white cord with which Ursula had been hanged. "And I wanna know who this belongs to."

"You don't think it was hers, sir?"

"It's the cord off an old-fashioned dressing gown, Azi, and if you've watched this I-Spy crap at all, you'll know that she was anything but old fashioned." With the mortuary attendants gone, Hoad set off down the stairs. "Come on. Let's get to it."

***

"In an updated statement, Detective Chief Inspector Frank Hoad of Chester CID says that Ursula hanged herself using the cord from a dressing gown belonging to Housey, Marc Ulrich, which she probably took from him earlier in the week. Although the police do not suspect anyone else of being involved in the incident, they are nevertheless questioning the Housies and the backroom team here at Gibraltar Hall."

His face a mask of frustration, Joe looked away from the latest television report from outside Gibraltar Hall, and instead fumed at the heavy traffic making for Chester city centre.

"Bloody rubbish," he growled.

Sheila drew her attention away from the TV news, and followed his gaze. "Rubbish, Joe? Chester, or the volume of traffic?"

"I-bloody-spy," Joe replied. "Suicide, my eye. She was murdered."

Sheila blanched. "Don't go saying things like that, Joe. You could implicate Brenda."

"That's not the reaction I'd expect from a police inspector's wife," Joe chided her. "Of course we know Brenda wouldn't hurt her, but that doesn't alter the fact that Ursula did not kill herself. Listen, Sheila, when we get to the hotel, can you handle everything while I get off down to Gibraltar Hall?"

Sheila tutted. "You don't seriously imagine the police will take any notice of you?"

"They will," Joe assured her. "They always do. Even your Peter, rest in peace, always listened to me when I had something to say. I'm telling you, that woman was in no state to commit suicide the way they've described it. I'll tell you something else, too, the investigating officer will keep the Housies on ice until he's through with his inquiries. We both know what Brenda's like. We know how tough she can be, but we also know how worried she'll be. I have to go down there and see if I can persuade the police to let me work with them." He checked the exterior again as Keith pulled into the forecourt of the Victoria. "Looks like we're here. You just handle the members, Sheila. I'll grab a taxi and go down there."

"You will keep me informed?"

Joe fished his mobile phone from his pocket. "Scout's honour. Let me check in first. I'll drop my bag in my room and get off to Gibraltar Hall."

Keith manoeuvred his vehicle around an ornamental fountain, to the grand front of the Victoria, where, the moment he braked, Joe leapt off, leaving Sheila to address the remaining passengers.

With no time to take in the functional, redbrick building behind the ornate concrete and plaster façade, Joe hurried in. By the time the bags were unloaded, he had already registered, and before his remaining members had checked in, he had left his suitcase in his room and was climbing into a taxi for the 20-minute journey to Gibraltar Hall.

Sat in the rear seat, he felt the knot of tension in his gut rising. Memories of Filey, where not one, but two of the club members had died; manslaughter and murder. Now here he was again, another outing, another member embroiled in a suspicious death.

When he eventually climbed out of the cab at the entrance to Gibraltar Hall Lane, he found his way barred by a police woman manning the barrier on the main road.

"I'm sorry, sir," she told him, "but there's been a suspicious death in the house and…"

"I know," Joe interrupted. "Why do you think I'm here?"

The young brunette frowned. "I don't understand."

"Then get your boss out here," Joe ordered. "You may not have heard of me, but I'll bet he has."

The girl backed off a little. And spoke into her radio. Two minutes later a smartly dressed Asian man appeared in the lane and marched across the barrier. "What's the problem, constable?"

"This gentleman insists that he's here because of the… because of what's happened, Sarge."

"Joe Murray," Joe declared. "The girl didn't hang herself.

She was murdered."

Rahman frowned. "And how do you know that, sir."

"Let me in and I'll show you." Joe frowned. "You are the senior investigating officer, aren't you?"

He peered at Joe through his thick lenses. "I'm Detective Sergeant Rahman, Mr Murray. Detective Chief Inspector Hoad is busy at the scene of the suicide."

"It's not a suicide," Joe repeated. "Now get your boss out here. If he has any doubts, tell him to ring Detective Chief Inspector Terry Cummins of the North Yorkshire police. Terry will vouch for me."

Rahman's irritation grew. "Just who are you?"

"Joe Murray. A better detective than you or your boss will ever make, son. Now do as I ask and speak to your inspector."

With an annoyed cluck, Rahman, ordered, "Wait there," then turned on his heels and marched back towards the house.

Joe shook his head. "How did he make a detective?"

The policewoman's features darkened. "Race and religion are no barrier to advancement in the modern police service."

Joe frowned. "Who's on about the colour of his skin or the god he prays to? I'm talking about those glasses he wears? He must be blind as a bat without them."

Chapter Seven

It would be a wait of almost fifteen minutes before the policewoman's radio bleeped for attention. She listened for a moment and then said, "Yes, sir." Then she lifted the barrier and said to Joe, "You can go through. Sergeant Rahman will meet you at the gates and take you in to see Chief Inspector Hoad."

Joe grunted his thanks, and to the click and whirr of digital cameras from nearby reporters, stepped through the barrier into Gibraltar Hall Lane.

His anxiety carried him quickly along the tree-lined road. From the fields beyond the trees, he could hear the sound of pop music, and he could easily imagine the crowds in front of the stage. It sent a hammer blow reminder of the last time he had walked along this same road. Then he had been jittery, but his concern was all for Brenda. Now he felt more nervy, and again, much of his concern was for Brenda, but he was keener to ensure the police did not dismiss this woman's death so easily.

Rahman greeted him at the cabin where Brenda had first entered the hall the previous Saturday. He ushered Joe in to meet an older man. Shorter, stockier than the sergeant, his dark hair was thinning on the crown and a bushy moustache curved down either side of a grimly set mouth. Joe could almost feel the burn of his eyes.

His gaze darting around the room, he rested a moment on the dressing gown cord in the evidence bag on the desk, and was satisfied that his original assumption was right.

"I'm Detective Chief Inspector Hoad, Mr Murray. You come highly recommended."

"You spoke to Terry Cummins?" Joe asked.

"I did, and he suggested I accept your help."

Joe smiled, but Hoad's next words wiped it from his face.

"However, I'm not with the North Yorkshire Police and I see no reason why I should let a private individual in on a simple case of suicide."

Joe shook his head sadly. "You're one of *those* chief inspectors, are you?"

"If you mean in control of the investigation, sir, then the answer is yes. Now if you'd like to go on your way, we'll…"

"Ask yourself one question, Hoad," Joe interrupted. "How could she hang herself when she was sound asleep?"

Hoad screwed up his face. "There are only two ways you could know that, Murray. You were either here, or more likely, someone who was here telephoned the information to you. Perhaps I should be speaking to your friend, Brenda Jump."

Joe took out his tobacco tin and began to roll a cigarette.

"And you can't smoke that in here," Hoad warned him.

"See, that's always the trouble with you cops," Joe said, spreading a thin line of tobacco along the paper. "You think everyone else is dumb. You think I don't know I can't smoke it in here. You also think that because you've been closest to Ursula Kenney's body, you have all the answers." He rolled the cigarette, licked the gummed edge of the paper and finished it off. "You're wrong on both counts, and when you're willing to listen, I'll be outside…" He held up the completed cigarette. "… smoking this."

He stepped out of the cabin, ignoring the chief inspector's protests. Once out in the sunshine, he took out his brass Zippo and lit the cigarette, drawing the smoke deep into his lungs and letting it out with a hiss of satisfaction.

Hoad and Rahman hurried out after him. "What the hell are you talking about?" the chief inspector demanded.

Joe took another drag on his wafer thin cigarette. "I don't watch much TV, but because Brenda is here, I've been following this crap all week. I was up late last night. Late

86

enough to see Ursula leave the ladies' dorm and make for the Romping Room. She was groggy; almost out on her feet. Staggering everywhere. I don't know what she swallowed every night, but I do know she took two pills before going to bed. She's been saying all week that they're strong painkillers. I'll tell you something else, too. Just now, I saw a dressing gown cord on the desk in there." Joe jerked his thumb backwards indicating the cabin. "It was fashioned into a slip knot. It's in an evidence bag, which probably means it was the rope she used to hang herself. Now you're trying to persuade me and everyone else that she could do it when she was zonked out of her mind? Never in a million years. What's more, when she left the dorm last night, she was wearing a flimsy nightie and a pair of stockings none of which left much to the imagination. So where did she get the cord? No, Hoad, it may look like a suicide, but when you get the autopsy report, you'll find she was murdered. I knew it the minute I heard it on TV."

With a frown, Hoad took out his mobile phone and jabbed at the number pad. "This is Chief Inspector Hoad at the outside cabin. Find me the video of Ursula Kenney going to the Romping Room last night, and pipe it to the TV in the hut. Keep running it over and over again until I bell you to stop." Putting the mobile away, he narrowed a gimlet eye on Joe. "Chief Inspector Cummins was right about you."

Joe grinned. "Was he?"

"Yes. He said you were a proper pain in the backside, but your mind moves faster than everyone else's and you spot things three weeks before other people even stop to think about them."

The smile faded from Joe's wrinkled features. "I must remember to ring Terry and thank him for the reference." He pulled on his cigarette again. "Chief Inspector, I know you have your ways, and I know you'll probably get there in the end, but one of my friends is in there, and even though I know she didn't do it, you'll have to question her. I'll counter that by going my own sweet way until I can prove to you what I'm saying. I won't interfere with your investigation, but why don't you accept my help in the spirit in which I'm offering it? Help, not hindrance."

Hoad considered the proposition for a moment. "Put your smoke out and come back into the office."

Joe dropped the cigarette, crushed it underfoot and followed them back into the cooler interior of the cabin where Hoad waved Joe to a chair and Rahman switched on the TV. When the screen came alive, it showed Ursula weaving her way along the landing and into the Romping Room. When she disappeared, the sequence ran again, starting with her departure from the ladies' dorm.

"Look at her as she comes along the landing," Joe said. "You can see straight through that nightie."

Sure enough as she passed beneath one of the overhead lights, she became silhouetted and the diaphanous nightdress all but disappeared. As she neared the Romping Room door, it became obvious she was carrying nothing at all.

"So where was the cord?" Joe asked.

Sat behind his desk, the chief inspector stared at the evidence bag as if it had betrayed him. Pushing it aside, he logged onto a laptop computer. After fiddling with the tracking pad, he turned it to face Joe.

"Photographs taken in the Romping Room when we got here," he declared. "You may find some of them distressing."

Joe pulled the machine towards him. The first few images were of Ursula's naked body hanging from the wall hook. Her feet were on the floor, but she had slumped low enough for the noose in the cord to asphyxiate her.

"I'm not a ghoul," he grumbled and skipped quickly past the early pictures.

The remainder were of the room in general; the pristine bed linen, the closed, secure hatch, even the closed door.

"Do you have a time of death?" Joe asked.

"Not specifically, no," Hoad admitted. "Some time after midnight. We know from the footage you've just seen,

88

which, by the way, we had watched before, that she went into the room at about eleven twenty. We guess she was contemplating it for a long time. Suicides usually do."

"Hmm," Joe muttered. "I'll tell you what suicides don't do, though. They don't make the bed before they hang themselves."

Both police officers started. "What?" the Detective Sergeant asked.

Joe turned the laptop to face them, its screen showing the bed linen neatly in place.

"She went in there at eleven twenty. She hung herself, according to you, forty minutes later with a dressing gown cord she didn't have. What was she doing in the meantime? There are no chairs in this room. So did she stand up for three quarters of an hour while she was thinking about it? The state she was in, she'd have been lucky to stand for five minutes. She probably lay on the bed, but that means the bed sheets should be rumpled, and they're not. Now, did she decide to make the bed before she hung herself? Given her general approach to this life as we can judge from this last week, it doesn't seem likely. Or did someone else make the bed to persuade you that she never used it, and instead went in there and hung herself immediately?"

"Hanged, not hung," Rahman pointed out. "But why would any killer make the bed? Once we realised it – sorry, Mr Murray, but I think we would have realised it eventually – it would only arouse suspicion."

"Joe is right," Hoad said. "You don't mind if I call you Joe? Good," he responded to Joe's nod. "He's right, Azi. If Ursula was either asleep or already dead when the killer moved her, the sheets would have shown signs of her body having been dragged from the bed."

"Correct," Joe agreed. "So he tidied up, knowing it would take you some time to realise that she had been deliberately hung."

"Hanged," Rahman corrected him again.

"I don't know if linguistic niceties matter to Ursula Kenney," Joe countered.

"In that case forget about them," Hoad said. "Joe, I can understand you want to clear Mrs Jump of any involvement, but what you've actually done is drop her deeper into it."

"How so?"

"I don't watch this stuff, but I know that Brenda had a hell of a row with Ursula the other night." Hoad smiled coolly, and with hands held up and open, shrugged. "Where you have a murder, you have to have a murderer and he… or she… has to have a motive."

Joe was about to protest but the younger officer beat him to it. "With all due respect, sir, Mr Murray, I don't see how she could have been murdered anyway. None of the backroom staff could get into that side of the house and, besides, according to the duty log, there were none of them here last night. The security officers were the only ones on duty. And to complicate matters, none of the other Housies could have done it without being picked up on the night cameras while they were leaving the dorm and making their way to the Romping Room."

"And yet she was murdered," Joe said. "Is it possible someone could have got in from the outside?"

"Totally *im*possible," Hoad argued. "Someone young enough and fit enough may have been able to get over the back wall, but they would have been picked up by the security cameras, and even if they were missed there, they have about twenty yards of garden to cross to the back door, and the gardens, too, are covered by cameras on the outside of the house. If, by some miracle they got to the back door without being detected, how did they get past the security guards?" Again he shrugged. "I agree with you, Joe. It looks like murder, but it's an impossible murder, so it must have been suicide, and if it was suicide, where did she find the dressing gown cord?"

"Sir," Rahman said, "I think we should speak to Marc Ulrich."

Hoad sat up. "Why?"

"The dressing gown cord is his, sir."

When both Hoad and Joe registered their surprise, the

sergeant went on to explain, "I said I've been compelled to follow the series, sir." He smiled bleakly. "Press-ganged, but I have seen a lot of it. Marc has worn a dressing gown several times this week, and yesterday he was complaining about having lost the cord."

"Was he now?" Hoad said, getting to his feet. "You never said anything earlier."

Again Rahman's smile was bleak, but this time apologetic. "Sorry, sir, but I only just made the connection when Mr Murray pointed out that Ursula wasn't carrying the cord."

"All right. "Let's get a word with him. Sorry, Joe, but this puts a new light on it, and it may very well be suicide."

Joe frowned. "How do you make that out?"

"Ursula was one of the most frequent visitors to that room. Suppose she took the cord and hid it there earlier?"

"I don't buy it," Joe said. "It still doesn't explain the bed linen, but all right, you talk to the Housey. While you're doing that, is there any danger I could speak to the backroom people?"

The police officers exchange glances, and Hoad nodded. "Don't see why not. What are you thinking?"

"That someone may have been able to get past the security and into the house to kill her."

Hoad laughed. "Yes, Cummins said that about you, too. Whenever you get a bee in your bonnet, you want the honey from it before you let it go."

***

Joe frowned in puzzlement. "Lemme get this straight. I thought you were working for the TV channel."

The production control room was situated in what had once been the servants' dining area, below stairs. Joe found himself confronted with a mass of electronic equipment. One wall consisted of a bank of monitors showing the view from any and every camera in the house. In front of them was a huge control bank with four seats set before it, and in the centre of the control board was a single monitor.

Helen shook her head. "No. We're the production company, Mr Murray." She leaned forward and rubbed irritably at her leg. "Sorry. Childhood scar," she explained. "Still gives me trouble. Now, what was I saying? Oh, yes. We're the production company. We're completely independent of the TV channel."

"But you call all the shots?" Joe asked, waving at the equipment surrounding them.

"That's the arrangement," Naughton agreed. "There's nothing unusual in it. If you take a drama series, it's usually made by an independent production house, which then sells it to the TV channel, but it's sold as is. Complete. We're reality TV, not drama, but the principle is the same."

"That's a debate I already had," Joe muttered. "More like invasion of privacy TV if you want my opinion, but that, too, is another argument. There's no one in here of a night?"

Helen, Naughton and Katy all shook their heads.

"Not cost effective," Helen explained. "The truth of the matter is, Mr Murray, there is very little happening in the house during the night. At that time, most of our viewers are online with a few thousand couch potatoes glued to their TV screens. Advertising income for the TV channel tends to be the bottom end of the market in the early hours, so they pay us the lowest rates and we have to economise where we can. We automate as many systems as possible. Motion sensors pick up the Housies during the night, so if there is anything happening anywhere, the computer will pick it up and direct the appropriate cameras."

"Not only nosy but cheapskate TV, too," Joe observed.

"If Brenda is to be believed, you're not the freest man in the country when it comes to money," Katy observed.

Joe dismissed the scathing tone of her accusation. "I'm a businessman, young lady. I cut costs where I can, but I don't advertise beefsteak and then serve scrag end." Switching his focus to Naughton, he asked, "How does the computer decide between rooms if there's a conflict?"

"It used to lead to problems," Naughton admitted. "If

there was movement in two rooms at the same time, the computer would switch back and forth like a strobe, but we solved that by putting a minimum ten-second hold on any camera that comes onto the main feed." He pointed at the central monitor on his console. "That hold is programmed into the computer."

"Let me get this straight, then," Joe said. "If someone wanted to get into the Romping Room from, say, the men's dorm, and there was movement in the living room, for example, he would have a ten-second window to get himself along the corridor and into the Romping Room. Is that right?"

Naughton and Helen nodded.

"Has Hoad been made aware of this? Because if there is a suspicion that Ursula was murdered…"

"Won't work, Mr Murray," Katy interrupted. "We may have a view hold on cameras, but not a record hold. In other words, if someone moved at the same time as someone in a different room, although their movement wouldn't transmit because of the view hold, we would still have it on record." She pointed to the vast computer servers surrounding them. "One of the first things we did after Anne found Ursula was check the footage from last night. After they all went to bed, no one moved all night."

"Besides, how would any of the Housies know that the cameras were on hold?" Naughton smiled and Joe felt the cockiness in the gesture. "Your murder theory is impossible, Murray. It simply cannot be done."

"Hmm. You know, someone once *proved* that if trains travelled faster than about twenty-five miles an hour, everyone in the carriages would suffocate. I wonder what British Rail would make of that."

"Not a lot," Katy retorted. "British Rail hasn't existed as such for quite some years."

Naughton gave her a small clap for her response.

"Smartarses, too," Joe commented and was pleased to see the irritation his remark brought. "Now, listen to me, all of you. I'm not interested in your cheap and nasty programme, or your fancy equipment. I will tell you that this woman was murdered. Hoad doesn't believe it yet, but he will when he has sufficient evidence. I know the Romping Room is the only room used by the Housies with no cameras, but I need to know how anyone could get in there without being seen."

Helen laid her hands flat on the console. "They can't," she said with great finality.

"The cops won't let us in the room until their scientific support people are finished, but Hoad showed me photographs," Joe declared, "There's some kind of hatch on the rear wall. Could someone get in through there?"

"Not big enough," Naughton argued. "It's about nine inches square."

"What's it used for?" Joe asked.

"Delivery of fresh linen," Katy replied. "And if you're wondering why they would need fresh linen–"

"I may be getting on," Joe interrupted, "but there's nothing wrong with my memory... or my physical abilities," he added hastily. "I'm not in Ursula Kenney's league but I can still... Never mind, we're getting distracted. You use this hatch to drop fresh linen into the Romping Room. Are there similar hatches in other rooms?"

"Every room," Naughton agreed. "Why?"

"And how do you get access to the hatch?"

"The backroom set up, Mr Murray," Helen told him. "Only the smallest part of Gibraltar Hall is given over to the Housies. Not just Gibraltar Hall, but any location we choose for I-Spy. Far and away the greater part of the house is used by the production and support team. Where do you think your friend, Brenda, got the ingredients for her meal last night?"

"A meal which, I might add, appears to have had an ill effect on all the Housies," Katy sneered.

"If Brenda's meal has upset their systems, trust me, it's the ingredients, not her cooking. She's worked for me for six years and I've never had a single complaint."

"We were about to look into that when Anne found Ursula," Helen admitted.

"Not interested," Joe dismissed her. "Let's get back to these hatches. Any chance I can see this backroom area you're talking about."

The three production managers exchanged glances. Naughton shrugged. "As long as the cops don't mind. Why?"

"Well it occurs to me that if you can reach through them and leave stuff in the rooms for the Housies, you can also reach in and take stuff out. Stuff like a dressing gown cord. Not only could you take it from the men's dorm, say, but you could leave it in the Romping Room for someone to pick up and use on Ursula."

"Or for Ursula to use on herself," Katy pointed out.

"True, very true," Joe agreed, "except that she didn't." Joe proceeded to explain what he had noticed on the footage of Ursula leaving the dorm. "Someone could have put that cord in there through the hatch."

"It's a nice theory," Naughton said, "but it didn't happen."

"And how do you know?" Joe asked.

Naughton again gestured at the screens and computer equipment around them. "Every feed from every camera is here. I'm not saying one of us would have spotted it, but whoever did it would know the danger of being caught, and he'd be an idiot to risk it. But even if you're right," he pressed on over Joe's attempted interruption, "you still can't get round the fact that no one followed Ursula into that room last night. She was alone. The other seven Housies, the only ones who had access to the Romping Room, were all asleep." Again he delivered that superior smile. "I repeat. Murder is impossible. It's suicide."

Chapter Eight

"How come you're all so bloody superior?" Joe asked as Katy led him away from the rear of the Romping Room and the access hatch, and towards the back stairs.

It had proved a fruitless mission. The areas behind each room were simply barren boxes with two, sometimes three, hatches built into the wall. The hatches could not be opened from the front, the Housies' side of the room. Behind the Romping Room, it was secured by a simple, sliding bolt, which meant that any theory Joe could construct would have to come from the technical side, and that would involve collusion with one of the Housies. Since that appeared to be impossible, and access was denied to the technical crew, it began to look as if Ursula really had committed suicide.

Joe slid back the bolt and pushed the hatch open. It was too small for him to see the entire Romping Room. At most he could make out the bottom corner of the bed. He backed away, a frown of deep thought etched into his brow.

"Something wrong?" Katy asked.

"Hmm. Maybe, maybe not." He took out his mobile and dialled. "Frank?" he asked when the connection was made. "It's Joe Murray. The initial report on Ursula? Did you tell me there were no signs of a struggle?" He listened to the chief inspector's reply, then said, "That's what I thought. Thanks. Catch you later." He hit the side button of his phone and locked it up.

"Well?" Katy asked.

"No struggle. It means that Ursula was probably asleep when the killer came into the room."

"And?" Katy tapped her foot impatiently on the floor.

"So how did anyone know she was asleep?" Joe asked.

"Maybe they didn't," Katy suggested.

"My feelings exactly. And that would mean that the killer knew she was expecting him, or her. Either that, or…"

Joe turned back to the hatch and examined the frame. There was nothing remarkable about it. He went further and examined the entire wall, but it was no more than a wooden frame covered with plasterboard panels. It had probably been erected in a matter of hours and could certainly be torn down in minutes. The hatch was no more than a wooden panel set into a small frame, with a shelf on the Romping Room side.

"Nowhere anyone could have hitched one of those tiny cameras," he concluded. "That means Ursula was definitely expecting her killer."

They came away from the room, making for the stairs again, when Joe passed his comment about their assumed superiority.

"It's not us, it's you, Mr Murray," she assured him. "You come with a built-in reputation, thanks to Brenda and some of the stories she's told about you this week. But here you're in TV land, and you're out of your depth. We have answers for everything, and because this hall is flooded with cameras, we can account for everything that's happened."

Joe stood his ground. "I'm not wrong. I know I'm not. Listen, Katy, call a truce for one minute and tell me, honestly, what did you think of Ursula."

The young woman shrugged. "What can I say? She was a whore, plain and simple. Celebrity behaviour, celebrity ambitions, and she went out to show the world just what she could be like."

"And that would win her the big prize?"

"Not necessarily," Katy admitted. "That's decided by a public phone vote. But it would certainly bring her to the media's attention. The tabloids will hand over cheques that make the I-Spy prize look like pocket money. And you can bet your last penny that there was some publicist out there with an army of ghost writers just waiting to pen her biography. She's not the first contestant we've had like that, and without exception, the others have made a fortune even when they haven't won the public vote." Setting off down the stairs, she went on, "People like her come on the show simply to manipulate the system."

A couple of steps behind her, keeping a firm grip on the banister as they descended the steep staircase, Joe noted, "You sound bitter."

The staircase turned back on itself halfway down. Reaching the tiny landing at the turn, Katy paused and gazed up at Joe. "It's not what we had in mind when we first thought of the programme. Our original idea was to bring in eight people, equally divided between the genders, but all of different ages, and let them make an effort to get on with each other."

"I don't watch a lot of TV," Joe confessed, as he reached the landing, "and I certainly don't watch this kind of rubbish, but it occurs to me that when you have someone like Ursula, it probably hypes your viewing figures. She pays your wages."

"Yes, well, right now she's probably put an end to my wages." Katy continued on her way down the stairs.

Falling in behind her, Joe asked, "How come?"

"She committed suicide, Mr Murray. Aside from the police investigation, there'll be an internal inquiry, and because of the health and safety implications, the company will probably decide that I-Spy is too risky, and that means I'll be looking for work again very shortly."

"And suppose she was murdered?" Joe asked.

Katy reached the ground floor and waited for him. "That makes it even worse. The other contestants could conceivably sue the company for failing to check the backgrounds of their fellow Housies thoroughly enough and putting them in proximity of a killer. Long before the legal battles start, the company will shut I-Spy down."

She led the way along the rear corridor which, Joe guessed, servants would have used at some time in the hall's history, to the security checkpoint at the rear door. A single officer sat in the small office, and before him were more TV monitors, but these were more familiar to Joe than the plethora of such screens in the control room.

Computer controlled, they were external CCTV screens and they showed only four views; the exterior of the house and rear garden from each corner of the building, and the view into the woods at the rear from each corner of the property's back wall.

While Katy explained that she and Joe would be going out to look around the gardens, Joe watched the cameras panning around their respective views. Using the garden's ornamentation as a guide, he guessed that there should be some overlap between the views, but there was not. An elephant shaped bush disappeared from one screen and there was a delay of almost two seconds before it appeared on the other.

"Right, Mr Murray," Katy said. "Let's show you the outside."

Joe took out his tobacco tin and rolled a cigarette. "Please call me Joe," he invited. "I've never liked formality."

Warm sunshine greeted them as they stepped out into the garden.

"Would you consider yourself a success, Joe?" Katy asked.

Breathing in the fresh air, hung with the tang of various scents from the riotous flowerbeds, Joe lit a cigarette and drew deeply on it.

"That's better. Nothing like a bit of good, old-fashioned pollution to set you up." His wrinkled brow creased even further. "A success? It depends how you define the word. I took over the running of the café when my father got too old to work it. I stamped my own personality on it. I'm mean, miserable, grumpy and tight-fisted, but everyone in Sanford knows me, and my place is a gold mine. The food is staple, working class diet, I suppose, but I have a large customer base, and they know exactly what they're getting. I end each year in profit. I don't make anything like the amount people think I make, but I'm happy with my lot, so from that point of view, I suppose yes, I'm successful." He took another drag on his cigarette. "What about you?"

Katy pointed up at the caricature of a head wearing a top hat. "The man who cut that from the bushes probably took the same view as you. He trained and trimmed that bush until he created something. He was probably paid pennies for doing it, but nevertheless, he would have been happy with it. He would have considered himself successful. I don't think I'm a success. I'm twenty-seven years old and unmarried by choice. I didn't want relationships to get in the way of my career. I came out of university six years ago, and here I am a production assistant on I-Spy. By my calculations, I should have been at least one more rung up the ladder." She smiled wanly. "Second unit assistant director on the next James Bond movie."

"I was reading James Bond on the way to Chester," Joe commented. "It's good to be ambitious, and you'll probably get there."

Katy shook her head. "There are others coming along behind me who will probably leapfrog over me. I haven't even got to work on a drama project yet. I piddled about with silly jobs on a few minor projects, and then landed I-Spy two years ago. If that goes, I'm back in the pool, scratching for work."

"Where is all this leading?" Joe asked.

"Ursula Kenney. She would have understood, Joe. She was a failed actress turned estate agent. Thanks to her, I'll probably be out of work, and maybe I'll end up as an estate agent, too. If you're looking for someone who might have murdered her, you could do worse than look at me. I had every reason to kill her."

***

Her whole body trembling, Brenda took the chair opposite the two police officers and drank from a bottle of water.

"A friend of yours has turned up," Hoad told her. "Joe

Murray."

Brenda cleared her throat nervously. "I knew he would the moment he heard the news. Has he, er, offered to help you?"

Hoad nodded slowly. "I've charitably permitted him to ask a few questions here and there, but made it clear to him that this is my investigation." The chief inspector sat back and nodded at his junior.

"Mr Murray insists that Ursula Kenney was murdered," Sergeant Rahman declared.

Brenda shrugged. "If Joe says that, then the odds are he's right. He always is."

"We don't think so," Hoad admitted," but we have to entertain the possibility because Joe is persuasive, and that's why we're talking to you."

The first inkling of alarm spread through her. She drank again from her bottle. "Oh yes?"

"We've just spoken to Marc Ulrich concerning the cord from his dressing gown, which he claims went missing sometime yesterday. That cord was used to hang Ursula."

Brenda recalled what Joe had always said about dealing with the police. *Maintain the initiative. Throw questions back at them.* Clearing her throat again, she put the principle into practice. "What does that have to do with me?"

"If we're dealing with a murder, and I stress 'if' then we need to think of a motive," Hoad told her. "You had a hell of a row with Ursula a couple days ago."

"Wednesday evening," Brenda agreed. "She goaded me once too often."

"And there was, as the chief says, a blazing row," Rahman reminded her.

"There was an argument. I told her where to get off. Not only her but the men, too, and the idiot who plays Master Spy."

"Do you often get angry, Mrs Jump?"

Brenda shook her head. "I'm like anyone else. Even tempered, easy going, but I do come to a point where I can lose it. Ursula reached that point on Wednesday evening."

It was another of Joe's canons. *Answer the question they ask don't supply answers to those they haven't asked.*

"I've had a brief look at some of the footage," Hoad told her. "After tearing a strip off Master Spy, you stormed out of the living room and went up to the Romping Room. Ben called on you afterwards and you told him to clear off, too."

"I was angry. I needed to be on my own to calm down."

"I can understand that," the chief inspector admitted, "but I have to ask, Mrs Jump, did you sneak into the men's dorm, take the cord from Marc's dressing gown, and keep it to one side."

"No."

"And did you then sneak into the Romping Room the following night after Ursula had gone there, and strangle her with it?"

"No, I did not." Brenda felt a rush of anger sparked by fear, running through her. She drank again from her bottle of water. "If you're so smart, you'd check the footage. I didn't leave my bed last night."

"We did," Rahman told her, "and we would agree. But your friend Mr Murray, doesn't. He admits that he doesn't yet know how it was done, but he insists that it was murder, and right now, Mrs Jump, you are the only suspect we have."

"Then in that case you're wrong, and so is Joe Murray." Brenda sucked on the bottled water again. "And when I see him, he'll wish he'd been suspended on the end of that rope."

***

After trying the solid wooden, rear gate and finding it locked, Joe raised his eyebrows at Katy.

"There's an entry call system," she told him. "Controlled from the security office. When we want access, we push the buzzer, security lets us in."

"And of course they have CCTV so they can check on your identity."

"Correct."

They moved on, circling the paved paths until they came to the high fence that separated the Housies' half of the garden from the production crew's access.

It was built of six-foot by six-foot waney lap panels, but they had been doubled up, one on top of the other, supported by a high, trellis-like framework.

"As a part of their contract, the Housies can have no contact with anyone outside the house," Katy explained. "To ensure that, and also to ensure that they can have access to the gardens, we need to put in a temporary divider. Rigging this up as we do provides the perfect answer."

Joe pointed to the rear wall. "That's not particularly high, though, and I noticed on the security cameras that it runs the length of the house at the rear and sides. What's to stop a reporter or a friend of one of the Housies getting over it?"

"CCTV for one thing," Katy said, "and have you tried getting through the woods to the back wall? We checked it out when we first arrived. It's like the Burma jungle out there."

Passing a piece of topiary shaped like a double-decker bus, they turned for the house once more.

"I'm surprised at you referring to the Burma jungle. Most people wouldn't know of it. Did you do world war two history at university?"

Katy laughed. "No. I took media studies. My great grandfather was in Burma during World War Two."

"Ah." Joe took a final drag on his cigarette and crushed it out in a planter. He stopped, turned and faced her. "Did you murder her?"

Katy did not appear surprised by the question. After a moment's pause, she slowly shook her head. "No, Joe, I didn't. I was simply pointing out that if she was, indeed, murdered, then there are plenty of candidates, and I'm only one of them."

"I've seen all I need to see here," Joe told her. "Let's go back inside."

While they walked on, Joe asked, "The access hatches? I

103

notice some rooms had as many as two or three."

"Technical access," Katy explained. "Our technology is good, but it's not perfect. Cameras do break down now and then. The kitchen camera has been a bloody nightmare this week. Always breaking down. Technicians can access the cameras through the hatches and remove and replace them as and when we need to. And of course, the lenses have to be cleaned daily."

"Cleaned?" Joe was surprised.

With a pleasant giggle, Katy gestured up at the clear, Cheshire skies. "It's summer, Joe. Hot weather and enclosed rooms like those in the hall? What does that produce? Dust, of course. Especially in areas where you have electrical equipment on the go, and that's just about every room because the lights are on twenty-four seven. The camera lenses are cleaned hourly throughout the transmission day. Eight in the morning until ten in the evening."

"So someone comes to the hatch, reaches in and gives the lens a quick once over with a tissue?"

"Specialist, static-free dry wipes to be really accurate," Katy corrected him. "We also use a dab of lens polish once a day. Not a lot. That stuff can create flares if you overuse it."

Joe paused at the entrance to the hall. "So how come I've never noticed this when I've been watching?"

"We have what are known as stock feeds," Katy explained. "We were here a month or six weeks before the Housies turned up, positioning cameras, putting up the partitions to create our technical areas. When the cameras were in place, we ran them and stored the footage. We can cut that stock footage in at any time during transmission. So when a technician goes to attend to a camera, or even just clean the lens, we run the relevant stock footage until the job is done."

"And us viewers, we don't notice?"

"It's done when there's no activity," Katy assured him, "and the process is seamless. No. You wouldn't notice. We would if we studied the recording closely enough, but you, the viewer, wouldn't."

"And how long could you run these stock feeds?"

Katy shrugged. "As long as you wish. We've been transmitting stock feeds since Ursula's body was discovered this morning."

"Now that is interesting."

He followed Katy back into the house, and paused at the security lodge. "Could you contact Chief Inspector Hoad and tell him Joe Murray would like a word?"

"No problem," agreed the security officer, and reached for the phone.

While he spoke to the police, Joe studied the CCTV coverage of the exterior. "Do you get this same footage?" he asked.

Katy nodded. "Security record it on their own database, but we take a recording of it, too. If there was anyone hanging around outside, there's a greater chance that we would spot it because we're studying monitors all the time. Security have other duties to perform…" she nodded at the security man talking quietly on the phone. "…like contacting the cops for you, and there's always a danger that they may miss something."

"Good," Joe said.

"Chief Inspector says he'll see you in their cabin at the main gates in a few minutes, Mr Murray."

"Yeah. Right. Thanks. Oh, hey, while I think, were you on duty last night?"

The security man shook his head. "I'm days, guv," he reported. "The night people are Ernie Bexley and Rebecca Driscoll."

"The same crew every night?"

"For the entire week, yes."

"Cheers." Finished with the security man, Joe faced his guide. "Well, that's been enlightening, Katy."

"I hope I've managed to persuade you that no one could have got in to kill Ursula."

He grinned. "Oh no. Exactly the opposite, in fact."

Hoad scratched his head. "You want to bring someone else in?"

"Just for a couple of hours, yes. See, I think I know how it could be done; I'm not fit enough to prove it, but I know a man who is."

"And who would this be?"

"An ex-army man. If I'm right, he'll show you what I mean, and it'll count for an awful lot more than me telling you. I promise, Hoad, he will be here for less than an hour."

"And how much evidence will he disturb?" the chief inspector demanded.

"None," Joe replied. "In fact, he doesn't need access to the Housies' side of things. Only to this room and the rear garden... the techs' side of the garden, not the Housies'."

"All right, if you think it'll help. But I'll want to see and speak to him before he does anything."

"Right." Joe checked his watch. "It's half past twelve. I'll have to go back to Chester and collect him. I should be back by two. What price I can take Brenda with me?"

Hoad shook his head. "Sorry, Joe. For the time being, the Housies stay put."

"Come on, man, Brenda didn't kill her."

"I don't think any of them did," Hoad retorted, "but if I'm wrong, Mrs Jump is my prime suspect."

Chapter Nine

"You want my help?" Les Tanner guffawed uncharacteristically. "If you were on fire, Murray, I wouldn't call the Fire Brigade."

Sat opposite him on the bar terrace, Joe fumed. Guessing that Tanner and his lady friend, Sylvia Goodson, would be out and about in Chester, Joe had rung Sheila while he waited for the taxi at Gibraltar Hall. By the time he got back to the Victoria Hotel, Sheila, Sylvia and Tanner were enjoying a drink in the sunshine.

The location was almost idyllic and did much to lift Joe's spirits. A view of the boat station across the river, where cruisers prepared to take trippers on a short journey along the River Dee, and on the river bank were hundreds of people simply enjoying the summer sunshine. Downstream, they could see the slow moving waters gather pace where they frothed over a weir. Beyond the river, in the background, was the city centre, with its streets of shops, many housed in buildings that were hundreds of years old, reminding Joe that two millennia back, this area had been a Roman fortress.

But if the view both relaxed and inspired him, Tanner's cynicism had exactly the opposite effect.

Not that there was any serious basis to their mutual antagonism. Back home in Sanford, aside from spending some of his free time as a soldier, Tanner worked full time for the local authority, supervising the clerks in the Payroll Office at the Town Hall. Joe, a taxpayer and a businessman, had long been a thorn in the town council's side, complaining about everything from street lighting and cleaning, to the exorbitant (in his opinion) local taxes.

Everyone at the town hall knew him; most of the elected councillors went out of their way to avoid him, and men like Les Tanner took great delight in each and every opportunity to snipe back.

Twice in the past, Tanner had challenged Joe for the Chair of the Sanford 3rd Age Club. Twice he had lost; something which Joe was never slow to mention, but Tanner was equally quick to remind the membership in general, Joe in particular, of the many and various inefficiencies which resulted from what he claimed was Joe's weak organisational skills.

"When it comes to organisation," he would often say, "Murray is a classic example of the famed booze up in a brewery."

Most of the time, Joe ignored it just as much as Tanner ignored his gripes at the town hall, but now was not the time for obduracy. Not with a mutual friend, Brenda, trapped at Gibraltar Hall by police procedures.

Tanner, on the other hand, saw it as the perfect time to see Joe grovelling.

"It's not for me," Joe complained. "It's for Brenda and the other Housies."

"Not interested, Murray. I'm sure the police will release Brenda as and when they realise she could never be party to murder. My only regret is that it is she who took part in this farce, not you. I'd love to see you wriggling on the end of the police hook and line."

Joe's temper began to get the better of him. "Listen, you brainless sod, I've already worked out how it could have been done. If I'm right, Brenda will be free to join us tonight, not cooped up in that house for another twenty-four hours. The trouble is I need someone who can help me prove it and heaven help me, that someone is you."

Sylvia touched Tanner's arm. "Let's hear him out, Les."

The Captain tweaked his moustache. "All right, Murray. I always knew there'd come a day when you couldn't handle reality. So tell me what is it you want?"

"You're ex army. Even if it is only as a toy soldier..."

"Joe, that is not fair," Sheila warned. "I've told you before, the Territorials receive the same training as regular soldiers and in an emergency they're called up first."

"Sheila is right, Murray. I'd give my right arm to have you under my command. You wouldn't be half so slovenly or loudmouthed."

"And you'd be crying in your pink gin in a week," Joe retorted.

"Joe," Sheila admonished him again. "You say you need Les's help. Insulting him is not the right way to go about it."

"All right, all right. I'm sorry." Joe chewed spit on the words. "Now for crying out loud, just shut up and listen, will you? That girl, Ursula, she was murdered. I know she was. Chief Inspector Hoad won't have it because he insists that there is no way anyone could get in the house without being seen on the CCTV cameras. I think there is, but you're the only person I know who might be able to demonstrate it."

Tanner gloated. "Well you're out of luck, Murray. Sylvia and I are planning an afternoon of shopping and a leisurely stroll round the city before dinner."

"Wait a minute, Les," Sheila said, suddenly swinging to Joe's aid. "This isn't just about salvaging Joe's pride or helping him solve a puzzle. It's also about Brenda. She's trapped in that house. The police won't let any of the Housies leave until the investigation is complete. She could be there for days, yet."

"And who was it that got Sylvia off the hook that time?" Joe pressed.

It was a reference to the killing of a young disabled woman named Kimberly Lowe. As one of Kim's unofficial carers, Sylvia had been amongst the last people to see the girl alive, and had been arrested by the Sanford police on suspicion of the killing. It was Joe who had proved she did not do it.

"Sheila and Joe are right, Les," Sylvia said. "If it hadn't been for Joe, I could have been in serious trouble over Kim Lowe. For Brenda's sake, we have to forget our own plans for this afternoon. Sheila will stay with me, just to ensure I don't have one of my turns, won't you Sheila?"

"Yes, of course," Sheila agreed. "And if you like, we could find an old-fashioned tea room where they serve proper toasted teacakes. Chester must be wallowing in them."

Tanner capitulated. "All right, Murray. Where do we go?"

"I'll get us a taxi from here to the hall. It's only about ten miles. Sheila, keep your phone on. I'll need to catch up with you when we get back."

***

There was no sign of Hoad, or Rahman when they arrived back at the I-Spy house, but the policewoman on duty at the end of Gibraltar Hall Lane allowed them access after speaking with the detectives via the radio.

Walking past the shed commandeered by CID as their headquarters, they carried on to the corner of the retaining wall, and turned left along the rear. Here the lane was even narrower, lined on the left by the redbrick wall, and on the right by dense thickets, the edge of the Gibraltar Hall Wood.

As they made their way to the rear gate, Tanner cast an appreciative eye over the wall, studied the CCTV cameras, and then ran his eye over the trees and bushes on the right.

"The immediate problem I can see is getting here without being picked up by the security cameras," he said, "but if there's a way through the woods from the entertainment field, I think it could be done. We shall have to investigate."

"What about getting over the wall?" Joe asked.

Again, Tanner ran his eye over it. Twin CCTV cameras at either end turning on their axes. As the eastern camera turned away, so the western one turned with it to cover the ground it was leaving behind.

"But you'll notice," Tanner said, "that there's a slight delay between the eastern one turning away and the western one following suit. Only a matter of a second or two, but provided the intruder was fast and sufficiently agile to get over the wall, it would be enough."

Joe stroked his chin, thoughtfully. "He'd have to be young and nippy to do that, huh?"

"Nonsense," Tanner argued. "I could do it." He cast an imperious stare over Joe. "You couldn't. You're too short. It needs someone tall, fit and active, Murray. Not a shortarse fed on meat pies."

"Steak and kidney pies, not meat," Joe corrected him. "I'm a Yorkshireman, not a Lancastrian. What happens when he gets over the wall?"

Tanner shrugged. "I'd need to see the garden to judge. But my impression from the TV coverage I've seen this last week is that there's sufficient shrubbery and ornamentation to give him cover right up to the house. Especially if he were familiar with the place."

Joe looked around them. "Plenty of cover here, too, so he wouldn't be seen waiting for the cameras to turn."

"Ample," Tanner agreed. "But like I said, it would depend on finding a route through the woods from the field beyond. Now, is that all? Only I'd like to get back…"

"No," Joe cut him off. "If I can arrange this with Hoad, would you be prepared to give it a go?"

"Murray, I came here for a relaxing weekend, not to play commandos on a garrison house."

Back on the terrace of the Victoria Hotel, Joe had explained what he had in mind, and Tanner had come dressed for the purpose. He wore a pair of denims, and a thick, army jumper, its green wool would allow him to blend almost perfectly with much of the surrounding foliage.

"Then why did you dress for the part?"

"To impress the police," Tanner reported and tapped the three pips on his left shoulder.

"So you're happy to let Brenda sweat it out?"

Tanner sighed. "Emotional blackmail. I never thought you'd sink that low."

Joe reached for the electronic entry-call button on the back gate. "Trust me, I can go a whole lot lower."

***

Hoad, when they met him in the production control room, was a good deal less than enthusiastic. "Who are you again?" he demanded of Tanner.

"Captain Leslie Tanner, Yorkshire Regiment. And I'll thank you to address me as sir, young man."

"I'm not sure that you actually outrank me," the policeman replied. "Forgetting the formalities, are you saying to me that it's possible for someone to get into the grounds without being seen?"

"That is my opinion, Chief Inspector," Tanner agreed. "What's more, I'm prepared to demonstrate it."

Hoad looked even more doubtful. "You're, er, a little old for such games, aren't you, sir?"

Tanner tutted and Joe, for once, agreed with him. "What is it with you people that makes you think age equals deadweight? Let him have a go."

Hoad shook his head. "Sorry. I can't take responsibility…"

"No one is asking you to take responsibility, Chief Inspector," Tanner interrupted. "Nothing will go wrong, but if Murray is right, it'll prove that someone other than the inmates could have broken in to kill this young woman."

Joe frowned. "Inmates? This is a TV show, Les, not a prison."

"No," Tanner argued. "It's a zoo. Perhaps 'inmates' was the wrong word. Let's call them exhibits."

"I don't care what you call them," Hoad grumbled. "Murray, you were the one who insisted that Ursula Kenney couldn't have committed suicide. Even if they could get over the wall like General Incompetence here insists, they still couldn't get into the house to kill the woman. There were security men on duty."

"And none of the animals could have done it," Joe retorted, picking up on Les's zoo theme. "They couldn't get past the cameras out of the dorms. You've seen that for yourself. It had to be someone outside."

112

"Or suicide," Rahman said. "I understand your objections, Mr Murray, but it still seems the only obvious conclusion."

"Not so," Tanner disagreed. "And if Chief Inspector Plod will permit, I'll demonstrate."

"Can we stop trading childish insults?" Hoad asked.

"You started it," Joe pointed out. "Look, Hoad, let Les show you what we're talking about. He needs to be on the outside and in the control room, not at the crime scene or anywhere the Housies go. Like I said earlier, he won't interfere with any of your forensic work."

With an exasperated sigh, Hoad yielded. "What is it you want?"

"I need to see the multiple screens in the TV and security control centres," Tanner told him, "After that I need to see the rear garden. Then I'll need a little while to plan my approach. Beyond that, I'll show you how it's done."

"All right," Hoad agreed. "I want a waiver. If you injure yourself, it's your own fault."

"That's the spirit," Tanner smiled. "Glad you weren't leading the troops in Normandy."

***

"Why is there a delay between the movement of east and west cameras at the rear of the house?" Tanner asked.

"Manual override," Scott Naughton explained. "Those two cameras belong to security, not us. They're not on our main feed, but we do use the eastern ones for mid shots when Housies are in their garden." He gestured at two separate monitors to one side of the control bank. "Katy explained to Murray earlier. We have them here so we can monitor them during the day, and the security people have them in their office for night duty. Like all our cameras the feeds can be altered manually. Under normal circumstances, the cameras would turn left, then right, and scan through their preset arc, but if the security guys, or one of us sees something suspicious beyond the walls, we can override the movement of either camera and focus on it."

"So what you're saying is that someone, at some point overrode the automatic movement of the cameras and that's why their movement is no longer co-ordinated?" Joe asked.

Naughton nodded. "When that happens, the whole system needs to be reset. A couple of buttons and the cameras will return to their azimuth position, then start to scan again." He reached for the console.

"Don't do that," Tanner barked and Naughton backed off as if he had received a shock from it.

"If someone had stopped the automatic movement of the cameras, would that be logged somewhere?" Joe asked.

"Yes," Naughton agreed. "And I can assure you we don't have it on our log. I keep it and no one asked me for it yesterday, nor this morning. Security officers may have logged it, but if so we haven't been informed." He smiled wanly. "Mind you, we've all been busy with other matters since first thing this morning."

"Hang on a minute here," Hoad interjected. "I asked you earlier if anyone could have dodged the cameras and got into the grounds, and you said no. Are you telling us now that they could have done?"

Naughton shook his head. "If one camera was stopped, the other would still be scanning. But even if they did get over the wall and into the garden, where are they gonna go? The garden is covered from the house and they wouldn't get past security."

"But the house cameras, like the wall cameras, are rotating, aren't they?" Tanner asked.

"At night when the house is closed up, yes. During the day when the Housies could be out in the garden, we control the feed, and I personally zeroed both cameras yesterday evening before I left." Naughton appealed to Hoad. "Chief Inspector, I know what you're driving at and I tell you it's impossible. No one could get into the grounds or the house during the night. Without being detected, that is."

Hoad jerked his thumb at Joe and Tanner. "Sherlock Bones and the chocolate soldier disagree."

"I'll thank you to have a little more respect, Chief Inspector," Tanner insisted. To Naughton, he said, "Show me the garden feeds on automatic scan."

They moved across the room to the main bank of I-Spy monitors. Naughton spoke briefly to his technician who flipped a few switches. The director turned his attention to two monitors set to the right hand side. "Okay, you're watching the cameras mounted on the house in security mode."

Joe watched as the cameras swung through their respective arcs, his eye darting from one screen to the other covering the whole of the garden from the rear of the house, a steeply angled view, to the rear wall.

"There's a big discrepancy between the scans," he noted. "They're covering the same areas for long periods."

"Up to five seconds," Les agreed with an eye on the sweep hand of his wristwatch.

"They've been altered during the night," Naughton said. "They must have been. We can reset them any time we want, but it's not been necessary. Want me to do it now?"

"No," Tanner replied. "I want everything as it would have been last night... or the early hours of this morning."

The room fell silent, Joe following Tanner's eyes as he watched the scene from the garden. Areas appeared and disappeared on the two monitors: the duck, the ballerina, the elephant, the fountain. At one point the fountain and the duck were visible on both screens before the scans parted and went their separate ways.

Tanner followed them for a long time before finally nodding his satisfaction. "I think it can be done, Murray. In fact, I'm sure it can. I'll need a small pair of field glasses and a little time to get ready at the rear of the house. I'll need you to record what happens from the cameras, Mr Naughton."

The director shrugged. "No problem. What are you going to do?"

Tanner smiled. "Get into the house without your cameras seeing me."

While Detective Sergeant Rahman waited at the rear gate, Joe and Tanner had made their way to the entertainment field, and from there, dismissing the protest of a steward, over a waist-high fence into the woods.

Joe was surprised that the field was still so busy. Thousands of people were crowded in there, singers and dancers still occupied the stage, but the giant screens now showed the stage action instead of views from the I-Spy house.

He was initially glad to be out of the field, into the wood. It muffled much of the noise, and as they made their way further in, so the sounds faded even further.

That was the upside. The downside was fighting their way through the riot of trees and bushes.

"How the hell do you know where we're going?" Joe complained once more. "I can't even see the sky."

The Captain pointed down at the flattened mosses over which they were walking. "Someone has been this way before. Many times."

After what seemed like eternity, the trees began to thin a little and Joe could make out the rear wall of Gibraltar Hall, with the ungainly partition fence strutting high into the sky the other side of it.

"You join the policeman," Tanner whispered to Joe. "I need to observe the cameras from here."

Joe checked and sure enough, above the wall, he could see the house-mounted cameras swinging back and forth through their arcs.

He stepped out, taking Sergeant Rahman by surprise. "Almost arrested you there, sir."

"Sorry, son. Les is playing hide and seek in there." He pointed into the woods. "Shouldn't be long now." Joe rolled a cigarette and lit it. "You don't mind me asking, Azi, but how come you're CID when your eyesight is so bad?"

"They couldn't put me in an office, Mr Murray, because I can't see well enough to concentrate on a computer screen for long. And they daren't pension me off, so they assigned me to CID," Rahman replied. "It's difficult, obviously, and I'm no use on, say, fingertip searches, so most of the time, all I do is question witnesses and take statements." He shrugged. "It's all a bit politically correct, if you know what I mean."

"I take your point. But you're a hero apparently, and you're right to milk it for all it's worth."

With a speed and agility that took Joe and Rahman by surprise, Tanner suddenly burst from the bushes, rushed forward and threw himself at the wall. In less than a second he was gone. Over the top and into the garden.

"How do you do it, you silly old sod?" Joe muttered. "Come on, Azi. We need to be inside." He led the sergeant through the rear gate and along the path to the rear entrance. Several times he looked around, seeking sight of Tanner but there was no sign of him.

When they arrived in the control room, it was to find Chief Inspector Hoad and Scott Naughton studying the monitors.

"When is he gonna show?" Naughton asked.

"He left about two or three minutes ago," Joe reported. "Over the wall like an Olympic pole-vaulter... without the pole. And he was in the garden before us."

Naughton buried his surprise, but not before Joe had noticed it. The director gestured at the monitors. "No sign of him here."

"And you obviously didn't get him on the rear wall cameras."

Naughton shook his head.

"Even if he makes it, Murray, he would still have to get past security," Hoad pointed out.

"Let's worry about that when he makes the back door, huh?" Joe suggested. "But I will say this. You'd better call the two night security people and get them down here. We'll need to talk to them."

He had barely got the words out when all hell broke loose from beyond the control room. Naughton leapt from his seat and hurried out, with Joe, Rahman and Hoad on his heels.

They emerged into the rear of the house to find a security officer wrestling with Tanner.

"Will you tell this moron to let me go," Tanner demanded.

"It's all right, Ray," Scott ordered. "We know about him."

"Sorry, Mr Naughton, but we don't even know how he got in."

"That was the point of the exercise, you blithering idiot," Tanner snapped.

Muttering apologies, Ray released the irate Tanner, who then stared triumphantly at Hoad.

"Still think I'm too old for the game?"

***

"I'm impressed, Les," Joe said as he and Tanner sat down in the control room with a cup of tea. "I never thought you could do it."

"It still doesn't get Brenda out of here, does it?"

"She'll be out by teatime," Joe promised. "You have my word on that."

Tanner grinned. "I think you're a complete waste of space most of the time, Murray. You're irritable, offensive and thoroughly inefficient, but I have to say you're persistent and your insight does you credit."

"Careful, Les or we may end up as friends."

Tanner laughed. "I hardly think so." He sipped at his tea. "So what now? You've proved that someone could have got in from the outside, but you haven't got them past security and into the house."

"That's the easy bit," Joe assured him. "Hoad is on the blower to the night security folk right now. They're going to be brought in for questioning. You go back to Sylvia and Sheila, and make sure you get a bill from the taxi driver. I'll reimburse you from club funds. I'll bring you up to speed at the hotel tonight."

Chapter Ten

"Sit you down, Ms Driscoll."

Joe guessed security officer, Rebecca Driscoll's age to be a shade under 40. Her dark hair was neatly styled into place above a lean, angular face. The slender shoulders and rough hands spoke of a woman who had worked all her life, and her confident stride and assured posture probably meant she had seen time in the forces. It was an impression borne out by the darting way her eyes shifted around the makeshift interview room.

With the time pushing 3:30, the strain of the day's events, a long and tiresome journey from Sanford, all the hassle of taxis back and forth between Chester and Gibraltar Hall, the constant round of arguments and debates with both police and the backroom staff, were beginning to take their toll on Joe. He needed to be back at the Victoria Hotel to sleep some of it off before dinner, but he could not leave Brenda in this hell hole for one more night.

"This is Joe Murray," Hoad was saying to the security woman. "He's not a police officer, but he is a specialist investigator, and he helps the police all over the country when needed."

Joe allowed the lie with only a smile.

"You're not obliged to answer any of Joe's questions," Hoad insisted, "but you are obliged to answer mine, and I have to advise you, if you don't answer him, I'll ask exactly the same question. You understand?"

Rebecca nodded and cleared her throat. "Am I under arrest?"

"No," Hoad said. "You're merely helping us with our inquiries."

"Over the bimbo what topped herself?"

"Interesting," Joe said.

Rebecca eyed him with even deeper suspicion. "What?"

"You seem convinced that Ursula hung herself. We're not so sure."

The security officer shrugged. "Couldna been anyone else, could it. They'd have been on camera."

"Not if they knew how to run stock feeds," Joe argued. "And we know they could have got in through the back door."

A visible shock ran across her features. A widening of the eyes, creasing her forehead. It was only fleeting and she was quick to suppress it, but Joe noticed it.

"Not possible," she declared. "They might get past old Bexley, but no way would they make it past me."

"Oh yes they would," Joe retorted, "especially during the time you weren't there."

There was no mistaking the surprise this time. "I work here all night, every night," Rebecca insisted.

"Then how come I saw you in the bar of the Victoria Hotel at half past eleven last night?"

The security guard shook her head. "No way. No way was I in the Victoria Hotel last night. You've got me mixed up with someone else."

Joe leaned back in his seat. "It was you. I wouldn't know you from Adam, but I know that uniform. I watched you leave the Victoria Hotel last night at just after half past eleven... oh, my mistake. It wasn't half past eleven. It was half past twelve. That's right. I was in my room, which overlooks the car park and I saw you getting into your car."

"Try again," Rebecca challenged. "I was nowhere near the Victoria Hotel last night. I was here."

"Joe and I both know that's not true, Ms Driscoll," Hoad insisted. "Now it could be that Joe was mistaken. And he didn't see you at the Victoria Hotel. But I don't believe he is. I believe he saw you there. If you weren't there, tell us where you were."

"I told you. I was here."

"That's not what your pal Bexley says," Joe lied. "He says you slipped out for an hour or two."

Her face flushed with frustration. "The bloody idiot. I told him to keep quiet or he'd drop us both in it."

Joe's relaxation was less forced this time. "Tell us what the arrangement was."

The security officer sighed. "It was private, right? Between me and him. He's a tired bugger, Bexley. Getting too old for nights. Has a habit of nodding off, and last night I had what I thought was an emergency, so we came to an agreement. He'd keep an eye on everything while I nipped home to sort it. I swear I was gone no longer than an hour."

"What was this emergency?" Hoad demanded.

"I got a call after midnight. One of my kids had been injured in an accident at home. I rang the house and got no answer. I was in a panic. I had to get home to sort it out."

"And did you?" Joe asked. "Sort it out, I mean?"

Rebecca's face fell. "No. When I got there, everything was all right. The reason I got no answer on the phone was both kids were in bed." She smiled weakly. "They would be, wouldn't they?"

"Let me get this straight," Hoad said, "you're working nights here and leaving two children home alone?"

"I had no choice. I did ask if I could have days, but they told me no, and I need the money, so I took it. "

Joe frowned. "What's Bexley's angle on this?"

"When I got back, I let him have a couple of hours' kip."

Joe leapt upon the admission. "But when you got back, he was already asleep, wasn't he?"

Rebecca nodded. "I rang the berk from the back gates so he could stop the cameras and let me get in without it registering on tape. He was dopey as hell. Just managed to stop the cameras. I got back in and he was asleep again. I had to start everything up."

"And that answers the how," Joe commented. "How you manage to get out and back in without showing up on the surveillance cameras."

"We pause them," she confessed. "Fix the view on one

121

end of the garden and hold the house mounted cameras just long enough for me to get back in."

"If anyone studied those recordings properly, you could have been in serious trouble."

"Different feeds," Joe said. "No one would question the rear wall cameras pausing on the same spot because all Driscoll and Bexley had to do was claim they'd seen movement in the woods. And the chances of anyone here rumbling that the house cameras were stopped at the same time would be slim because until Les Tanner demonstrated it earlier, everyone was convinced the place was impregnable."

"Is that right, Ms Driscoll?" Hoad asked.

The security guard nodded. "It's just about the way me and Bexley figured it. Look, you don't get this, do you? We were never put on this gig to stop people getting in. According to the TV bods, that's impossible anyway. We were here to stop the Housies getting out. That would be a breach of contract. I guarantee no reporter could get into the place, but there was always the danger that one of the Housies had a contact with the press and maybe a mobile phone hidden in the garden." She raised her hands slightly upwards in a gesture that took in the whole house. "The odds of these muppets winning the big prize are, like eight to one, so the TV company figure that they might wanna shorten the odds by selling stories to the papers. You get it? That's why we're here. Nobody in their right mind would wanna break into this gig, but the Housies might wanna break out."

"Let's put that aside," Hoad said. "What time did you leave last night?"

"About half past midnight, I got back at one forty. But Bexley was on the job. No one could have got in… or out."

Joe shook his head. "Bexley was asleep. I'll stake a week's takings on that."

"Was there anything unusual when you got back?" Hoad asked. "Anything out of the ordinary?"

She shook her head miserably. "Apart from dipstick

Bexley being asleep again, no."

"Was it normal for him to be that sleepy?" Joe demanded.

"No," Rebecca replied. "He's a tired old git, granted, but he usually managed to stay awake when he need to."

"And aside from that, there was nothing?" Joe demanded. "You didn't see anyone else in or near the hall?"

She shook her head again.

"Right. We'll speak to Bexley," Hoad said. "Sergeant Rahman?"

"Sir?"

"Take Ms Driscoll out, and show Bexley in. Then while Mr Murray and I are talking to Bexley, you can take a formal statement from this lady."

Rebecca clucked. "You'll get me fired."

"That's not my problem," Hoad replied. "Detective Sergeant Rahman rang you this morning and over the phone you maintained that you never left your station all night. You lied, madam, and that lie could have compromised my investigation were it not for the help of Mr Murray. Your employer may have more to say on the matter, but that's your lookout. All I need from you is a statement of the truth. And I'll want your home address and the name of your eldest child so I can confirm all this."

"Aw, come on, man…"

Hoad held up a hand for silence. "Not interested. Rahman."

The sergeant led Rebecca out, and Hoad half turned in his seat to face Joe.

"How did you guess?"

"Short of either her or Bexley killing Ursula, it was the only way it could be done," Joe insisted. "And I did see a security guard at the Victoria Hotel. He was wearing the same uniform as these people here, so presumably works for the same company. He was having a drink in the bar. Dunno whether he was working or not, but I figured if he was, then he was stealing the company's time."

Hoad laughed. "You weren't even in Chester last night."

Joe grinned by return. "No. It was this lunchtime when I

went back for Tanner." His face became more serious. "The question we have to ask ourselves, Frank, is: did Rebecca Driscoll or Bexley kill the girl? It seems unlikely. Not only would they need access to the TV feeds which they don't have, but they'd also need to know how to use them. I think that eliminates them. So if not one of them, then it's a member of the crew, and that, in turn, means it's someone who knew Rebecca's number, *knew* her kids would be in bed and also knew that Rebecca was the kind of mother who would run for it if the kids were in trouble."

"We'll know about that when Rahman checks out her statement."

The door opened and Rahman ushered Bexley in.

He could not be more unlike his partner. Short, tubby, his hair almost gone on top, Joe judged him to be in his early sixties, a man coasting to retirement. Carrying a bottle of water in his dumpy hands, he stared around the room like a man suspecting a trap.

"Sit down, Bexley," Hoad invited, and while the chubby man took his place and gulped down a mouthful of water, the chief inspector introduced Joe the same way he had introduced him to Driscoll.

"There's no great pressure," Joe said at length. "We just want to know how come you fell asleep last night while Ms Driscoll was out attending to her kids."

"I, er, I don't know, er, I'm not sure…"

"Before you try to lie your way out of it," Hoad interrupted, "your colleague has just told us exactly what went on last night. She also told us that you were supposed to keep your eyes open to cover for her, but last night you were asleep again by the time she got from the back gate to the security room."

"I, er, I dunno. I was tired, I reckon."

"More tired than…"

Joe interrupted Hoad before he could complete his question.

"What's your usual routine, Ernie? From coming on duty, I mean."

Bexley shrugged and drank from his bottle of water. "We come on shift at ten. First job is to sign the production crew off and give them back their mobile phones."

Hoad suppressed his irritation at Joe's interruption. "Give them their mobile phones back?"

Bexley nodded. "No one's allowed a mobile phone while the live feeds are going out with commentary. That's from seven of a morning until ten at night. Through the night, there's no commentary and no crew on duty, y'see, so it's not a problem."

"So as the crew come in during the day, they hand their mobile phones in to security?"

Bexley nodded and drank more water.

"Once you've signed the crew out at ten, what next?" Joe asked.

"We just settle down and watch the monitors. All night. Unless something happens, like. Then we have to deal with it, but nothing ever happens."

"Boring job?" Joe asked, and taking another swallow of water, Bexley nodded.

"Sleep a lot on duty, do you?" Hoad followed up.

This time Bexley shook his head. "Not really. Look, at my time of life, I get a bit tired during the night. Right? We work a ten-hour shift. On at ten and we don't get off until eight in the morning. So Rebecca, see, she lets me have an hour's kip."

"And last night, she had to call in the debt," Joe suggested.

"She was panicking," the security man agreed. "As far as I can see, there was no harm. Like I said, nothing ever happens here during the night... well nothing we can do anything about."

"But something did happen, Bexley," Hoad said. "Last night, while your mate was out checking on her brats, and you were sleeping, someone sneaked in, killed that poor lass, and sneaked out again."

That was the signal for Bexley to take on more water. When he removed the bottle from his lips, he gasped in his breath and shook his head. "Not possible. It can't be done. The cameras…"

"It can be done," Hoad interrupted again.

"Do you drink a lot of water, Ernie?" Joe asked.

"Not normally, no. Normally I drink tea."

"But a lot of it?" Joe insisted.

"Not really. I like a brew but in a ten-hour shift I wouldn't have more than three or four cups." He looked down at the bottle and then back at Joe. "Just thirsty, that's all."

"Nerves?" Joe asked.

Again Bexley shook his head. "Don't think so. I think I'm sickening for something. Been thirsty as hell all day."

"Just like the Housies," Joe murmured.

"Can we stick to the subject?" Hoad demanded. "What time do you normally take your kip?"

"There's no fixed time," Bexley replied. He fiddled again with the bottle as if he were reluctant to take a drink after Joe had questioned him.

"But it's always when Rebecca is there to cover for you? It's not, for instance, when she's in the lavatory, or touring the gardens?" Joe asked.

Bexley nodded. "We don't tour the gardens or the building."

"Whatever. Last night it went wrong, didn't it?" Joe challenged. "You fell asleep while Rebecca was out. You couldn't keep your eyes open, could you?"

Jitters getting the better of him, Bexley sucked on the bottle again. When he had satisfied his thirst, he pleaded, "I told you. I think I'm sickening for something."

"And while you were giving out zeds, someone sneaked past you and murdered that girl," Hoad snapped.

"I tell you, that can't happen," the security officer pleaded.

"Leave us to worry about that, Ernie," Joe said. "Can you say with any certainty what time you nodded off?"

Bexley's shoulders slumped. For long moments he stared at the floor, his tubby features working, worrying or trying to remember. "The company could fire me for this."

"Your pal has already said that," Hoad told him, "and I wasn't interested. Just answer the question."

"I felt sleepy not long after we came on shift," he admitted. "I was struggling to keep my eyes open. Especially after the crew had gone home. You know, when there's less to do. But I was awake when Rebecca left. I had to be. I had to pause the house and wall cameras so she could get out. She left about half past twelve. I reckon I must have stayed awake for another, I dunno, fifteen, maybe twenty minutes. Next thing I knew was Rebecca ringing me to let her in. That was about twenty to two."

Hoad looked to Joe who gave the slightest of nods as a signal to the chief inspector that he was through.

"All right. You can leave. You'll need to give a full statement to Detective Sergeant Rahman before you go home. And you won't be needed here tonight."

They watched him leave.

"Well?" Hoad raised his eyebrows at Joe.

"The killer had a forty, maybe fifty-minute window in which to get in, kill Ursula and get out again. It has to be one of the crew."

Hoad stood up. "*If* she was murdered."

Joe tutted and shook his head. "She was murdered, right? The bed and the cord are telling us that."

"I prefer to rely on the post mortem." Hoad strode to the window and looked out at the hall. "But I'll indulge you, Joe. Tell me how it happened."

"Someone slipped something into Bexley's tea. Notice he said he's been thirsty all day? Classic sign of having taken a powerful sleeping pill. Our killer knew plenty about this pair. He gave Bexley the sleeper and then waited until Driscoll left by the back gate. The killer then waited a while longer, until he was sure Bexley was asleep. It wouldn't matter if he wasn't. The killer, because he was a member of the crew, would have some excuse ready. Anyway, he's out there in the woods, waiting. The time's right. He dodges the cameras the way Les did earlier, comes in through the back door and finds Bexley asleep. He then makes his way to the control room, stops the cameras, goes to the Romping Room where he finds Ursula asleep, probably because she's doped up to the eyeballs, too, on those painkillers of hers. The post mortem will tell us that. He hangs her, then leaves the same way he came in, using the disparity in camera sweeps to cover his tracks. All up, I'd reckon it would take a fit man, or woman, less than half an hour."

Hoad said nothing, but continued to stare into space.

While he waited for the chief inspector to speak, Joe concentrated on his netbook and brought his notes up to date. Eventually, he saved the document and shut down the computer.

"Well?" he asked.

"It's too wild and there are too many unanswered questions," Hoad replied turning from the window. "I don't have the post mortem results yet, so I don't really know that we're dealing with anything other than suicide." He pressed on as Joe opened his mouth. "Yes, yes, I know about the bed and the cord, but we both know there are other possible explanations for both. I need more evidence, Joe, before I can call it a murder investigation."

"What kind of evidence?" Joe demanded, folding the netbook away into its travelling case.

"I don't know. Signs of a struggle; bruising to indicate she was manhandled; something in her blood. I really don't know."

Joe checked his watch. "Almost four o'clock. What time do you expect the post mortem results?"

"Any time now," the chief inspector said. "Look, Joe, you've demonstrated that someone could have got into the house, but there are questions you haven't answered yet. There are about 150 cameras covering every cubic inch of this house. There are two on the first floor landing to get to the Romping Room, our killer would have to disable those two at least. Possibly more. If that had happened, every nerd following the online streaming would have been up in arms. Our preliminary view of the overnight footage indicates no break in transmission. How are you going to get round that?"

"Stock feeds, I think." Joe chewed his lip. "Katy gave me a rundown of them when we were out in the garden, but we need to know more. What say we talk to this director, Scott Naughton?"

***

Back in the control room, Joe marvelled once more at the morass of monitors, computer drives and the massed control panel. "How the hell do you sort all this out?" he asked.

"It's not difficult when you know how," Naughton replied, with a gesture at the large, single monitor. "This is our master feed. It's what the viewers see at home. I can switch feeds from any of the cameras at any time."

He scanned the bank of monitors and homed in on a view of two Housies in the kitchen. Turning to his assistant, he said, "Switch to 33."

The scene on the large monitor switched from the lounge to the kitchen.

"So that's what the viewers are seeing at home, right now?" Joe asked.

"No." Naughton shook his head. "It's what the viewers would be seeing. We shut down within five minutes of confirming that Ursula was hanging. As far as I'm aware, the channel is now running old John Wayne movies."

Joe grunted his approval. "Good for them."

Naughton put on a face of pure agony. "Come on. John Wayne?"

"I know what you mean," Joe said, "but he's still preferable to the garbage you're putting out."

"I have a mortgage to pay," Naughton told him. "I can't afford altruism."

"Yeah, right. I know what you mean. Even I buy frozen pies during busy times, too. Katy mentioned something about stock feeds earlier. Tell me, what do you do in the event of a breakdown? I mean, I know this stuff is reliable,

129

but don't tell me you don't get technical problems with the cameras now and then."

"True enough," the director agreed. He waved again at the monitors. "For each of our cameras, there's a technical hatch where we can reach in, remove a camera and replace it if it goes on the blink."

"So I've been told," Joe reported, "but what about your web surfers? They can access any view at any time so I'm told. They'll see the technician at work, won't they? And if the Housies are nearby it means they're having contact with the outside world which is against the rules."

Again the director shook his head. "That is precisely when we run the stock feeds. If we have a breakdown the Housies are ordered away from the room and we run a stock feed until the camera is swapped."

"And you have those stock feeds to hand?" Hoad asked.

"They're a part of our backup recordings."

"Ah. I wanted to ask about that," Joe said. "I know you techie guys. You always back everything up. That's like me putting two Yorkshire puddings in the oven just in case one doesn't rise."

Naughton frowned. "I suppose so." His brow creased further. "Do you do that? Put two Yorkshires in the oven? As a backup?"

"Do I hell as like. My Yorkshires always rise. I was just pointing out the futility of it. You store backups in case something goes wrong, but it's rare that anything actually goes wrong." Joe took out his tobacco tin and began to roll a cigarette. "So, how do you store these backups? Videotape or DVD or something."

Naughton's face turned to one of sour disdain. "Stick to your Yorkshire puddings, Murray."

"No, no, I mean it. I want to know."

"You're living in the Stone Age," Naughton told him. "They used Videotape on the Ark and Columbus played with DVDs on the Santa Maria. Everything these days is digital. We store the feeds as digital files."

"You mean like the ones I see on YouTube?"

"Correct," Naughton assured him.

Joe looked around the room and down at the floor where several tower units appeared to be working.

"If I wanted to make a DVD of some of your backups, could I do it?"

"If you knew what you were doing, yes," Naughton agreed. "But it would take a long time. These are high definition files. They take up an enormous amount of memory."

"So I couldn't do it in secret?"

"Only during the night, when everyone has gone home, but even then you'd need to get past security and into here to do it."

Joe stroked his chin and gazed again at the morass of equipment. "All right, Naughton. Let's imagine the camera on the landing outside the Romping Room breaks down. How quickly can you switch the view to your stock feed?"

Naughton shrugged. "Me? I could do it in maybe five seconds. Helen probably could, and maybe Katy, too. Most others, I'd guess, would take a good minute, maybe longer. They'd have to search the computer folders looking for the correct feed. I know where it is." He sat forward in his seat and spun away from his control board. "What are you getting at, Murray? You think someone switched the feeds so they could get into the Romping Room without being seen?"

Joe nodded. "Hmm. Maybe."

"Impossible," Naughton declared.

"Why?"

"Because there are other feeds your supposed killer would have to switch. The main entrance hall, for instance. There was no access to the upper landing from the back stairs. It was sealed off until the police got here. And there's a second camera on the landing, at the other end. We can watch the landing from either end, and that covers dorms, bathrooms and the Romping Room."

Hoad's eye gleamed with triumph. "You see, Joe. There is no way anyone but one of the Housies could have got into that room, and we know from studying the footage that they didn't."

"So when your post mortem results come back and they tell you she was murdered, which way will you go then?" Joe demanded.

"If she was murdered, I'll sell my missus into slavery," the chief inspector insisted.

"Then give me a price," Joe retorted. "I could do with a cheap kitchen hand."

***

"What about Brenda and the other Housies?" Joe asked as he and Hoad stepped out of the house into the hot, sunny afternoon.

"We've done with them for now, so I think we can let them go," Hoad agreed. "As long as they agree to stay in the area." He slipped his jacket on and dug into the pockets for his mobile phone. "If you want to hang about, I'll give them the good news and your lady friend can go with you back to your hotel."

Joe smiled broadly. "Good man. I'll bell for a taxi and be waiting outside for her. You'll let me know about the post mortem results?"

"Yeah, no problem. Tell me, Joe, what's your thinking now? That one of the production crew came in, set up stock feeds to cover their movements while they did the business?"

"You said you don't think it could be done?"

"It would need a lot of planning and careful timing," Hoad ventured. "And there's one other ingredient missing, isn't there? Motive."

"Well, my experience is that the victim will tell you all about the motive."

"I'll be in touch," Hoad promised.

Chapter Eleven

After fighting through the rush hour traffic on Grosvenor Road, the taxi circled a roundabout and turned onto the final leg of its journey, along a narrow road, lined either side with terraced houses.

Contrary to her usual, garrulous self, Brenda had been silent throughout the 25-minute journey from Gibraltar Hall. Joe had wittered, telling her how the café and the Sanford 3rd Age Club had missed her for the past week, and how they were looking forward to having her back in the fold for a celebratory dinner in just a few hours.

Small talk, he thought to himself. Neither of them wanted to broach the subject of Ursula Kenney.

They had confronted death, even murder, a number of times in the past, and Brenda had personal experience. She lost her husband, Colin to cancer some years back. It was a subject that touched her, worried her, even frightened her sometimes, and in Joe's opinion, it helped explain her free and easy approach to life and love. She, more than any of them, was acutely aware of her own mortality, and there was a burning need to bury that fear under a life in pursuit of mild hedonism.

This time, however, she had been implicated in a death, no matter how slightly. The grilling she had undergone from Chief Inspector Hoad and Sergeant Rahman had unnerved her.

On the way into Chester, they had been surrounded by the sights, sounds and smells of an English city in full summer flow. An August sun blazed onto the crowded pavements, T-shirts and shorts, lots of bared, often burned flesh, the call of the bars and shops, the chatter of the shoppers, the glare of the sun from the flat calm river, all conspired and called to the sense of freedom which went with a summer's afternoon. Yet Brenda sat locked in a nightmare of murder (despite Chief Inspector Hoad's hesitancy, Joe remained convinced that Ursula had been deliberately killed) where she was a possible suspect.

Now the shops and restaurants had thinned out, becoming this faceless row of terraced houses, and the cacophony of summer faded to the muted peace of suburbia.

Joe felt a sudden urge to take Brenda's hand. The two women had worked for him for over five years and all three had been friends since childhood, but he was careful to maintain a discreet distance. A kiss at Christmas, friendly lips touching at birthday parties; they were the sum total of intimacy between them. Joe wanted nothing more of either Sheila or Brenda, but he felt she needed support and if holding her hand would lend it then...

As his gnarled hand wrapped around hers, she smiled wanly. "Thank you, Joe."

The moment did not last. The driver turned into the Victoria Hotel's forecourt, skirted the fountain and its surrounding rockery and pulled up to the entrance.

While Brenda climbed out of the car, Joe paid the driver and retrieved her suitcase from the boot.

"You'll have to register," he told her as the car pulled away again. "You're expected but we couldn't book you in until you actually arrived. You're billeted with Sheila and once we get you signed in, I'll take your bags up to your room."

Escorting her into reception, Joe again noticed that she said nothing. She was bottling it up and he knew the flood would come. He would prefer not to be there when it happened. Women who cried always made him feel guilty, and anyway, Sheila had spent many years as a school secretary. She was better equipped to handle the inevitable flood of tears.

He had rung Sheila from Gibraltar Hall as they climbed into the taxi, warning her to expect them, and she was there, waiting in reception for their arrival. Looking into the bar beyond her, Joe could see the Staineses, Owen Frickley and George Robson at a table close to the entrance. He guessed that the whole of the Sanford 3rd Age Club contingent would be in there, everyone on pins, waiting to see their heroine.

Brenda spent a few moments filling in the registration card at the reception counter, then crossed the carpeted lobby to chat briefly with Sheila. Joe waited patiently for the two women to move towards the lift, the signal for him to tag along with Brenda's suitcase.

Without warning Brenda fell into Sheila's arm and began crying. Feeling useless and helpless, Joe concentrated on a display of leaflets for boat trips on the River Dee. Why did women always have to cry?

Sheila hugged her friend for a long moment and then gently guided her to a seat. Sitting alongside her, the two women dissolved into muted, serious conversation, Brenda dabbing away her tears with a tissue, Sheila holding her hand. Joe took out his tobacco tin and rolled a cigarette. When it was completed, he tucked it into his shirt pocket, and looked to the two women again. A thin smile had broken across Brenda's pained features. Sheila doing what she did best, he diagnosed; quietly, gently encouraging her best friend.

Dragging Brenda's luggage with him, Joe made his way to the bar entrance and looked in. Expectant faces greeted him. Across the room, by the windows, he could see Sylvia and Tanner, sat with Mavis Barker and Cyril Peck. Tanner raised inquisitive eyebrows. Joe gave him the thumbs up. Close to him, George Robson and Alec Staines stood with the obvious intention of approaching. He frowned and shook his head in a gesture that said, "Not yet," and the two men sat down again.

Joe backed out. His sole purpose had been to allow his two companions a moment or two alone so they could reconcile Brenda's distress.

The two women stood up. "Right," Sheila announced

briskly. "If you're ready, Joe, let's get Brenda's belongings upstairs."

"About time, too," Joe grumbled. "I'm gasping for a smoke and waiting for you two…"

Brenda bestowed a smile upon him that was almost loving. "Has anyone ever told you, Joe, that you're a wonderful man?"

"Yes, well, don't go spreading it about. I have a reputation to live up to, you know."

***

Sat on the rear terrace looking over towards the boat station, Joe drew on a cigarette and let the smoke out slowly. With the afternoon sun dipping behind the distant city centre, Joe, Sheila and Brenda sat with tea enjoying the cool evening shade, watching the sightseers and early Friday evening revellers, making the most of their time, and Joe felt more at peace than he had done all day.

After changing into a conservative dark skirt and white blouse, escorted by her two friends, Brenda had made her way down to the dining room for just after seven, where a rousing cheer from the STAC members almost reduced her to tears again. She received their gushing reception and personal messages of goodwill with modest reddening of her cheeks, causing Joe to comment, "I never thought I'd see the day when Brenda Jump blushed."

Eventually, after an excellent meal of lemon sole, still carrying a glass of white wine, she joined Joe and Sheila on the terrace, and declared, "It's nice to know you have such friends."

"We were all rooting for you, Brenda," Sheila told her.

"What will the TV company do with the prize money now?" Joe wanted to know.

"It's also nice to know that some things never change," Brenda teased. "As I understand, Joe, we're sharing it, all eight of us. Ursula's share will be paid to whatever family she had, or if they can't find anyone, they'll donate it to a charity." She drank from her glass and demanded, "Tell me the truth, Joe. Was it suicide?"

Joe shook his head. "It was murder. By the time I'd done with Frank Hoad, he was all but convinced, and the only good news is that you Housies are all in the clear. There is no way any of you could have done it. You'd need access to the control room to get out of the dormitory to the Romping Room."

"I know I didn't do it," Brenda said, downing another large swallow of the house white. "But that bloody detective, that Hoad, swore blind I had a grudge against the girl. Me? When do I bear grudges?"

"You did have some arguments with her, dear," Sheila pointed out.

Brenda aimed an accusing finger at Joe. "I argue with him six days a week, but I haven't minced him up into the steak pies yet."

"I like the way you left the option open," Joe said. "Brenda, tell us about Ursula."

"You haven't been watching?" Brenda sounded affronted and Joe felt secretly pleased that she was coming back to her old self.

"Of course we have," Sheila replied, "but I think Joe's hinting that even watching you for twenty-four hours, day and night, you don't get the same, er, *feel* for a person as you do when you're with them."

"Sorry," Brenda said. "I can't help thinking that the poor girl…" She trailed off, tears sparkling in her eyes, and drank more wine to settle her nerves.

"Brenda," Joe insisted, "I know you don't like to speak ill of the dead, but in this case, we need to know everything we can about her. Listen to me. Someone murdered her. I'm sure of it, and when he gets the post mortem results in, Hoad will be too. The only way we can get justice for her is to find her killer, and the only person who can give us a hint is Ursula. She's dead, so we need to get those hints from people like you. So come on. I don't need you to speak ill of her. I just need you to be honest."

Brenda remained silent for a while, staring out across the river to the far bank where couples walked hand in hand. Her eyes focussed again and narrowed on Joe. Pulling in a deep breath, she let it out with a sigh.

"She was a little tart. There. I've said it. A cow of the first order. She spent all week playing up to the men, looking for a fight with the women so she could show that she was the celeb, the alpha-mama." Brenda sighed again in an effort to ease her anger. "If she was murdered, and I stress, if, then a lot of people will say she got what she deserved. But you know me, Joe. It's not true. It was a front, all of it. She was fond of telling us she'd been an actress some years ago, and she was using whatever acting skills she had to put it all on. She wanted that prize money and she actually said more than once that it was as good as hers."

"Because she was so sure she could out-perform you all," Sheila commented.

"Or did she know something the rest of you didn't?"

The two women stared at Joe.

"That's impossible, Joe," Sheila said at length. "The winner was to be decided by a telephone vote."

"And only the TV company would know the outcome of that vote," Joe pointed out. "Let's just play devil's advocate here. Suppose, just suppose, she had an arrangement with someone high up in the company headquarters. What's to stop them fixing the vote? I don't know enough about the safeguards to really comment, but it must be possible."

"There have been cases in the past," Brenda murmured, "but I don't know that they actually affected the outcome."

"Were you given any indication at any time of your ongoing popularity?" Joe asked.

"Not in so many words," Brenda said. "When you went into the video room, they would say, your popularity has risen today after... whatever you did. Or it might go the other way. Your popularity has slipped today because of... again, whatever it was you did." Brenda finished her wine and pushed the glass to one side. "Joe, I can see what you're driving at, but according to our best information, the vote was impossible to rig. You'll probably have to argue this out with the TV company or the police, but I don't think it could be done."

Joe chewed at the stub of a cigarette. Digging into his pockets, he pulled out his Zippo and lit it. "Then why the hell was she killed?"

"If she really was murdered, only she would know that."

"The killer would, too," Joe pointed out. He glanced at his watch. "A quarter to eight. The disco is at nine. What say we take a walk along the river bank?"

"That is the best suggestion you've made all day," Sheila replied.

"I'll second that," Brenda agreed, "and I've only been here a couple of hours."

***

"Frank's here," Joe said to Sheila. "Do you wanna handle the disco while I see what he wants?"

To the sound of the Monkees trying to take *The Last Train To Clarksville* filling the lounge bar, Chief Inspector Hoad entered, looked around, spotted Joe on the podium and waved.

Sheila nodded, Joe gestured to the terrace and as Hoad made his way round a dance floor crowded with members of the Sanford 3rd Age Club, Joe stepped outside and rolled a cigarette.

"You're a DJ, too?" the chief inspector asked as he sat down.

"Only for the club," Joe confessed. "My choice of music is a bit limited for Radio One... Radio Two as well, come to think. Bitta fifties, lotta sixties and seventies. Nothing later than Abba." Joe dropped his tobacco tin in the side pocket of his gilet. "So, what can I do you for, Frank?"

"I have to hand it to you, Joe, you got it spot on," Hoad said. "Ursula was murdered. Post mortem leaves no doubt."

Joe jammed the pipe-cleaner-thin cigarette between his lips, took out his Zippo and lit up, his face briefly illuminated in the early evening light. Blowing smoke into the light breeze, he invited, "Go on."

"Pathologist's preliminary report says her bloodstream contained large doses of Zopiclone. It's a short term tranquiliser, marketed under the trade name Zimovane. A sleeping pill."

Joe frowned. "So what does that prove? Everyone who watched her on TV saw her taking pills before she went to bed every night." Joe smacked his hand against his forehead. "She told everyone they were Dihydrocodeine Tartrate. And they were Zimovane?"

Hoad shook his head. "It's more complicated than that, even. Everyone who watched her on TV saw her taking chalk before she went to bed every night. Her pills, which she claimed were powerful painkillers, were ordinary paracetemol capsules. Headache stuff nothing more. And as far as we're aware, she had no need to be taking them. She was putting on an act, Joe. So where did the Zimovane come from? When we found out, we asked for urine and blood tests from Ernie Bexley. We're waiting for the results, but we think he may have been doped with the same stuff, and it was you who put us onto it."

"All right," Joe agreed, "so it begins to look more like murder. You still don't know for sure?"

"Yes we do. The post mortem also reports that on close investigation there are two ligature marks round her neck. The one was caused by the cord she was hanged with, but it was post mortem. She was already dead. The other, the one that really killed her, was caused by something a lot finer and not plaited the way the cord was. A nylon stocking or something similar." Hoad drummed his fingers on the table. "She won't have known much about it. The Zimovane would have knocked her out by the time the killer came. She was asleep and she just never woke up." He frowned again. "We searched the Housies' effects yesterday, looking for Ursula's pills – alleged strong painkillers – and a few of the women had tights and stockings in their bags."

"No way, Frank." Joe puffed on his cigarette. "Remember

what I said earlier? It has to be one of the crew. They're the only ones who could get at the control room to pause all the cameras or change the feeds." Like Brenda earlier, he too stared across the river as if seeking inspiration. "Have you watched the internet feeds from the appropriate time?"

"Ha!" Hoad's laugh dripped contempt. "Do you know how much of it there is?" He shook his head and lit a cigarette. Blowing a white cloud of smoke into the air, he went on, "We've downloaded most of it from the appropriate cameras, and I have a team of people going over it as we speak, but I don't hold out much hope. It could take days. According to Scott Naughton and Helen Catterick, any shift from live feed to stock is near seamless. They're on standby to help if our people pick up anything at all."

"Katy told me the same," Joe said, "and it's great them offering to help but if it's one of them, they're not going to go out of their way to point it out, are they?"

Hoad's features creased into a frown. With cigarette smoke steaming through his nostrils, giving Joe the impression of a fabled dragon, he asked, "What do you mean?"

"We're looking at the crew. Catterick and Naughton and Katy... whatever her name is, are members of the crew aren't they? Listen to me, Frank, you can't eliminate anyone just because they're higher up in the management scales."

"I'm not," the chief inspector said, "but do you seriously imagine that Helen Catterick could get over that back wall? Scott Naughton or Katy Flitt might do it, but she wouldn't. She's too old."

Joe tutted and took another pull on his cigarette. "Les Tanner is, I think, sixty. He had no problem getting over it. And don't rule out that other one, either. That Marlene Caldbeck. False leg or not, she can go some. She trained with the Paras in one series. Did you see it?"

"Nope. Don't watch much telly. Haven't time."

"She was proving someone with a disability can do it just as good as someone who's fully fit," Joe reported and crushed out his cigarette.

"And did she?" Hoad wanted to know.

Joe promptly took out his tobacco tin and rolled another cigarette. "Did she what?"

"Did she prove that she could do it just as well as someone who's fully fit?"

"I dunno," Joe admitted. "I didn't watch it. Like you I don't have much time for TV."

Frustration shot across Hoad's tanned features. He, too, crushed out his cigarette. "Then how do you know?"

"I read about it in the *Daily Express*," Joe replied.

"It's a little thin, Joe," Hoad said, "and it's contrary to what you just said. Neither Caldbeck nor Rivers are members of the technical crew. They're front people."

Sheila and Brenda stepped out of the bar onto the terrace. Joe frowned. "Who's looking after the disco?"

"I put on some mood music, Joe," Sheila told him. "*Nights In White Satin*. The full version. A good five minutes worth. Most of the dancers went to the bar."

Brenda grinned. "But Alec and Julia Staines are only just short of having it off on the dance floor."

"As long as you don't leave the music too long." Joe concentrated on the chief inspector. "Don't kid yourself, Frank," Joe said as the two women took seats either side of him. "Caldbeck and Rivers may be actors, but I'll bet they know their way around the production system. You can't eliminate any of them."

Hoad bestowed a thin smile on Brenda. "And for that same reason, I can't eliminate any of the Housies."

She glared at him. "Are you accusing me, Chief Inspector? Again?"

Joe noted that she was better in control of herself than she had been earlier. That, he concluded to himself, was the more dangerous Brenda.

Hoad appeared equal to it. "No, Mrs Jump. However, I can't eliminate you either. Because of certain facts which have only come to light late this afternoon, I have to question everyone again, starting tomorrow. I'm sure Joe will bring you up to speed, but I'll need another statement from you."

"So it's definitely murder?" Sheila wanted to know.

Hoad nodded slowly, grimly. "Even if we say that she took the sleeping pills herself – which we very much doubt – the underlying ligature indicates that she was already dead when she was hanged."

"The killer hung her to try and hide the strangling," Joe declared.

"Hanged," Sheila corrected him.

Joe scowled and lit a fresh cigarette. "Pardon my grammar. Hanged, hung, what's the difference? The girl is dead."

"She was a human being, Joe, not a piece of meat," Hoad said. "And I have to know who may have left the dormitory, Mrs Jump."

"During the night, you mean?" Brenda asked. "I didn't. We know Ursula did, but I can't say for the others. As far as I'm aware, no one left, but then I slept all the way through until the alarm was raised this morning."

"We're checking the overnight footage now," Hoad told her, "but as Joe pointed out at the hall, we don't know how reliable it is."

Brenda gaped. "You mean even though it proves no one could have gone into the Romping Room, someone may have done." She glared at Joe. "How come you never said anything in the taxi? You must have known. He's just said so."

"You were upset," he pleaded. "I didn't want to make you worse. I figured the last thing you'd want to talk about was Gibraltar Hall."

"Yes but…"

"Joe's right, dear," Sheila cut in. "You didn't need any of that adding to your woes." She turned to Hoad. "Will Brenda be allowed a representative with her when she's questioned, Chief Inspector?"

Hoad nodded. "All suspects are permitted a representative." He smiled encouragingly. "And Mrs Jump is not really a suspect. However, I will still have to question

143

her and take a formal statement."

Sheila took Brenda's hand. "Joe will be with you. Won't you, Joe?"

"Yeah, course I will. It's no sweat, Brenda. We know you didn't kill her, but like Frank says, he has to speak to everyone."

Hoad stood up. "Twenty to ten. Time I was going home or the missus will want to know where I am. If you could make your way to Gibraltar Hall some time tomorrow, Joe, Mrs Jump, and you're welcome, too, Mrs Riley, I'll see you all there."

He bid them a cheery good evening, and left.

"Pleasant man," Sheila said.

"You wouldn't have thought so when I first met him," Joe replied.

"And you wouldn't have thought so when he and his pal, Rahman, were interviewing me this morning," Brenda concurred. She, too, stood up. "Is it time we were checking on our dancers, Sheila?"

"Good idea. We'll see you in a few minutes, Joe."

Joe nodded and dragged on his cigarette again. Staring out across the river once more, his mind tumbled over the day's events.

It was his habit to keep a journal on his travels, and he had ample notes on his netbook, but notes, as he well knew, were only indicators. The real difficulty came in stringing the observations together to account for all that had happened.

Even as he thought about it, he realised that his notes would be inadequate. Something had happened which, he knew, should be pointing him in a direction, but it had not yet gelled, and he knew the answer did not lie in the notes. It had happened since he returned from Gibraltar Hall with Brenda.

"Come on, Joe," he muttered to himself. "Slide your brain into gear."

That, too, would not work. It was the kind of thing that, the more he thought about it, the harder it would be to pin it down. What he needed was to take his mind away from it, and it would occur naturally.

Sitting alone, looking out over the boat station, taking in the sounds of a busy English city in early evening, he allowed a sense of peace to wash over him. The noise of the fairground reached his ears, the happy screams of those on the rollercoaster, the delighted cries of children playing on the stalls, music coming from a nearby bar, the hum of chatter from the restaurant next door, mingling with the smell of Tandoori, all conspired to mellow him.

The stresses, strains, irritations large and small, of running a café 80 miles to the east, dissipated as they were supposed to do, and it was in that contemplative state, that the answers would come to him.

He loved a puzzle. He loved a challenge. He detested murder, but enjoyed the pursuit, tackling the carefully laid plans of the killer, pulling them apart thread by thread until the whole lay bare before him.

The evil that had been worked at Gibraltar Hall would not beat him. It would take time, but he would win.

Chapter Twelve

"I think a spot of retail therapy is just what I need to get over the shock," Brenda said as they approached the entrance to the Grosvenor Shopping Centre just after half past nine on Saturday morning.

Joe eyed a nearby bench. "This is not what I had in mind," he argued, "And we're getting short of time."

"Chief Inspector Hoad didn't give us a time to be there, Joe." Sheila told him.

"Just get on with it," he ordered. "I'll sit out here, have a smoke and enjoy the sun."

"You fit, Sheila?"

Sheila was not listening. Her gaze was focussed on a café to their right. "Joe, isn't that Rachel?"

Joe spun his head round to look.

The café was sited beyond the shopping mall, where Pepper Street met Newgate Street, in sight of one of the old city gates, a red stone arch spanning the road. A number of the café's customers had elected to sit outside and, like Joe, enjoy the morning sunshine with their food and drink. One woman sat alone, checking her mobile phone. She had no plate or cup in front of her, and Joe guessed she was waiting for her husband or partner to join her from inside the café.

There was no mistaking her identity. The blonde hair may have been turning a shade of silvery white, the tanned hands manipulating the tiny keys on the phone, may have been older, more wrinkled, and the square set of the shoulders may have developed a slight stoop, but Joe would have recognised her anywhere. As if to confirm her identity (not that he needed any such confirmation) Derek Varley came out of the café carrying a tray of tea things and joined her.

Joe stood up again. "You two go ahead. I'll have a chat with them."

"Do you have to, Joe?" Sheila asked.

He frowned. "Listen, when news gets out that Joe Murray is looking into the death of Ursula Kenney, they're gonna know I'm in Chester, and they'll come looking for me. I may as well get it over with now."

Brenda wagged a finger at him. "No arguing, Joe. Rachel was never worth the hassle, and you know it."

Joe drew on his cigarette and blew a cloud of irritated smoke into the air. "Unless Rachel has something to complain about, I've no axe to grind. Bell me when you're ready for going to Gibraltar Hall."

Sheila and Brenda moved on and Joe sat, finishing his cigarette, his memory drifting back over the years and a family feud that had never quite gone away.

In the early eighties, Joe's older brother, Arthur, had upped sticks and gone to Australia, taking his family with him. Whilst Arthur had always been considered the black sheep of the Murray clan for his refusal to come into their father's café, Joe always believed that he went to Australia largely at the insistence of his wife, Rachel.

For Arthur, it was the right move. He had stayed there, set up his own plumbing, heating and air-conditioning business and according to the occasional communication was still doing well. But Rachel had come back to Sanford in less than five years, and brought her son, Lee, back with her. When the boy left school, she badgered Joe into taking him on at the café, Joe agreed and put Lee through catering college. But the lad also played as prop for the Sanford Bulls Rugby League team, and had a promising career ahead of him. When a severe knee injury ended his hopes, Rachel all but abandoned him and moved to Leeds, where she eventually met and married Derek Varley. Her disinterest in Lee, his life, his marriage and his son, Danny, rankled with Joe.

Stubbing out his cigarette, he crossed the paved area fronting the café, moved behind the pavement screens which marked out its seating area, and sat opposite Rachel.

Alongside her, Derek's eyes darted back and forth between the pair. A tall, slender, balding man who had been in the employ of Leeds City Council until his retirement, he had also been under Rachel's thumb for as long as Joe could recall.

"Just when I thought Chester couldn't sink any lower than I-Spy, you had to show up," Joe announced.

Rachel appeared comparatively unsurprised to see him. She delivered a thin smile. "Hello, Joe. How are you?"

"No better for seeing you," he replied with deliberate candour. "How are you, Derek?"

"I, er, I'm fine, Joe. Just wonderful." Derek waved a hand at the air. "All this sunshine, fresh air. Couldn't, er, couldn't wish for more."

"Bit of a coincidence seeing you here," Joe rambled. "We're here to pick up Brenda."

"We?" Rachel's eyebrows rose. "You and Sheila Riley?"

"Me and the Sanford 3rd Age Club," Joe corrected her. Quickly changing the subject, he asked, "Have you seen Danny, lately? The kid's growing up, you know. Gonna be big and strong, just like his dad. A real chip off the old block."

"Thick as a brick, you mean?"

Rachel's insult was deliberate, and Joe knew it, but it nevertheless sent a spear of anger through him. "Lee might be a bit slow on the uptake, but he's a fine lad. Hard working and, unlike his mother, completely dedicated to his wife and son."

She took a sip of tea. Joe noticed her hand tremble and scored himself a point.

"Don't start, Joe," she warned. "We came here for a few days of pleasant downtime, me and Derek. Not to look for fights with you." She put the cup down. "Have you heard from Arthur recently?"

Joe shook his head. "Not since last Christmas. He sends a card and money for Danny. He's still enjoying life in Melbourne."

"He should."Again Rachel smiled. "Of course, you've never met the little tart he was screwing while I stayed home looking after Lee, have you?"

"That's not the way Arthur tells it."

"It's the way I tell it, Joe," Rachel shot back, "because it's the truth."

"Shh," Derek urged. "People are listening." Again he gestured aimlessly around them.

"Joe never worries about other people eavesdropping, do you, Joe?" Rachel commented with a cynical smile. "As long as you get to say your piece."

"It's why I don't suffer any problems up here." Joe tapped his temple. "I'm just saying I don't like the way you cut Lee out of your life. You dragged him away from his dad, brought him halfway round the world to a country he'd forgotten, and encouraged him to play rugby, but the minute he had to give the game up, you shot off out of his life. You forgot all about him and yet, when he and Cheryl are going to Leeds to see you, he's as excited as a big kid."

Rachel shook her head. "When he had to give up playing rugby, it coincided with me meeting Derek. Aren't you the one who always says things are never what they seem on the surface and it's what's underneath that counts? I don't forget Lee. He knows where I am and he knows he's welcome anytime."

"As long as he rings in advance to let you know he's coming." Joe's contempt burst through his words. He recalled Brenda's advice and before Rachel could pick him up again, he asked, "So, what brings you to Chester?"

"It's not a coincidence," Rachel admitted. "We've been following Brenda on TV so we thought we'd come over for the big finale." She smiled again and irritated Joe even further. "Show some support for a fellow Sanfordian."

Joe suppressed a cynical laugh. "And there was me thinking you never cared about the old place."

"I don't," Rachel agreed. "But that doesn't mean I've forgotten those people I used to call friends. You've always criticised me, Joe. Supporting your Arthur, I suppose, although I can't think why. I know he's blood and all that, but when he refused to work for your dad in the café, he condemned you to a life of bacon sandwiches and full English breakfasts, and you've spent most of that life taking it out on everyone else, including your customers. Well your dad had it right. Arthur was selfish. I never did anything wrong other than bring my son away from a country where he would have grown up lonely and friendless." She drank her tea. "At least he made friends in Sanford, and he had you to look out for him."

Joe could not be bothered with the argument. "Well, it's been, er, interesting seeing you both, but I have a life to lead. Got other people I need to snipe at. I wouldn't hang about for D-Day at the I-Spy house, Rachel. What with this Ursula being killed, it ain't gonna happen."

Shock travelled across Rachel's face. "Killed? I thought she committed suicide?"

Joe chuckled. "Oh dear. Let the cat out of the bag, haven't I? Not to worry. The cops will be announcing it on the news before the day's out. She was murdered. I think it might have been her ex-husband's brother. See y'around."

"Yes. See you, er, Joe," said Derek as Joe tromped off.

Disgruntled by most of what Rachel had said, Joe ambled into the Grosvenor Shopping Centre, and had barely gone through the entrance, when his mobile tweeted for attention. He pulled it from his shirt pocket and checked the menu window. *Unknown number.*

With a wolfish grin he put it to his ear. "Morning, Frank, how's it going?"

"How did you know it was me?" Hoad asked.

"Educated guess," Joe replied. "What do you know?"

"A lot that I didn't know yesterday, or even late last night. Any interview with your friend is likely to be very short, but she may have a lot of information to give us. How soon can you get here?"

"The women are shopping right now," Joe said, "so how about we plan for noon?"

"Fine. I need to speak to the other seven Housies,

anyway. But make sure it's not too long after."

Joe agreed and rang off, then dialled Brenda and arranged to meet the women at the main entrance on Foregate Street, in sight of the old clock tower sitting on its ornate arch.

An hour later, after dropping their purchases at the Victoria Hotel, they were on their way to Gibraltar Hall.

"Chief Inspector Hoad didn't say what he'd learned?" Sheila asked as the driver pulled out of the hotel grounds and onto the single track Old Dee Bridge to cross the river.

"No." Seated up front with the driver, Joe half turned in his seat to look at Brenda. "Marc wore that god awful dressing gown at breakfast most mornings, didn't he?"

"Every morning as far as I can recall," Brenda said.

Joe noticed she had suddenly become more reserved. "Look, Brenda, I know this isn't easy for you, but let's think on the positive side, huh? Frank doesn't suspect you. He has to take a statement, true, but you're not in the frame. All we can do now is help find this woman's killer. She may have been a grade one slapper, but she didn't deserve to die like that."

Brenda drew in her breath and nodded.

"That's the spirit," Joe smiled. "Now, I'm wondering, when did anyone take that cord from the dressing gown. In fact, I'm wondering *did* anyone get that cord from the dressing gown."

Brenda gawped."You think it may be Marc? Come on, Joe. He's as gormless as young Lee. I don't think he'd have the guts, never mind the gumption."

"Brenda, you've only known him a week. You've been in a false situation, and all you really know about each other is what you're told by each other. He tells you he's a… what is he?"

"An accountant from Northampton."

"Right. He tells you he's an accountant from Northampton, but you only have his say so for that. He plays the part right down to the wire, letting everyone think he's a gawp but for all you really know, he could be a… well I don't know. An actor from Musselburgh."

"Why Musselburgh?" Brenda asked.

"It was the first place I thought of."

"And why an actor?" Sheila demanded.

"So he could play the part," Joe responded. "Anyway, Ursula was an actress and if he was an actor, he might have known her from the past."

***

When they arrived at Gibraltar Hall it was to learn that Chief Inspector Hoad was locked into a conference call between himself, his superiors and representatives of both the production company and the TV station. Seeking out Helen Catterick, Joe suggested they take a walk in the garden, were he could enjoy a cigarette while they talked.

Agreeing to his request, she said, "I'm not sure what I can tell you that I haven't already told the police."

"We have different methods, Helen, and sometimes one of us sees things others don't."

They stepped out into the garden where workmen were already busy removing the high fence that separated the two halves.

"The police authorised it," Helen explained. "It takes us several weeks to set up properly, but when the show is over, which it would have been today, we have one week to restore it to its former condition. Ursula's death has terminated the show early, and we thought we may as well get on with it."

Joe drew on his cigarette. "It's bad for you, isn't it?" he commented. "This whole business." He mentally rebuked himself for his lack of small talk. Helen was dressed in a dark jumper and skirt that reached below the knee, and she would have made a perfect date, if he ever felt comfortable talking to such women.

"We don't know what the ramifications will be," she said. "It could mean the end of I-Spy altogether."

"Or at the very least more careful selection of Housies," Joe suggested.

With a nod, Helen leaned forward and rubbed at her leg.

Joe followed the movement and picked out a three-inch scar of white flesh over her tanned calf. He caught her watching him and felt the colour rush to his cheeks. "Sorry. I wasn't... you know... the scar."

She laughed good-naturedly. "It's all right, Joe. May I call you Joe?"

"Better than the names some people call me."

Helen rubbed the leg again. "An accident in my childhood. I think I was about three years old when it happened. Nothing really, but I remember making such a fuss at the blood. It doesn't hurt, but when I have a tan – did I tell you I'd recently had a holiday in Crete? – it really annoys me."

"Scar tissue," Joe said. "It never tans. I have a similar one on my right knee, but it's only tiny. Fell on a broken bottle when I was a kid."

Silence fell and they savoured the glorious sunshine and hot, morning air.

"You've demonstrated that our security team could be at fault," Helen said suddenly.

"What?" Joe emerged from some of the more dangerous meanderings of his mind which involved legs. "Oh. Yes. It was all obvious to me from the start." He grinned sheepishly. "My brain's wired up differently, you know. I knew that whoever got in had to get past security and that told me one of them was probably absent and the other asleep."

Helen frowned. "It doesn't surprise me. The younger one, Driscoll is she called? She was pestering me from day one about getting time off for her children. I told her to take it up with her employers, not me. We're not responsible for them, you see. They're contractors." Her eyes narrowed on Joe. "Someone on the inside must have spotted it and used it to their advantage."

"It's more complicated than that. Someone called her and tricked her into leaving the house." Joe crushed out his cigarette. "And I'm sorry, but yes. The finger does point at

153

your people."

She shrugged. "We can't help the, er, actions of our colleagues, can we?"

"No. No, we can't." Joe gazed at the trees beyond the rear wall, and birds flittering to and fro between them. "How well do you know the people who work for you?" he asked.

"As well as I can, I think. Scott's ex-army who feels his job is beneath him, Katy is a frustrated director who doesn't want to wait until she's fully matured within the industry."

"She's twenty-seven," Joe countered, "And she looks pretty mature to me."

"You're talking physical maturity. I'm talking professional. She has only five or six years in the industry. I waited over twenty years before I got my major break."

Joe shrugged. "Well, you know your business. Tell me, how fit are they both? We're looking for someone who's nimble enough to get over that rear wall and then make their way to the door without being seen."

"I should imagine either of them could," Helen speculated. "I'm not sure whether *I* could. I keep myself fit, certainly. I'm a member of a gym near my home and I work hard to keep myself in good, physical condition. Scott, as I said, is ex-army so I should imagine..." she trailed off. "Come, Joe, you don't seriously imagine that either Scott or Katy had anything to do with this business, do you?"

Joe took out his tobacco tin and began to roll another cigarette. "We don't know anything really, other than she was murdered, and I knew that much the instant I heard of her death. It's only when we began to ask deeper questions that it became apparent it was one of the crew." Licking the cigarette paper, completing the smoke, he put it between his lips and lit up. With a crooked smile, he told her, "Hoad will get there. And if he doesn't, I will. I have a lot of experience dealing with this kind of crime, and trust me, all killers make mistakes. Soon as I spot that mistake, we'll have our man."

They ambled on around the garden, and Joe paused to

154

studied some of the topiary.

"Are you married, Joe?"

Her question took him by surprise. "Divorced. You?"

"The same," she replied.

"Is it relevant to anything?" he asked.

"Hmm." Helen nodded vaguely. "I think you and I are as much alike as we are different, and the both of us are like the man who created this." She aimed her arm up at the bush carving. "Whoever he was, he had no distractions. It takes a wealth of patience and time and absolute dedication to produce something like this. I think he had no wife to distract him, and you're like that. So am I. You run your business, you become involved in crimes such as this and you have no wife in the background pestering you to take her shopping or decorate the back bedroom. That's why you're so good at it."

Joe grunted; a noise that could have been anything from a complaint to a laugh. "I've a feeling my ex-wife would agree with you, only it wasn't decorating the back bedroom with her. It was fancy, foreign holidays."

"So what happened to her?"

"She left me and took a permanent foreign holiday," Joe confessed with a sigh. "She lives in Tenerife these days." He drew on his cigarette. "Tell me about Marlene Caldbeck and Ryan Rivers."

"I don't know them terribly well," Helen admitted, "but I do know that I don't particularly like either of them. They were not appointed by me, or even my bosses, but by the TV station. They cost a fortune and to give credit where it's due, they hold the show together quite well. But neither of them are particularly easy to work with."

Helen frowned and for a moment Joe wondered if she were simply screwing up her eyes against the strong sunlight.

"You know…" her face relaxed. "No. I shouldn't say anything. It's not right."

"Helen, if you know something you have to speak up," Joe assured her. "Ursula may not have been everyone's cup of tea, but she has a right to justice."

"Well, it's just that... On the..." Helen stopped, turned and faced him. "On the day before the Housies came in, we had our final meeting, and for a brief moment, it looked as if Marlene recognised one of the Housies. I tore her off a strip for it, but she insisted she had made a mistake. She didn't know them. It's important, you see, to us. None of the presenters, no member of the crew, can have had any dealings with the Housies at any time in the past. If they do, it automatically disbars them from working on the programme, and that would have cost Marlene money."

If the eyes really were windows to the soul, then all Joe could read was honesty. "You're thinking if she did know one of them, it may have been Ursula?"

Helen nodded. "It's an intriguing thought, isn't it?" The producer looked back at the garden wall. "But how would someone with Marlene's disability get over that?"

"She might have been able to do it," Joe said. "But if she did, would she know how to work the stock feeds, how to knock out the cameras and stuff?"

"Oh, yes," Helen assured him. "Both her and Ryan are quite conversant with the technical side. Ryan produced his own one-man show for long enough, and Marlene has done all sorts of work on TV, including assisting the post-production editing staff."

Joe stroked his chin. "Interesting. Thanks, Helen. You've given me food for thought."

He followed her back inside to the control room where Sheila and Brenda sat off to one side talking with Katy, and Naughton was skimming through the day's newspapers, most of which concentrated on Ursula's death and the damage done to I-Spy.

"I'm told you're ex-army," Joe said after scrounging a chair and sitting with the director.

"What about it?" Naughton demanded.

The slightly confrontational attitude Joe had found in previous encounters with him was stronger now, as if he found Joe's very presence an irritation.

Joe met him head on. "You must have heard we're looking for someone who not only knew how to operate all this gear," he said flinging his arm out at the morass of equipment surrounding them, "but also someone fit enough to get over that back wall. Someone who's maybe ex-army."

Naughton nodded cynically."Oh. Right. And I fit the bill. Wrong track, Murray, try again somewhere else."

"Why should I?"

"Because it wasn't me."

"You say. Where were you the other night between say midnight and two a.m."

"At my hotel," Naughton snapped, "and if you want to know whether anyone can confirm that, the answer is no. I was alone."

Joe backed off a little. "Sounds like your life is as sad as mine."

"No. It's sadder. At least you do what you want. I do what I have to."

"What? And you don't like it?"

"You want the truth? I'd rather be back in the army. All my life, all I ever wanted was a career in the military. I made it through Sandhurst, did my first two years and got my second pip. Lieutenant Scott Naughton. Had a certain ring to it. Then there was an argument in the officer's mess. It turned to a fight. I was court-martialed. Can't have an officer who couldn't control his temper."

"So you were cashiered?"

"It's called dismissal these days," Naughton said.

"What was the argument over?" Joe wanted to know.

Naughton scowled. "A woman."

"Some things never change, huh. So how come you ended up working in TV? Did you have a special bent for this stuff, or what?"

"I got lucky, is all. I had no background and no qualifications in film, TV or even theatre, but I landed a job as a gopher on a movie, and I used the money I earned to get myself a little training. That was twenty years ago, but it was enough. Listen to me, Murray, everything I have, I've worked for, and I mean worked. Like a dog. I wouldn't throw it away for a little tramp like Ursula Kenney."

"Did you know Ursula before she came here?" Joe persisted.

"Not that I'm aware."

Joe was puzzled. "Not that you're aware? What the hell is that supposed to mean?"

"Do you know how many people I've worked with over my years in TV?" Naughton demanded. "Thousands. Maybe hundreds of thousands. Ursula claimed to be an actress, but no one here can recall anything she ever appeared in. No one on the crew here could remember her. It's possible that she was an extra in a crowd scene when we put together a drama documentary on the sermon on the mount, ten years ago, but there were about a hundred such extras in that programme. Helen asked, the day before we went live, whether any of us knew any of the Housies, and the answer from all of us was no."

"Not according the Helen," Joe retorted. "She said Marlene was having second thoughts."

"Marlene is a bigger cow than Ursula, but she's a professional. Yes she hesitated for a moment because she thought she recognised one of the Housies, but I don't know that it was Ursula. Whether it was or not, Marlene eventually said she was wrong and she did not know any of the Housies."

"Let's think about Thursday night," Joe suggested. "You said to me that if and when you needed stock feeds, you could locate and run them in a matter of seconds. Anyone else would have to find them first."

"Therefore I'm the chief suspect," Naughton sneered. "If you listened, Murray, I also said that both Katy and Helen could do it. I know neither of them did, and I didn't either, so where does that leave your theory?"

"Nothing wrong with the theory," Joe replied, "because I don't have to believe you. I showed you how it was done. All I'm saying beyond that is you, Helen and Katy are the people who could have done it most efficiently."

"There's so much more you don't know," Naughton snapped back. "Everyone can see the sense of what you're saying, but to get where you think the killer got wasn't simply a case of jumping over the wall and past security. Do you know how awkward it is to go from this backroom area to the Housies' side of things?" Naughton got to his feet. "Come with me."

He led the way from the control room, along the lower corridor to the security station by the rear entrance.

"Morning Ray," he said to the officer on duty, the same one as had been there the previous day. "Can you open the key cupboard, please?"

"Certainly, Mr Naughton." Ray got to his feet, unhooked a key chain from his waistband, and reached up to a wall-mounted cupboard on the back wall. He opened it and Joe studied the contents with a growing sense of annoyance.

It was packed with keys, some long, some short, some deadlock, some mortise, others obviously designed for lockers or cupboards.

"I don't know how many keys there are," Naughton said to Joe, "but the theoretical killer would have needed three. One for the control room, one for the lower door to gain access to the stair case, and a third to get off the staircase into the Housies' area once he got to the first floor." He glared at Joe. "How long could he risk hanging around in the security office, here? It could have taken him anything up to twenty minutes to find the right keys unless he knew *exactly* which ones to take, and I'll tell you something else, I wouldn't know which ones they are, and neither would Helen nor Katy."

Joe shot a glance at Ray, then back at Naughton, and finally Ray again. Taking out his mobile phone, calling up the stopwatch, he barked, "Get me those three keys now."

Ray began to sort through the keys, checking the labels on each one. At length he chose a key, then a second, then a third. Finally, he passed them to Joe.

"Less than a minute," Joe said. "The theory holds, Naughton."

Chapter Thirteen

Joe was in the garden again exercising his mind and enjoying another cigarette when Hoad found him.

"Sorry about the delay, Joe," the chief inspector apologised. "Bloody politics."

"What's the problem?" Joe asked.

"The production company and the TV station want to use the hall for the final goodbye this afternoon," Hoad explained.

"D-Day," Joe translated.

"Whatever they like to call it," Hoad sneered. "Can't allow it, especially after what we've learned overnight. I have scientific support going over the Housies' area with the traditional fine-toothed comb. We've had a bit of argy-bargy over it. They even rang the Chief Constable, but I'm sticking to my guns. I can't have anyone, not even the Housies now, disturbing anything in the Romping Room or the upper landing. Not until forensic have finished their work."

Stubbing out his cigarette under a rhododendron bush, Joe fiddled with his cigarette lighter. "So what's this stuff you learned overnight that's so important?"

"That's the reason I wanted to see you. We've been looking into Ursula Kenney, and it turns out that little miss viper was even less of an angel than she made herself appear," the policeman explained.

"That," Joe observed, "would be difficult considering her performance this week."

"Precisely. Let me tell you the tale. Twenty years ago, when she was about eighteen, there was an, er, incident. A man named Victor Prentiss was found dead in Hogshead

Wood, about five miles from here. It's part of the Delamere Forest. Prentiss was seen with Ursula Kenney and another, unidentified women, in and around a Chester nightclub in the week leading up to his death, and according to the pathologist at the time, he'd been dead about three days before his body was found."

Excitement beginning to grip him, Joe took out his tobacco tin and rolled a fresh cigarette. "Was Ursula questioned?"

"She was," Hoad nodded. "She admitted being with the man at the nightclub, but it was *four* days before he was found, not three. She seemed to think that would finalise her innocence, but, of course, pathology can be quite hazy on such matters, so she was brought in for questioning. Although Prentiss' death was not natural, there was nothing suspicious about it, either. He had a leather belt wrapped around his throat and he died of asphyxiation. The coroner's verdict speculated that he was indulging in auto-erotic asphyxiation. I don't know how much you know about the practice, but basically it involves..."

"Oxygen deprivation to heighten orgasm," Joe cut in. "It's also known as scarfing." He smiled thinly at Hoad's suspicious surprise. "Don't look at me like that. I may live alone but I'm not suicidal, and I don't indulge, but I do know about it."

"Yes, well, Prentiss' friends all told the police that he *did* indulge in it, which is how come the coroner reached his verdict."

"So, what does this have to do with Ursula Kenney?" Joe asked. "If she insists that she was with the guy but left alone, was there any evidence to the contrary?"

"Regarding Ursula, no," Hoad admitted. "But there was plenty of evidence to suggest that Prentiss wasn't alone when he died. His body had been quite badly dressed. Shirt buttons done up wrong. And the body was found half buried under leaves and branches in the woods. It had been there about three days when it was found. Secondly, one of those branches had recent blood on it. It wasn't Prentiss' and it wasn't Ursula's."

"So where is all this leading?" Joe asked.

"The investigating officer's notes indicated that he was never entirely happy with Ursula's story. He said she was nervous and fidgety throughout the interview, even though there was never any suggestion that she was involved in Prentiss' death. There were no traces of her ever having been to his place, and nobody ever suggested that she had. Questioning her was purely a matter of routine, in order to establish what had happened in the hours leading up to his death. The feeling was that Prentiss choked to death getting his jollies, and the woman, or *women* who were with him, moved his body to make sure they could never be linked to him. So it begged the question: why was Ursula so jittery at interview?"

"The police have that effect on some people," Joe pointed out.

"True, but you don't know the whole story yet. Y'see, Prentiss was a film producer and at the time, Ursula was a struggling actress." The chief inspector shrugged. "You see how easy it would be to put a scenario together?"

Joe was already ahead of the game. "Prentiss is putting together a movie, Ursula wants a part in it, so she uses her best attributes, like free-fall knickers, to try and land the part. Prentiss insists he can only get off by scarfing, it goes wrong and Ursula moves his body to this wood."

"But not alone," Hoad insisted. "She was barely eighteen years old, and the DVLC tell us she didn't even have a driver's licence at the time. If Ursula was involved, she had to have an accomplice. But like I say, there was absolutely no evidence to implicate her other than the fact that she had been seen with him a few days before he was found. So that leaves us looking for an accomplice."

"The mystery woman or women from the nightclub?"

"Neither of whom ever came forward and who, so she insisted, Ursula knew nothing about." Hoad, too, lit a cigarette. "Tempting, isn't it?"

"But hard to prove at the time and after twenty years,

you'd never do it," Joe said. "What's more, with Ursula dead, you're no nearer knowing who the second woman was and you'll never find her."

"Not necessarily," Hoad suggested. "You see, back then, Ursula wasn't working under her real name. She had a stage name. Xavier Armandez, and she appeared in one or two minor roles with another actress named Margaret Billingham, better known these days as Marlene Caldbeck."

Joe's eyebrows rose. "Now that is interesting. But Marlene would have been so obvious even then, with that false leg."

"Would she?" the chief inspector asked. "Let me paint you another picture, Joe. Suppose Marlene didn't have that missing limb then. Suppose she and Ursula were working this guy in the nightclub. They went back to his place, got it on, his lights went out instead of burning a bit brighter, the two girls panicked and decided to shift his body twenty miles away. While they're hiding him in Hogshead Wood, Marlene slices her leg open on a stray branch, septicaemia sets in and she loses her lower leg."

Joe considered the possibility. "Everything is hunky-dory for twenty years, then suddenly, out of the blue, Ursula turns up on I-Spy under her real name and puts the screws on Marlene."

"Ursula is still unknown," Hoad agreed, "but Marlene is a household name. Ursula isn't blackmailing her for money. Instead she's insisting on the I-Spy prize. Twenty-five grand. If Marlene can't swing it, Ursula goes to the papers with all the gory details of Prentiss' death, and how she and Marlene covered it up."

"I can see one immediate problem," Joe said. "We're pretty sure that the killer got in over the rear wall. Marlene only has one leg. How the hell did she do it?"

"Well, it was you who pointed that out, but there again, you did say you didn't see it on telly."

Toying with his Zippo lighter, Joe shook his head. "I'd rather pull my fingernails out with pliers than watch TV. It's more entertaining. What are you getting at?"

Hoad smiled. "You speak as a man who isn't married. I don't watch telly myself, but the missus and kids have the damn thing on all the time. Anyway, that doesn't matter. I didn't know about it until you mentioned it the other day, and this morning, I checked up on it. You said Marlene Caldbeck appeared on a reality programme with the Paras. Not quite right, Joe." The chief inspector leaned forward to stress his next point. "Two years ago, Marlene appeared on a reality programme called *Commando*. She was put through a training regime with the Royal Marines, not the Parachute Regiment. Disabled or not, she cracked their assault course in record time for a civvy. And she could climb like Spiderman." The chief inspector leaned back again. "She plays on her disability, Joe, but her performance on *Commando* proves that it doesn't hold her back half as much as she makes out."

Joe pursed his lips to demonstrate he was impressed. "So what are you going to do?"

"She told us she didn't know Ursula Kenney, she told the crew here, that Helen Catterick woman, that she didn't know Ursula. It was a lie. Rahman is on his way over to the entertainment field right now. I'm bringing her back here for questioning. Because it's a formal interview, ten to one she'll call her brief, and he won't let you sit in on it. But the live feed will be on so you can watch it all from the control room. We can discuss it afterwards... assuming we don't get a confession, that is."

Now Joe shook his head. "If she set fire to hell, she'd deny it with the devil as her witness. No way will you get through that ego."

***

"Ms Caldbeck, we've called you back today because there are certain, er, anomalies in the statement you gave us yesterday," Hoad explained, "and I'd like to clear them up."

"If I can help." She smiled, but Hoad could not help mistaking it for the grin of a hyena stumbling across the remains of a dead zebra.

"Your current working name is Marlene Caldbeck, but your real name is Margaret Billingham. Is that correct?"

Marlene checked with her solicitor who nodded. "That's right," she said. "There's nothing illegal about that. I file my tax returns under my real name. Marlene Caldbeck is purely a stage name, nothing else."

"Of course," Hoad agreed. "When we questioned you yesterday, you told us you had never met Ursula Kenney and you did not know her. Do you remember saying that?"

Marlene did not bother checking with her a lawyer. "It's true."

"We'll see about that in a moment," Hoad warned her. "Have you ever heard of a man named Victor Prentiss?"

Again she wasted no time checking with her solicitor. "No."

"He died about twenty years ago," Hoad told her. "Autoerotic asphyxiation."

Marlene laughed. "Strangled himself getting off? What does that have to do with me?"

"He was a film producer," Hoad told her. "He was a local man and, of course, you're from this area, aren't you?"

"More Manchester," Marlene replied. "But I still don't see what he has to do with me."

"He had a habit of bedding young actresses."

The change in her attitude was as rapid and abrupt as it was unsurprising. Her face twisted into a mask of pure anger, and her tones matched it. "He didn't bed this actress."

"That's something else we'll discuss in a moment," Hoad advised. "Let's come back to Ursula Kenney. You say you'd never met her, and yet according to our information, you and she appeared in a BBC drama production together. That, too, was about twenty years ago. A few months before Victor Prentiss died, as a matter of fact."

Marlene shrugged. "If you say so. I don't remember every part I've played. And anyway, even if we were cast in this thing, there's nothing to say that we actually met. We

165

may not have been in the same scenes."

"You were," Hoad told her. "We checked. She wasn't called Ursula Kenney then. Like you, she had a stage name. Xavier Armandez. She played your sister in a drama production entitled *Happy Families*." He glared at Marlene. "Now do you remember her?"

Marlene's features drained of colour. She looked at her solicitor and he merely shrugged. Her eyes blazed at him, and he sat forward.

"Chief Inspector, may we ask where this is leading?"

"It's leading, Mr Underwood, to the murder of Ursula Kenney. A woman who, we believe, knew a secret about a member of the production team here, and was blackmailing that person." Hoad's stare swung back to Marlene. "When we looked into you, Ms Caldbeck, we found several, er, shall we say explanations, for your disability. A childhood disease, a car accident when you were aged about ten, a car accident when you were in your twenties. And yet, when we looked at footage from that production of *Happy Families*, your leg appeared to be intact. I'd like to know right now, when and how you lost your lower leg and unlike the paparazzi, I want the truth."

"Well you can sod off," she snapped. "I'm telling you nothing." She nudged Underwood. "Tell him."

Underwood sighed. "What relevance does this have?"

"It's relevant," Hoad assured him. "You see, Mr Underwood, we believe that Victor Prentiss died when he was playing bedroom games with two actresses. We're pretty sure that one of them was Ursula Kenney, known then as Xavier Armandez. The identity of the other has always been a mystery, but we believe it may have been your client."

Marlene's mouth fell open in outraged astonishment. Before she could speak, her lawyer spoke for her.

"I still don't see the relevance of my client's disability."

"You wouldn't," Hoad agreed. "No one ever suggested that Victor Prentiss was murdered. He had a penchant for these kinds of games. His death was, in all probability, accidental. However, the two actresses with him decided that they could very well be implicated in the matter, and that would mean the end of their budding careers. So they chose to move his body about twenty miles and half buried it in the Delamere Forest, probably hoping it wouldn't be found for years. Unfortunately for them, it was discovered after only a few days. Other evidence at the scene indicated that your client could have lost her lower limb as a result of an accident while helping to conceal the body." Hoad's powerful stare rested, again, on Marlene. "We also believe the Ursula Kenney was blackmailing your client because of it."

Marlene leapt to her feet. "You're out of your mind, and I'm out of here."

"Sit down, Ms Caldbeck," Hoad ordered.

"Go to hell."

"Sit down or I'll have you arrested."

She leaned across the desk, towering above him. "You can't speak to me like this. I'm…"

"Sit down," Hoad ordered, his tones now the stern rebuke of a headmaster. He waited, maintaining eye contact refusing to look away.

Her fist clenched, then unclenched. The fury worked at her slim features. The small room held its collective breath waiting to see who would win in this battle of wills.

"Sit… down." Hoad punctuated his words with a long gap.

Marlene checked with her solicitor who again nodded and she slowly resumed her seat.

The chief inspector pointed a warning finger at her. "I'm not interested in your reputation, lady. I don't care who you are or who you *think* you are. Mess with me and I'll throw your arse in a cell so fast, your knickers will come off." He swung on the solicitor. "Now, Mr Underwood, I demand that your client answer the question."

"Tell him," Underwood instructed.

"No. I won't. It's part of the mystique that…"

"Marlene, tell him," Underwood interrupted.

167

She huffed out her breath and looked away. There was a long silence. Hoad noticed the sparkle of tears in her eyes, but remembered that she was an actress. These people, he reminded himself, could turn emotions on and off at the flick of an internal switch.

At length she turned back, removed an ostentatious gold and sapphire ring from her finger and began to play with it.

"I was filming in Australia about fifteen years ago. I was swimming in the shallows off Bondi Beach. I was at the southern end, where the surfers congregate, and that's where it happened. A surfer came in, I saw him too late and ducked to avoid him. He hit my leg and came off his board. He was furious with me, but I was in too much pain to care. My lower leg was totally mangled, and the surgeons took it off."

"And you were held responsible?" Hoad demanded.

She nodded. "I shouldn't have been swimming there. The film company were up in arms, too. They had to strike me out of the movie and reshoot." She sighed. "They needed a woman with both legs intact."

"Nudity?" Hoad asked, and again she nodded. "I'll need to confirm this."

"Listen, you idiot, I've told you the truth. It's a story we've been keen to suppress ever since I made my name. I can't have this getting out now."

"This interview is confidential, Ms Caldbeck," Hoad assured her, "and no details will be released to the media unless charges follow."

"Well, whatever, I had nothing to do with Victor Prentiss' death."

"But you did know him and you did know Ursula Kenney under her stage name?"

"Yesss," she hissed.

"Then why did you deny it yesterday?"

Another sigh. "According to the terms of our contract, if we know any of the Housies, we're supposed to say so. The Housies would not be removed, but we would. That includes me, Ryan, and the production crew, including Helen and Scott Naughton. Times are tough, Mr policeman, for all of us. I needed this gig. When I saw the lists of Housies, her name meant nothing, but when I saw her photograph, it registered right away and I thought, why should I lose the fees, the kudos of presenting I-Spy, just because I worked with the uptight little tart twenty odd years ago? She couldn't act then and if this week has proved anything she hasn't improved over the years. So I kept quiet. When you asked me yesterday, I maintained that silence. If I opened up about it, you could get me into all sorts of trouble with I-Spy."

"The same goes for failing to report a death, twenty odd years ago," Hoad retorted. "And even if we learn that you did lose your leg as you say you did, it doesn't alter anything. Until I prove otherwise, you are still in the frame for covering up Victor Prentiss' death and for murdering Ursula Kenney in order to keep it under wraps."

Marlene let loose a string of invective.

"That kind of language won't get you anywhere, Ms Caldbeck," Rahman told her.

"I'm talking to the butcher, not the block," Marlene snapped.

"Haranguing a police officer won't do you many favours, either," Hoad told her. "Detective Sergeant Rahman is a long serving, highly respected officer. If you'd had to work half as hard as he to get where you are, you would probably appreciate him."

"He's a…"

"Don't add racism to the possible charges," Hoad cut her off.

"I was going to say, he's a lackey," she replied. "A gopher, a jobsworth, and I don't answer to gophers."

His anger barely subdued, Hoad told her, "You disgust me. You and everyone else like you. You think your fame and your money can buy you anything, get you out of anything. Well right now, little miss fortune, you are under caution. Rahman, tell her ladyship her rights."

***

Enjoying the fresh air and sunshine of the gardens, puffing contentedly on a cigarette, Joe expressed his doubts.

"You made a mistake, Frank. You let her goad you into action, and I'll bet she'll have even more lawyers lining up to sue you for false arrest."

"She's not under arrest," Hoad corrected him. "Merely cautioned for her behaviour during the interview. She deserved it, Joe."

"Couldn't agree with you more. I was thinking of you."

"Yes, well, let me worry about that, eh? What did you think of the bits we got out of her?"

"I think we're skating on very thin ice," Joe admitted. "You established a connection between her and Ursula. You established that she'd lied, not only to you but to the TV company when she said she didn't know the woman. But that's all you've done. You can't tie her to Victor Prentiss, you can't tie her to climbing over the wall here, and if she can vouch for her whereabouts on Friday night, Saturday morning, you've lost her."

He gazed beyond the garden wall. Away over to the west, ominous, heavy cloud was building. The threatened end to the heat wave appeared to be materialising.

Joe frowned. "There's something about this whole scenario that isn't quite right."

"It was your thinking that led us along this route," Hoad complained.

"I don't mean that," Joe said. "Someone did come over the wall and interrupt the live feeds. It's the only way it could be done. No, it's the Marlene Caldbeck thing I'm talking about." He puffed agitatedly at his cigarette. "Think about it. Ever since the movies were invented, the casting couch has figured large in the legend. I don't know how much it's been blown out of proportion, but you have to think it went on sometimes. Now, suppose we go back twenty years. Marlene is a struggling actress and she's looking for the big break, yeah? She offers to jump Prentiss, he accepts. What difference would it make to her now if it all came out? When he croaked, why would she go to the trouble of trying to cover it up? Why didn't she and Ursula just pack up and leave and let someone find him in his own place?"

"We don't know that he was in his own place," Hoad replied. "He could have been at her place."

"All right, I accept that." Joe puffed on his cigarette, learned it had gone out and dug his Zippo from his pocket to relight it. When he could take a satisfactory drag from it, he went on, "But come up to date. On the surface, Marlene is the champion of the disabled, but she's also slept with more men than I've turned out egg and chips. And she doesn't care who knows it. Why? It's the old adage; there's no such thing as bad publicity. All this bed hopping keeps her name on the front pages of the tabloids and celeb magazines. So why would she give a hoot about Ursula Kenney threatening to tell what happened to Victor Prentiss twenty years ago? You already said, your boys never suspected murder, and Marlene could make a packet out of the story." Joe described speech marks with his fingers in the air and put on a high-pitched, squeaky voice. "I was young and silly, but all I really did was try to protect my reputation." He reverted to his normal voice. "See what I'm saying? She's an actress. If she threw in a few tears, the disapproving public would soon take her side. And even if you pressed charges for failing to report Prentiss' death, she'd get no more than a slap on the wrist. It just doesn't make enough sense." He stared at the clouds again. "Unless Prentiss was murdered."

Hoad disagreed. "Post mortem at the time said there were no signs of violence on him. If someone had strapped that belt round his neck with the intention of killing him, he would have struggled, and there would have been indications, but the pathologist found none. The only prints on the belt were his, too. After twenty years, it would take a bloody miracle – or a confession – to prove it, Joe."

"Have you checked Ursula's home yet?"

The chief inspector nodded. "We searched it yesterday. Nothing untoward. A laptop, but nothing on it that would hint at any involvement with Prentiss. No journal, no diary, and no documents addressed to anyone on this show threatening them with exposure. Rest of the flat turned up nothing… well, nothing of any importance. The usual stuff for an actress. Publicity stills, CV. That kind of thing."

"No houses for sale?" Joe smiled.

"Yes, one or two," Hoad replied. "You don't think it's important, do you? Her employer told us she took work home now and then."

Joe's smile faded. "To be honest, I was joking. Listen, Frank, is there any chance I could see this laptop?"

Hoad shrugged. "Don't see why not." He frowned. "You do think there may be something important on it, don't you?"

The clouds took Joe's attention once more. "I don't know. But it would be interesting to look it over."

"I'll have Rahman bring it to you." The chief inspector stood up. "I can see your point, Joe, but Marlene bloody Caldbeck is not out of the woods, yet. I'll keep the little bitch hanging on until I can clear her, at which point I'll probably let her off with a caution." He grinned. "Teach her a lesson."

Joe laughed. "It's one she'll never learn, and next week, she'll be on breakfast TV telling the world what a gang of Nazis you people are."

"So what's your master plan, now?" Hoad asked.

Joe shrugged and tossed his cigarette away. Crushing it underfoot, he said, "We're at a loose end, really. Maybe I should do some digging on this Prentiss guy, huh?"

"As you wish," Hoad said, "but I don't know what you'll learn that we couldn't."

Joe laughed. "I have my ways."

Chapter Fourteen

"Why do I keep seeing lights flashing on the screen?" Joe asked.

He had spent an hour staring at footage from the dorms taken at around the time of Ursula's death. The monitor showed the familiar monochrome view from night vision cameras, tinged occasionally with light which showed a pale green in colour. But frequently there were other, transient flashes of light. Earlier, Joe had been irritated by one from Anne Willis's bed and he had just spotted another from Greg Ingham's end of the men's dorm.

He re-ran the scene for Scott Naughton's benefit.

"Any number of reasons," the director said. "Tiny flickers of light getting in from somewhere, a lens trying to adjust the focus, anything. It's one of the problems with night vision cameras."

Naughton's attitude had not mellowed significantly, but when dealing with the technical aspects of movie-making, Joe nevertheless found him enthusiastic and happy to explain.

"You see," the director went on, "night vision cameras don't rely on infrared, which actually traces heat, not light. And, contrary to what most people think, cameras can see nothing in total darkness. So they emit a tiny light of their own, which allows the camera to focus. If that light impinges on something else, maybe a speck of dust in the air which reflects it back, it tricks the camera into believing there's more light that there actually is. It switches modes for a fraction of a second, but it's enough to give the fuzzy, out of focus effect that you see."

"And there's no way round it?" Joe asked.

"Only by manual focussing, but we can't focus them manually because there's no one here during the night."

Joe paused the video and spun his chair round to face Naughton. "Is that usual? You know. Having no one present, not even a technician, during the night?"

A deep frown etched itself into the director's brow and he chewed his lip. "No. It's not. In fact, this is the first time it's ever happened. In previous shows, we've left one or two guys here overnight, but Helen, who as producer is responsible for bringing the show in on budget, made the decision after that budget was cut."

"Save her much money?" Joe asked.

"Over the duration of the program, no, but if you take the long view, say over the year, it will probably cut fifty thousand off the wage bill. Come on, Murray, there's nothing sinister about this. These are tough times for the country as a whole. Most employers cut back on staff first."

"Which is why TV turns out so much of this cheap and nasty crap, isn't it?" Joe grumbled.

Naughton sighed. "Reality TV is what the public wants."

"And even if it doesn't, reality TV is what it gets," Joe riposted. "You can churn out this dross for pennies at the cost of, say, a major drama series. Am I right?"

"Yes, but there's nothing strange about that either if you think about it." Naughton paused a moment to gather his thoughts. "TV production is labour-intensive. It takes a lot of people to produce quality drama, and I'm not talking about the big stars with their giant egos and expensive entourages. I'm talking backroom bods. We don't need so many for reality TV, especially on a show like I-Spy because we can automate so many of the processes. You don't need a man behind each and every camera. We run a hundred and fifty lenses in the I-Spy house. Can you imagine the cost of 150 cameramen? It's automated, and they can be driven from these boards by two or three people."

"Let's leave the ethics aside for a moment," Joe suggested. "Let's talk about cutting in stock feeds instead.

Earlier, you told me that they're stored on these computers." He waved at the set up. "If they're cut in for whatever reason, would the computer have a record of that?"

"A manual record, yes. I checked and there is no record."

"Could that record have been tampered with?" Joe asked.

"Yes. Anyone of a dozen people could have erased it, but if anyone were up to no good, it would be simpler not to log it."

"But there's another log, isn't there? An automatic one on the computer."

Doubt crossed Naughton's features. "I'm not, er, sure."

"I wasn't asking," Joe said. "I was telling you. There are these, er, *things* in computers called event logs. They record every tiny thing that happens from switch on to shut down."

"Ah, I see what you mean. Yes, it would be in the event logs, but you'd never trace it. Well never in less than a year."

"Why?" Joe demanded.

"Because the event logs track thousands of items every second." Naughton pointed to the server. "What you're looking for, Murray, is in there, but it's one event in millions, and you can't narrow down the time sufficiently to narrow down the search. At best you can get it to a half hour gap on Thursday night, Friday morning. Do you know how many events the machine will have logged in that time frame? I'm telling you, it's millions. You'd be here until doomsday." The director checked the time. "Now, if you'll excuse me, I have to cover the D-Day ceremony from the entertainment field."

"Yeah. Sure. No problem… oh, Naughton?"

"What?"

"Is there an internet connection I can hook up to in here?"

The director shook his head. "Sorry. No. We can't have web interference from here. We beam by satellite back to the TV channel, and they put out the web content."

"Right. No problem." Joe shut down the monitor. "I'd better join Sheila for D-Day."

Under normal circumstances, the Housies would celebrate D-Day from the studio where they first entered the house, but as Hoad had told Joe, because of Ursula's death and the continuing police work in Gibraltar Hall, it had been transferred to the entertainment field. The Housies were driven round by bus, and also because of the unusual circumstances, family and friends, who would normally greet the Housies at the gates, were permitted to wait offstage in the arena.

"But we have to make our own way here," Joe grumbled as they fought through the crowds to the front of the stage.

Hoad had briefed the Housies earlier and had been quite specific in his instructions. "Like last night, you're permitted to leave the hall but not the area. Certain facts have come to light over the last twenty-four hours and we may need to recall any of you at short notice, for further questioning. You'll be allowed to return to your hotels only, at least for the time being."

"And how long will we be held, Chief Inspector?" Ben Oakley asked. "I have a business to run, you know."

"A matter of forty-eight hours, sir. No more, unless something else comes to light."

By 2:45 Joe and Sheila were stationed in the wings on the entertainment field, with friends and family of the other Housies, waiting for Ryan and Marlene to take the stage and begin the closing ceremony. Joe occupied his time trying to second guess who would be greeting whom. It was an engaging, if pointless exercise. The large woman in the ill-fitting business suit was of the right age to be Mrs Oakley, but then he remembered that Ben was a widower. The slimmer one in the dark trousers and white blouse would not look out of place alongside Greg, and the down at heel man in the scruffy jeans was almost certain to be Anne Willis's husband.

The Housies would come from the far side of the stage as their names were called out, but before that, Ryan and

Marlene had their bit to do.

"Coming through, get out the way," Marlene ordered pushing her way through the crowded offstage area.

Joe ignored her but nodded to Rivers as he passed.

There was a huge crowd in the field, greeting the presenters with loud cheers as they took to the stage. Joe noticed that although the side stalls were still selling food and souvenirs, the fairground rides had ceased doing business and were in the process of dismantling.

"Hello Chester," Ryan roared into the microphone. He was greeted by another rousing cheer from the audience.

"Well, it's been another startling week for I-Spy, hasn't it Marlene?" Ryan went on when the cheering subsided.

"A remarkable week, Ryan," she responded, and Joe marvelled at her ability to mask the bitchiness that underscored her persona. "Marred with tragedy, unfortunately, and you know, I think now would be the appropriate moment to show our respects for poor Ursula."

"That's right," Ryan agreed, marching about the stage. "We thought about a minute's silence, but we know you lot. No way could you ever be quiet for longer than five seconds, so what we'd like you all to do is join with us in a minute of applause for Ursula Kenney, who, before her tragic death, lit up our lives for the last week."

Joe noticed a quick movement of Ryan's hand, switching off his radio mike, before he and Marlene led the clapping.

As the applause died out (Joe reckoned it to nearer thirty seconds than the full minute) Ryan reach to his ear again, presumably to switch his microphone back on, while Marlene took front and centre stage.

"Ursula's death has shocked everyone on I-Spy, not least her fellow Housies, so let's have another round of applause for her friends from the house, Tanya, Greg, Brenda, Ben, Marc, Anne and Dylan."

As their names were called out, the Housies walked onto the stage to be greeted by more cheers from the vast crowd.

When the applause died down, Ryan took up the story. "As you know, we usually present the winner with their

177

cheque at this stage of the proceedings. This time, because of Ursula's death, the phone poll was suspended and there is no winner. So it was decided that each of the Housies should be presented with a cheque for three thousand pounds and that *four* thousand would be paid to Ursula's family. Right now, we haven't been able to trace her family, but we'll continue to look and if we don't find anyone, the money will be handed over to various charities."

This received another round of applause but Joe noted that Ryan did not specify which charities.

There was a brief interlude while Ryan and Marlene took it in turns to hand over the cheques and deliver the standard theatrical air kiss, and then the two presenters stood in front of the Housies, to work the audience once more.

"Ladies and gentlemen…" said Ryan.

"Boys and girls…" said Marlene.

"That's the end of this series of I-Spy." Ryan concluded. "So join us again in two months when we're in the fine city of Norwich."

"In the meantime, for the last time, let's say goodbye to the…" Marlene paused and then raised her voice. "I-Spy Housies."

The theme tune from I-Spy burst from the speakers all over the stage and the field, the two presenters stood to one side, leading the applause, and the Housies filed from the stage, waving to the crowds.

Pleased that the farce was, at last, all over, Joe was equally pleased to see that at least one of his deductions was correct. The woman in the trousers and blouse was Greg's wife or partner. The large woman, however, turned out to be Marc Ulrich's mother and the scruffy young man was not, as he anticipated, Anne Willis's husband, but Tanya Drake's brother.

"Your husband didn't make it, Anne?" Brenda asked.

"What? Oh. No. One of the kids is ill," she replied. She smiled weakly down at her cheque. Not to worry. The minute that policeman says we can go, I'll be home a few hours after, and this will make up for it?" She kissed the cheque.

"We have a big party on at the Victoria Hotel tonight," Brenda said. "You're more than welcome to join us, isn't she, Joe?"

Joe snapped out of a puzzled reverie. "What? Oh. Yeah. Sure." He smiled encouragingly. "Guest of honour. Listen, girls, I have to get back to the hotel. I've had wind of another angle on this business and I want to follow it up." He felt the presence of another and swivelled his neck to find Dylan standing behind him.

"Sorry, mate," Dylan said. "Just wanted to say goodbye to Anne and Brenda."

"Carry on," Joe invited and backed off a pace.

"Information?" Sheila asked while Dylan got into conversation with the two women.

"There was something iffy with a producer about twenty years ago," Joe explained. "Hoad thinks Ursula was mixed up in it. Might be significant, might not, but I thought I'd best check it out on the web."

"I don't see how it could have anything to do with this week," Sheila speculated.

Joe shrugged. "You never know."

With a final hug, Dylan wandered off and Brenda said to Anne, "How about it? Tonight at the Victoria."

Anne smiled weakly again. "I'll see how I feel after I've spoken to my husband and had some sleep."

"Talking of which," Joe said to Sheila and Brenda, "I could do with some kip myself. Why don't you bid *au revoir* to your chums, Brenda and let's get back to the hotel?"

***

It had turned half past four by the time Joe finally got back to his room, and fatigue was threatening to overtake him.

"I don't have time to sleep yet," he said to himself.

Taking a shower, he shook it off and seated himself at the

179

table beneath the window, connected his netbook to the free wi-fi connection and while he waited for it to hook up and open the browser, he gazed through the windows at the summer sunshine on the river.

Frequently when working on such puzzles as this, Joe relied on hunches. Many times they proved worthless, but just as often, they hit the mark. This time, he knew the moment he Googled Victor Prentiss that he was onto something.

There were many entries, but at the top of the list were two that took his immediate attention. The first was a video of an interview with Prentiss, and Joe watched it with growing interest.

The interviewer was a well-known, feminist journalist and she was clearly haranguing Prentiss on his habit of sleeping with as many women in the movie industry as he could. Despite the interviewer's (and Joe's) increasing irritation, the man remained unrepentant.

He was a large man, tall and muscular, and Joe guessed him to be in his early fifties. His thick head of dark hair, complemented by similar thick matting on his strong forearms, showered over his head in an unruly manner perfectly at ease with his couldn't-care-less attitude.

Checking the date of the video, although it had only been uploaded to the web within the last six months by someone hiding behind the handle Xarm, the programme from which it had been taken was over 20 years, and Joe guessed it must have originally aired just a few weeks or months before his death.

"We all know that success comes at a price," Prentiss said. "I've made many young women stars in their chosen field, whether TV, movies or the production side of the business, and I extract a price for that."

"You coerce them into your bed?" the interviewer suggested angrily.

Prentiss laughed. "There's no coercion involved. Suggestion, certainly, but not coercion. I don't force these women. They know who I am, they know I can probably do them some favours and they're willing to trade their favours in exchange. It's a business deal. What's wrong with that?"

"What happens to those who won't, shall we say, come across?"

The big man shrugged. "Nothing. I told you, there's no pressure."

With the bit between her teeth, the presenter pressed the point. "Name me one actress you have helped who refused to jump into bed with you."

He shook his head. "I can't do that anymore than I can name you one actress who did jump into bed with me."

It did not surprise Joe when Prentiss went on the attack a little further into the interview. "Your trouble is you're inconsistent. A few weeks ago you were clamouring for prostitutes to be allowed the right to ply their trade as long as they were not coerced into it."

"That's a different matter entirely," the interviewer raged. "I'm arguing for such women to have the right to choose."

"And I'm saying the women who come to me, seeking my help, have a choice. They can say no. I don't hold that against them."

Joe stopped the video at that point. He had already decided that Prentiss was a thoroughly disagreeable man. "And if he accidentally throttled himself trying to get off, it's exactly what he deserved," he announced to the empty room. "Cosmic justice."

Returning to his Google results he picked up the second link, this time to Dan Wellesley, retired entrepreneur, and again what he found captured his immediate attention.

The site was interspersed with photographs spanning several decades during which, if Joe understood it, Wellesley, a financier, poured a lot of money into movies and TV, as a result of which, he was quite friendly with Victor Prentiss.

Most people found Vic Prentiss a self-centred misogynist, but I have to say, I enjoyed his company, and over the years I had a lot of fun and made a lot of money working with him.

It was a homemade site, the kind anyone could build with minimal knowledge of the internet, the kind most internet service providers offered to their subscribers. There was nothing fancy about it. Pages of text, detailing his life and times as a venture capitalist, the movies and TV programmes he had invested in and profited from, were littered with photographs of well-known and some not so famous actors and actresses, faces Joe might be able to link to I-Spy, but he was not certain. Right-clicking the mousepad, he downloaded several into his photograph folders for later study.

Prentiss was not the only producer Wellesley had worked with, but he was obviously Wellesley's favourite. In contrast to the interview Joe had watched the previous day, Wellesley spoke in fond terms about the man.

It has to be said that Vic used people; especially women. He could never get enough of them and he was quite blatant about it. "If you want what you want," he would say to them, "you give me what I want first." And they did. That was the wonderful thing about it. These people were so eager, hungry for their share of the TV and movie exposure, that they were happy to jump into bed with him.

Vic was a man who liked to share, and he often shared these starlets with his friends. Do I speak from experience? You would have to work that out for yourself. I'm not one to kiss and tell.

Joe knew right away that Wellesley had 'shared' some of Prentiss' women, and the money man went down in his opinion, sinking almost as low as Prentiss.

There was always criticism that Vic had ruined as many women as he made. That was unfair. He did his best for them, but sad to say, when a girl with no talent still cannot make anything of herself, even with Vic's help, then she would be quick to blame him for it. And there were a number of such women. One took herself off home to London, claiming to be pregnant by Vic. The last I heard, she had had the child and committed suicide a few years later.

There was always some doubt about Vic's death, too. Sure he indulged in scarfing, but he was careful. He never did it while he was alone. So did the two women who were with him that night leave him to die, or did they actually tighten the belt around his throat? Or did they simply not know what was happening. These are questions I can't answer, but there was a young actress from Liverpool who claimed to know the truth.

Joe seized upon the latter. Ursula came from Liverpool. Was Wellesley hinting at her?

Skimming through the pages of the website, Joe found an email address, put a message together and sent it. He did not expect a quick response, so left the computer on the table and crossed to the bed, intent on taking a nap before dinner.

He had barely flopped on the mattress when the machine beeped to let him know there was an incoming message.

With an irritated tsk, he returned to it and opened up the message. *"You want to know about Vic Prentiss? Bell me. We'll arrange to meet."* The message ended with a phone number.

Taking out his mobile, Joe rang right way.

"You're Murray?" a thick, Liverpudlian accent asked.

"You're Wellesley?"

"The same. You want to know about Vic Prentiss?"

"I want to know whether he knew a woman named Ursula Kenney. Don't know if you watch much TV, but…"

"She was all over I-Spy until she topped herself yesterday," Wellesley interrupted. "Yes, Vic knew her. She's not the only one, either. Why not come out to my place? Mollington. A few miles out of Chester."

"No car," Joe replied. "You say Prentiss knew others on I-Spy. Who?"

"Not yet," Wellesley replied. "I need to check my facts, first. Can you get out here tomorrow morning, then?"

"Sure," Joe replied. "Tell you what, I can probably hire a car for the day. Gimme your address." Joe wrote it down as Wellesley dictated it. "Do you think your information may throw some light on Ursula's death?"

"Can't swear to that, sport" Wellesley replied, "but I think I can throw some light on Vic's death. About eleven tomorrow morning. Is that okay?"

"I'll be there." With a wolfish grin he cut the connection and then called up the internet on his netbook to seek out local car hire firms.

***

With the Sanford 3rd Age Club disco in full swing, Joe sat on the podium close to the terrace exit, and surveyed the scene. It was a familiar sight and one which always gladdened him, even if he chose not to say so.

Everyone was aged fifty or over, but he would be hard pressed to find anyone in the throes of middle-aged lethargy or depression.

"If life's a game of two halves, then this lot are well into the second half," he said to his companions while the crowd jigged to John Fred & The Playboy Band's *Judy in Disguise*.

"It's a grand way of getting over the last few days," Brenda commented. "So wonderful to think I have all these friends." A semi-sly grin crossed her features. "And I have money in me pocket. What say we go out and splash some of it tomorrow morning?"

"Cheshire Oaks isn't far," Sheila said. "What about it, Joe?"

Joe, still busily scanning the dance floor, snapped out of it. "Huh? What? Oh, I have to be out at some village called Mollington, at eleven tomorrow morning. I rang a car hire firm earlier and I've arranged a car for the day. I can drop you off, if you like, then go on to my appointment."

The women exchanged teasing smiles. "It would be better than having him trailing along and moaning," Brenda suggested.

"And he'd still be there to fetch and carry for us when we're ready to come back here," Sheila agreed.

"All right, Joe, you're on," Brenda said.

Busy selecting the next track, Joe did not register their comments. Tapping his microphone, he faded *Judy in Disguise* and announced, "There you have it, people, John Fred and The Playboys Band from about 1968... give or take. It's a lively weekend here in Chester, and we have one of our best friends back with us. Let's hear it for Brenda." A cheer went up, followed by a smattering of applause. "As you know, Brenda's been away on I-Spy, and with spies in mind, here's something a bit slower from 1963. It's Matt Munro and *From Russia With Love.*"

While the music started, Joe sat down again.

"Very clever, Joe," Brenda approved. "Linking I-Spy with James Bond."

"Not really," he replied. "I was reading the book on the bus."

Brenda frowned, Sheila laughed and Joe took a healthy swallow of lager.

"So what's this appointment, Joe?" Sheila asked. "About Victor Prentiss?"

He had told them the tale in the taxi on the journey from Gibraltar Hall. Now he nodded. "A shot in the dark and it turned out it was a good shot. Y'see, the one thing you have to think about is motive. Ursula was murdered. That's pretty well established, even though Frank Hoad keeps wavering on it. We know how, but we don't know why and until we establish that, we're groping in the dark."

Brenda smacked her lips. "I used to enjoy a good groping in the dark."

Joe scowled at her. "You need your backside tanning, you do."

"Don't, Joe," Sheila laughed, "or you'll end up with tales to make your hair curl."

"My hair's already curled," he growled. "Anyway, like I was saying, we have to establish a motive. I know Ursula was a bit of a tart..."

"A bit of a tart?" Brenda's eyes widened. "Joe, she had a ripcord fitted to her knickers and I'm surprised she didn't carry a price list round her neck."

"All right, all right, so she made you look like a nun. But is that any reason to hang her? Is it any reason to even slap her about? This is the twenty first century, for god's sake. People do that kinda thing. But as Hoad suggested, suppose Ursula was about to go public on what happened to Victor Prentiss? Suppose Ursula knew who the other woman was, the one the cops never traced? When I spoke to Wellesley, he told me he could throw some light on Prentiss' death. Maybe that will give us an insight into Ursula's, too."

Sheila heaved out a sigh. "That poor woman." She caught Brenda's gimlet eye. "Oh, I know what she was like, Brenda, but no one, no matter how flighty or antisocial they are, deserves to die like that."

"And you said as much to me when I brought you back here yesterday," Joe reminded Brenda.

"All right, all right, yes. I know what you're saying, but honestly, when I think of some of the tricks she got up last week, it makes my blood boil. You saw the way she belittled the men? Hinted that they were all, er, lousy lovers? I spoke to both Ben and Greg in private about it, and both assured me that when they were in the Romping Room with her, nothing happened."

"She'd turn me off, too," Joe said.

"No, that's not what I mean," Brenda said. "I mean, literally, nothing happened. Ursula wasn't interested in them as potential bedmates. They just talked. I don't know about Marc, and we all figured Dylan was giving her what for every day, but it was the same with Greg. Both Greg and Ben got the impression that she lured them into the Romping Room with intention of making it appear that something happened, so she could deliberately deride them in front of the cameras."

"And did it bother them?" Joe asked. "The derision, I mean, not the non-event."

Brenda waited while Joe attended to the laptop and ran Billy Fury's *Like I've Never Been Gone* in order to keep the dancers happy.

"No," she said when he brought his attention back to her.

"Not in the slightest. Greg insists he's happily married and Ben said he's at an age where he doesn't care what others think."

"He sounds like a good match for you, Joe," Sheila commented.

"No," he disagreed. "I didn't wait until I got to this age."

"No. You've never given a stuff what others think, have you?" Brenda declared.

"Let's stick to the subject, huh?" Joe suggested. "So we know what Ursula was like, but is that any reason to murder her?"

Brenda considered the question. "Where Ben and Greg are concerned, I'd guess no. I can't say for Marc, though."

"He seemed a very shy young man," Sheila said. "He didn't look as if he had the gumption to kill anyone."

Joe took out his tobacco tin and began to assemble a cigarette. "Still waters. You can make friends with wolves, but you wouldn't want to meet a hungry one out in the wild. And let's not rule the women out of this." He eyed Brenda. "Present company excepted. Ursula had a proper go at you all last week, and sometimes anger can build and build and build until…" He completed the cigarette. "But I think we're on the wrong track, here. I think Ursula's murder was planned before the I-Spy house ever opened for business."

"If it really was murder, then it makes sense," Sheila agreed, "but how will you prove it?"

"I won't until I've spoken to Dan Wellesley tomorrow." He stood up. "If anybody wants me, I'm outside having a smoke."

Chapter Fifteen

Sat on the rear terrace, Joe was enjoying the Sunday morning sunshine and its promise of another hot day, when Hoad turned up.

Joe had already been out and collected his hire car, a tiny Fiat, and was looking forward to a day out and about in Chester.

Hoad was less sanguine. "Bad news, I'm afraid," he announced taking out his cigarettes and lighting one.

"I'm used to bad news. Especially when my accountant rings me for the annual tax bill." Joe, too, lit one of his hand-rolled cigarettes. "What's the problem?"

"The chances of one of the crew members murdering Ursula are so remote we can forget about them."

Joe was in the act of drawing in a lungful of tobacco smoke and almost choked on the news. Enduring a long coughing fit, when he eventually calmed his breathing, he gasped, "What?"

"Scientific Support went through that landing and the Romping Room yesterday like a curry going through a dog with the trots. They found traces of every Housey, as we expected. They'd all used the room at one time or another, including your friend Mrs Jump. And obviously, they were all along the corridor many times. But no one from the Housies' side of things went anywhere near the exit door at the far end. The door that leads to the production side of the building. The only traces of the Housies we found were near the *bottom* door, which was the way they went into the house when they first arrived. Even then, those traces are from the Housies alone, and all traces of the crew who had been there before the series began, had been covered by them. I guarantee you that no one from the crew has been in the Housies' half of the hall since before the series began."

"It has to be one of the Housies, then," Joe said.

Hoad shook his head and took a deep drag on his cigarette. "Joe, how could the Housies get down to the control room to stop the cameras without getting caught on the cameras in the first place? And if you're going to say that they were working in league with one of the production crew, fine, but how did the crew member get word to them that Ursula was asleep and it was safe to move? None of the Housies had a mobile phone, and even if they had, notwithstanding the effects of any Zimovane, they would have disturbed the others, and obviously, they would have been caught on camera answering it. The only one who had any contact with the Housies was Master Spy and on the night Ursula was murdered, she went off duty at ten along with the rest of the crew, but again, I-Spy have all that taped. There was nothing untoward in any of the conversations Master Spy had with the Housies."

"No potential code?" Joe asked.

"Anything is a potential code, Joe, but where do you start to find it, never mind crack it? We're in a bizarre situation, Joe, where there is so much we can't explain. The Zimovane, for example. We know that Ursula was taking paracetemol and claiming it was Dihydrocodeine Tartrate. So do we assume that one of the other Housies had the sleeping stuff with them, pretending it was something else? If so, how did he or she get it to Ursula and the other Housies and how did the security man, Bexley, end up taking it … he did take it, by the way. The urine sample confirmed it. None of the Housies had any contact with him. The Housey in question would have to be working with someone from the outside, but as I've just pointed out, that's impossible. They needed to communicate and they couldn't."

"What you mean is, you haven't worked out how they did it, yet," Joe said. "What have you done about Marlene Caldbeck?"

"Nothing. She's still under caution, but she'll get away with a warning." Hoad shook his head sadly. "We're working a different angle now, Joe. We're thinking suicide again, only this time, we believe it may have been accidental."

"How can you accidentally commit suicide?" Joe demanded.

"Hear me out," the chief inspector insisted. "I told you about Victor Prentiss yesterday, yeah? We know that Ursula was one of his female associates. Suppose she got into scarfing while she was, er, you know, with him?"

Joe put his cigarette out. "I thought most victims of autoerotic asphyxiation were men."

"They are," Hoad agreed, "but it's not unknown for women to try it out. It might account for the older ligature mark on her throat and it would explain so many of the inconsistencies we've come across."

"Except that it wouldn't explain why the security man was doped up," Joe pointed out.

"It could be that it's not related." Hoad did not sound convinced and he was not convincing Joe.

"You know, Frank, I bumped into my brother's ex-wife yesterday. She lives in Leeds, yet here she was in Chester. I thought, 'what a coincidence' but of course it wasn't. She's originally from Sanford and she came to watch Brenda coming out of the I-Spy house."

"Your point being?"

"I don't like coincidences when they're too coincidental," Joe replied. "Someone chooses to dope up the security officer on the very same night that Ursula, the biggest tart to hit British TV since they dramatised Lady Chatterley, kills herself while getting her jollies? I don't buy it."

"It could be that Bexley has been on these pills all along and decided not to say anything to anyone for fear that he'd lose his job," Hoad pointed out. "His pal, Driscoll told us he was a tired old bugger. We'll be checking with his GP tomorrow."

"And Ursula was on exactly the same pills?" Joe asked.

"Another coincidental coincidence. I'm sorry, Frank, but this is all too pat, too simplistic. I stick to my guns. She was murdered and if you say there was a Housey involved then it means you have him or her working with someone on the outside, most likely one of the crew. They worked out a way to communicate. That's all. Find that and you'll find the killer. Find him… or her… and you'll find the one on the outside, too."

Hoad hedged his words with caution. "I don't know… Common sense tells me you're right, but how? Who?"

"I don't know." Joe concentrated on rolling a fresh cigarette for a moment. "I've hired a car and we're going out to Cheshire Oaks this morning… Well the women are. I have an appointment with a man who claims he can throw some light on Victor Prentiss' death."

Hoad was surprised. "Who?"

"Man named Dan Wellesley," Joe replied. "I found him on the internet yesterday afternoon, emailed him, he got back to me, I rang him and he's happy to talk to me. In his seventies now, but according to his website, he worked closely with Prentiss up until the guy's death. He lives at Mollington, somewhere north of the city."

"Follow the Liverpool signs and branch off just out of the city centre. You're following the university and Hoylake signs. The A540. It's a bit out in the wilds, mind."

"I'll drop the girls at Cheshire Oaks then go and have a chat with him." Joe lit his second cigarette. "He wouldn't tell me anything over the phone. Said he needed to check his facts, first, but the way he was talking, Prentiss' death wasn't quite the accident you hinted at."

"So he's saying it was murder?"

Joe shook his head. "No. He's not saying anything right now, but I'm seeing him at eleven. I'll bell you the minute I'm through with him."

"And what do you think he's gonna tell you? Aside from Prentiss' death, that is. He may just be yanking your chain."

"He didn't sound like it on the phone," Joe grinned. "And I've not only seen Wellesley's website but I've seen videos of Prentiss. Maybe Wellesley can tell us just how close Ursula was to Prentiss and whether that had any bearing on her death."

***

Joe found himself driving out of the suburban areas into quieter, more rural roads. The houses were gone and he was surrounded by open fields, occasionally blurred by bushes and trees or the odd small copse.

He had driven for about a mile and began to worry that the rented car's satnav had failed him, when houses began to appear intermittently, all hidden behind tall laburnum or larch. As the satnav informed him he was nearing his destination, he slowed down.

He need not have bothered. The house was instantly recognisable from the number of police vehicles parked outside; two patrol cars, a white, Scientific Support van and Hoad's car.

Joe pulled into the road side, and put his hazard flashers on. Climbing out of the unfamiliar Fiat, he hurried along the bumpy grass verge until a uniformed constable stopped him at the gate. He explained who he was and while the constable got on the radio to Hoad, Joe strained to see what lay beyond the high fence. All he could make out were the redbrick chimney stacks of a bungalow, but even from this disadvantaged viewpoint, the place had an air of affluence about it.

"Chief Inspector Hoad says you can go through, Mr Murray. He'll meet you at the door."

"Thanks."

Joe hurried in, barely taking in the pristine lawns either side of the neat gravel drive. The football pitch smooth grass was bordered by tall trees and several dwarf conifers, which hid an enormous and fine, white fronted bungalow, with red brick interspersed in the pebbledash front to lend a contrast. Double bay windows sat either side of the teak front door, where Hoad waited on the terracotta tiles.

"Did you say you were meeting Dan Wellesley, Joe?" the chief inspector greeted him.

Sweat breaking on his forehead, Joe nodded. "He's dead, isn't he?"

Hoad nodded grimly. "I got the call about half an hour ago. I tried to ring you, but you must have been driving or something."

"I was taking Sheila and Brenda to Cheshire Oaks, like I said," Joe replied. "What happened?"

"The next door neighbour noticed that the patio windows were open at the rear, and the glass was smashed out of them. Came over to see if the old boy was all right, found him dead. Head caved in with a small bronze statue. It's laid alongside him covered in blood." Hoad chewed spit. "I can't let you in there, Joe. Not while Forensic are doing their bit."

"So what else can you tell me?"

With a nod, Hoad led him around the side of the house and to the rear, where another vast expanse of lawn and trees greeted him. Beyond the far boundary of the property lay miles of open Cheshire countryside, and in the distance, the hills of North Wales, while away to the southwest, standing stark in the morning sunlight, were the more rugged mountains of Snowdonia.

Alongside the open patio doors lay a shower of glass, and a piece of the brilliant white frame on the paved area beneath it.

"Made to look like a break-in," Hoad said, "but all the glass is on the outside."

"Meaning it was smashed from inside, which in turns means Wellesley let him in, which probably means the killer was known to him. Anything stolen? Anything obvious, I mean."

Again Hoad confirmed Joe's question with a slow, grim-faced nod. "Yes. The tower hard drive from his computer."

"That figures," Joe said.

"Now you're going to insist that it's all linked, aren't you?"

"You don't think so?" Joe demanded. "I found Wellesley through his website yesterday afternoon. He hinted that he could tell me a lot about Victor Prentiss' death and maybe something about Ursula Kenney, although he wouldn't commit to that. Judging by the look of the website, it was home made. He was probably a hobbyist. Now where would he keep all his information if not on his computer?"

"All right," Hoad conceded. "Who knew you were coming to see him?"

"The girls, Sheila and Brenda, obviously, but I was talking about it while we were in the wings at the D-Day ceremony yesterday, and half the production team were there. If they mentioned it to anyone, it means the whole of Gibraltar Hall would know." Joe gazed again at the hills across the Dee estuary as if seeking inspiration from them. "Any idea of the time of death?"

Hoad shrugged. "Some time in the early hours is all the doc will say. Post mortem will be tomorrow, so we won't know anything properly until then. Do you think it matters?"

"Not really," Joe confessed. "It's the logical time to carry out an attack like this. I noticed there was a gravel drive at the front. No sign of tyre tracks or footprints."

"No tyre tracks," Hoad admitted, "and as for footprints, there's nothing obvious. We'll have to wait until forensic have finished their work. Even then, I'm not hopeful. The next door neighbour walked over the drive, and our people have been tramping all over it all morning."

"I don't think there's much I can do here," Joe said. "This is a job for your people. I'd better get back to Cheshire Oaks."

"Joe…" Hoad fell silent.

"What? What is it?"

"Look, I don't like having to ask this but…"

"Where was I during the night?" Joe grinned. "It's no sweat, Frank. I was at the hotel and there's absolutely no one who can confirm it after about one this morning. At that time, Sheila, Brenda and I were packing away my disco

194

gear."

Hoad nodded. "It's all right. I believe you. It wouldn't make sense for you to kill him, anyway, but there's something more worrying."

"What?"

"If you're right and this is tied to the murder of Ursula Kenney, when you get too close, you may be next."

Joe laughed. But it was hollow, without humour.

***

"We'll protect you, Joe," Brenda said. "Won't we, Sheila?"

"Of course we will. We can sit in your room playing poker while you sleep."

"We'll need guns, though," Brenda laughed.

"I'm glad you two find it funny, but Hoad has a point. Whoever it is has demonstrated he doesn't give that for a human life." Joe snapped his fingers. "It also means I'm getting too close for comfort and that could just make me a target." He gave them his sternest stare. "And it's not just me. It's you two as well.

They were seated outside the Cheshire Oaks branch of Costa, enjoying the noon sunshine and a cup of coffee. As usual, Sheila and Brenda were laden with purchases, while Joe was burdened with perplexities.

Unlike most shopping precincts, Cheshire Oaks was more of a village than an enclosed mall. The streets sang to the sound of summer Sunday and the shops were crowded with visitors. Most places offered famous brands at advantageous prices; something the two women found hard to resist.

Joe had no such problem. "I never see the logic in paying hundreds of pounds for a pair of trainers. I get two years out of my cheapos from Sanford market, so I'd want thirty or forty years out of the brand names."

"And I've told you before, Joe, it's not about wear and tear," Brenda scolded him. "It's about looking the part. It's about how others perceive you."

"In the same way that our killer perceived this poor man, Dan Wellesley, as a threat, whether he was or not," Sheila added.

A light came on in Joe's brain. "No. You're wrong, Sheila. The killer didn't perceive Wellesley as a threat. He really was one. Our killer is not stupid. He knows the risks, and he was smart enough to get rid of Ursula. Now, just when that's calming down, he goes after Dan Wellesley. Why? Why take that risk if Wellesley didn't know anything. He went out to see Wellesley, realised the old man knew something and decided to shut him up for good."

"Even if you're right, Joe, what can you do about it?" Brenda asked.

"Plenty," Joe replied. He drank off his coffee. "Come on. I need to get back to the hotel because what I have to do I can't do here."

"Not so fast," Brenda said, and handed him a carrier bag. "This is for you."

Suspecting some kind of practical joke, he peered first at her and then into the bag. He reached in and pulled out a brand new, quilt-lined gilet. Again his eyes fell on Brenda, silently questioning her.

"It's a thank you, Joe," she said. "For everything you've done over the past few days."

He tutted. "You don't have to do this, you know. I have enough money of my own without you spending yours on me."

"Good old Joe," Sheila said with a fond smile. "He can't even accept a gift with good grace."

"It's not that," he protested. "I am grateful, believe me. It's just that…" He trailed off not sure what to say.

"You've been a rock this weekend, Joe," Brenda said. "No matter what doubts anyone else may have had about me – that Chief Inspector Hoad, for instance – you fought my corner. You're worth it." She grinned naughtily. "Course, if you need a bigger thank you, I can come to your room after lights out."

"Thanks, but I'll stick to the gilet." Joe stood up and tried the cream and navy gilet on. "Good fit," he said. "And plentya pockets." He took it off again. "Too warm for summer, though. I'll save it for the colder weather." A glazed expression came over his eyes as he removed the garment. "How could I be so stupid?"

"I should think you find it very easy, Joe," Sheila said, taking the new gilet from him and folding it correctly.

He scowled. "Marc Ulrich," he said. "It's been hot as hell for the last month or two."

"One of the best summers we've ever had," Brenda agreed.

"So what kind of nerd hangs around in a dressing gown in that kinda heat? And it was his cord used to hang Ursula."

"He said it was lost," Brenda argued.

"What would you expect him to say?" Joe demanded. "Hey, gang, here's my dressing gown cord. I'm just off to throttle Ursula with it."

"He'd probably have got a round of applause if he did," Sheila observed.

For once, Brenda sounded cautious. "Joe, you're running off on a tangent, here, and Marc is not the kind I would describe as a killer."

"Besides," Sheila told him, "You've been saying all along that this murder was planned."

"Oh, it was planned all right," Joe agreed, "but I also told you not to lose sight of the killer's ability to hide himself. That nerdy front could be just that. A front. And," he stressed "Marc was there, with us yesterday afternoon, when I told you I needed to research Victor Prentiss."

"You didn't actually name the man," Sheila said. "You just said a producer."

"And that makes a difference? I think I said, 'something iffy with a producer twenty years ago'. Let's work this out. Ursula had problems with Prentiss. Maybe Marc and someone else, someone on I-Spy was in the frame, too. This someone else and Marc killed Prentiss then shifted his body to hide it. That would fit in with the hints Dan Wellesley gave me. Ursula wangles her way onto the show because she knows this someone else, who then drafts Marc in to shut Ursula up. He comes in, playing the gormless sod, but when he's alone with Ursula, he comes on heavy. She tells him to get stuffed, so Marc and the someone else go back to plan A, put you lot to sleep for a few hours, then murder her. As you're all coming out on D-Day, he overhears me telling you about Ursula and a producer and he puts two and two together, so last night, he and this someone else went out to see Dan Wellesley to shut him up. It all fits."

He looked at the two women, his eyes burning brightly, willing them to accept his idea.

"It holds together, certainly," Sheila admitted. "Superficially, at least. But you'll have an awful job proving it."

"Leave that to me," he promised. "They always make mistakes. All I have to do is spot it. Now are we going back to the hotel for lunch, or what?"

"Oh. Food." Brenda smiled gleefully. "Let's go."

Chapter Sixteen

At three o'clock, Joe left the Victoria Hotel, this time alone, and using the satnav to guide him, found the Ferry Path Inn on the eastern outskirts of Chester, close to the M53, and soon found himself sat in the beer garden with Marc Ulrich and his mother.

For Joe, the location was perfect. They were surrounded by open countryside at that time of year when the landscape became a patchwork of greens and beige as the fields yielded their crops and the trees their fruit. To the south lay the astonishing stark and steep hill of Beeston Castle, and to the north, the fields and mudflats of the Mersey estuary, the weather was pleasantly hot, the lemonade (Joe had to remind himself that he was driving) ice cold.

"It's closer to Gibraltar Hall here," Marc explained. "In case that policeman needs us back."

As Brenda had promised and as Joe had seen for himself on TV, Marc portrayed an air of uncertainty, as if he expected a comeback on every word. It did not take long to work out why.

His mother, Sonya, whom Joe judged to be about 65, was one of those forceful old matriarchs on which the empire had been founded. The kind of women it would be worth joining the army to avoid. The kind who would suffer no rebuttal to her forceful opinions.

"One cannot understand the attitude of the police," she declared. "It's perfectly obvious that my son would never hurt a fly, and to think they imagined he would be mixed up with this trollop. It's disgusting. If they knew anything at all about police work, we wouldn't be in this ridiculous position."

Joe opened his mouth to argue, but he was not fast enough.

"And who are you?" she demanded. "You're not a policeman. Why are you asking questions?"

Again Joe opened his mouth to speak, but she beat him to it.

"What gives you the right to harangue my son like this? He's done nothing wrong."

"That's as may be," Joe replied, relieved at last to get a word in. "And who am I? I'm a private individual helping the police clear my friend's name, that's who I am."

"Friend?" ranted Mrs Ulrich. "One of those strumpets, I suppose."

"Mother. Please," Marc begged, his ears turning bright red.

"My friend is also my employee," Joe insisted, "and whoever killed Ursula was male."

"Well, it was not Marc."

Joe elected to ignore her and concentrated on the man. "Marc, you complained on Thursday that the cord to your dressing gown, the one used to hang Ursula, was missing. Can I ask, what were you doing with a dressing gown, anyway?"

"What an absurd question." Marc's mother raged. "Everyone wears a robe when they're getting ready for bed or when they've just got up."

"Not in my world they don't," Joe argued, "and not when it's hot as hell like it has been the last month or two."

"We are not of the lower classes." Sonya barked.

Forcing his patience, Joe let out an exasperated sigh. Now he understood why Marc had brought the robe with him. "You met Ursula once in the Romping Room, didn't you? Brenda tells me you said nothing happened –"

"Of course nothing happened," the mother interrupted again. "What on earth do you take Marc for?"

Joe rounded on her. "You know, Mrs Ulrich, I usually find being rude to people very easy, but right now, I'm on my best behaviour, so I would appreciate it if, just for once, you shut your mouth and let Marc answer me. I'm the only one standing between him and a murder charge, so do me a favour and button it."

Sonya gaped and Marc blushed a deeper crimson.

"I've never been spoken to like that in all my life."

"Then you should get out amongst the lower classes a bit more." Joe fumed for a moment and then confronted Marc again. "No one's accusing you of anything, and you don't have to go into any gory details, but what happened with Ursula in that room?"

"Nothing." Marc was almost pleading. His eyes darted from Joe to his mother and back again. "I swear to you nothing happened."

Joe wondered who he was trying to convince and decided it was his mother.

"We just talked... well, she talked and I listened most of the time." Marc fidgeted with his glass of lager. "She asked where I came from, what I did for a living, was I married, the usual stuff. And that was it."

"But then she belittled you as a lover," Joe said.

"Well, not in so many words," Marc disagreed.

Joe shook his head. "I've seen the video. She may not have come right out and said it, but it's what she meant. What I want to know, Marc, is how that made you feel. Angry?"

"Well. Er, irritated I suppose."

"Irritated enough to strangle her later that night."

Sonya, who had been bursting to interrupt, leapt to her son's defence. "How dare you? How dare you sit there and accuse him of this crime?"

"It actually takes less guts than you might think," Joe told her. "And I didn't accuse him. I asked."

"Well, I'm sorry, Mr Murray," Marc said, "but you're wrong. I never moved from my bed on Thursday night."

"Neither did anyone else to look at the videos," Joe said, "but we know they've been rigged."

"I had nothing to do with Ursula's death," Marc insisted. "We had dinner together, all eight of us. Afterward we sat around chatting and suddenly, I felt very sleepy. I went to bed. And I wasn't alone. I think Ben was there when I got to the dorm. I washed, brushed my teeth, and got into bed. The next thing I knew it was Friday morning and everyone was getting up."

"And there was nothing odd about Friday morning? Apart from Ursula not being in the living room, I mean?"

"No… wait. Yes there was. I was ill… well not ill, but I had a raging thirst."

"I'm not surprised," said Sonya. "Unsanitary, that's what it is, all those men sleeping in the same room."

Joe disagreed again. "No, Mrs Ulrich. It was unusual, but it had nothing to do with sanitation." He got to his feet and finished his soft drink. "That's all I need to know for the time being, Marc, but remember the police may need to speak to you again. I'll bid you good day."

From the Ferry Path, Joe drove back into Chester and a boarding house on the river's edge where he met with Greg and Dylan. Both told him similar tales to Marc. Ben Oakley, too, echoed the story.

Joe left Ben's digs at half past four, drove the car back to the rental company, and then sat by the river bank, enjoying the lazy afternoon heat and sunshine while he smoked a cigarette and stared across at the Victoria Hotel.

Sunday afternoon and most of the shops were now shut. Joe was certain that his two closest friends would be back there now and despite her public face of caution-to-the-wind jollity, Joe knew without retail therapy to distract her, Brenda would be worried sick. He knew that she was not the murderer. He knew that the murderer was, *had to be,* a man. And one of those men had lied to him. One of them had feigned drowsiness, one of them had arranged for the stock feeds to cut in, one of them had crept along to the Romping Room, strangled Ursula, then hung her to make it look like suicide.

But which one?

After finishing his cigarette, he ambled along the riverside, beneath older city walls, up a shallow incline and turned left over the old Dee Bridge towards Handbridge. The bridge, a triple arch crossing the river west of the weir, was also a single track road controlled by traffic lights at either end. A stone wall bordered the right as Joe crossed, but railings stood on the left, the side with the pedestrian footpath. Both sides were recessed every so often. Joe moved into the centre recess and leaned on the railing looking out over the river, deep in thought.

The Dee flowed only slowly, but fifty yards away, the water tripped and tumbled over the weir, frothed and eddied briefly, before settling again. It seemed to Joe that it mimicked his thought processes; jumping, bubbling, tumbling here and there, then settling for a long, slow journey to the truth, before hitting another weir and falling all over themselves again.

Looking further along the river, at the bank from which he had just walked, one of the pleasure boats was making a sweeping turn, bringing its passengers back from their excursion.

Why couldn't the Gibraltar Hall investigation behave like that boat? Know where it was going, and simply get there.

Earlier, he had persuaded himself that Marc Ulrich was the killer. Now, having met the formidable Mother Ulrich, he was not so sure, and the other men, with the possible exception of Dylan, had some motive for killing her. He needed something to tie one of the male Housies to a crew member, and maybe then he could avoid the weir and follow the pleasure boats.

He detached himself from the railings and moved on, asking himself what of Dan Wellesley? Why had he chosen to wait before seeing Joe? Would he have been alive still if Joe had seen him Saturday night?

"I need to check my facts, first."

What did he mean by that? If he knew something, he must have known it for twenty years or more. Why did he need to *"check... facts"* now?

Twenty minutes later, feeling hot, uncomfortable and grimy, he stepped into reception and the clerk handed him his key.

"Oh, Mr Murray, Detective Sergeant Rahman stopped by earlier and left this for you." The clerk handed over a laptop computer. "He said it belonged to the young woman who was killed at Gibraltar Hall."

"Right. Thanks." Joe took the laptop and made his way to the lifts.

Maybe this would provide some clues.

***

With the time coming up to seven o'clock, Joe, showered, shaved and ready for dinner at eight, sat at the table beneath his window, and connected his netbook to the hotel wi-fi.

Opening the browser, he went straight to Dan Wellesley's website and the page concerning Victor Prentiss.

"You wanna know about the killer, Joe, you've got to look at the victim," he reminded himself, while he waited for the page to appear.

Error 404: page not found.

With a curse, Joe refreshed the page, but got the same message. He tried simplifying the URL to take him back to the site homepage, and when that did not work, he Googled Dan Wellesley's name and tried to access the site from there.

Eventually, with a cynical smile, he gave up.

"So what's going on?" Sheila asked an hour later when they settled down to their evening meal?

After such a large lunch, the Victoria put on a carvery for Sunday evening. Joe had chosen various cold meats and supplemented them with salad vegetables. His two companions had also chosen salads, but slightly less conventional than Joe. Sheila had opted for nothing but vegetables, and Brenda had chosen a slice of quiche to go with hers.

"Someone stole the computer hard drive when they murdered Wellesley in the early hours of this morning," Joe explained while he chewed on his cold cuts. "They've been busy wiping out the site."

"Don't you need passwords and stuff for that?" Brenda asked.

"Wellesley was a smart man once over," Joe said. "He must have been or he wouldn't have made his money. But he was also an old man and the internet is a comparatively new phenomenon. He was savvy enough to build the site, but where would he store his passwords?"

"Not on the computer, surely?" Sheila said.

"Not directly, no," Joe agreed. "But any computer can store your login details for any site. And he will have stored them there. That way, when he visited the site, it would come up with his user name and his password would be a line of dots in the box beneath it. All our killer had to do was click on the 'OK' button and he'd have access to Wellesley's entire site. It would allow him to delete the lot in a matter of minutes."

"Do you know who it is?" Brenda asked.

"No. Fortunately, I made a few notes when I was checking Wellesley's site yesterday, and I downloaded a few photographs, so that may guide us, but I'm hoping there may be a clue here." He reached down and patted Ursula Kenney's laptop.

"Which is why you brought it to dinner," Sheila observed.

"It ain't leaving my side until I've had a good look at it," he promised them.

"You surely don't imagine the killer could simply walk into this hotel and steal it, do you?" Brenda asked.

"No, but how do we know the killer isn't *staying* at this hotel?" Joe gestured across the dining room where Helen Catterick, Scott Naughton and Katy Flitt were dining.

"It seems unlikely," Sheila said.

"Why?" Joe wanted to know. "Listen to me for a minute. Ursula's murder has its roots in the past. Twenty years ago. Don't look at those three as they are now, think about them as they were two decades back. That Helen, she'd have been, how old? Thirtyish? Naughton would have been in his

205

teens, and Katy would be…"

"About seven." Brenda interrupted, "and that lets her out."

"Does it?" Joe asked. "Think about the tale Wellesley told on his website of some young kid who got pregnant and later committed suicide. How would that child feel if all that came bubbling to the surface again? Especially if Ursula were threatening blackmail with the story. How would you feel if someone tried to drag Colin's name through the mud?" He swung his attention on Sheila. "Or someone threatened to expose Peter for something that was not his fault?"

"Angry, certainly," Sheila agreed, "but not angry enough to commit murder."

"That's because you're you," Joe pointed out. "We're not the murdering kind, are we? But does that apply to Helen, Katy, Scott? We don't know and until we're sure, this laptop stays with me."

Brenda pushed her plate away, gulped down a mouthful of white wine, and smacked her lips. Casting her eyes towards the carvery, she said, "They have a rather delicious looking lemon tart with a meringue topping, and it's calling to me."

"What's it saying, dear?" Sheila asked.

"Take me and eat me." Brenda grinned. "You want some, Sheila? Joe?"

"Just a little fruit cocktail for me, please," Sheila said.

"I'll pass," Joe replied. "An infusion of nicotine is what I need."

"Back in a jiff," Brenda said and wove her way through the tables to the self service queue.

"More like the old Brenda," Joe smiled after her.

"She's coming back to her usual self, Joe," Sheila agreed. She sipped from her wine glass. "And she has you to thank for it. She's had a lot to put up with over the last week, and especially over these last three days, but she never doubted that you would get to the bottom of it."

Taking out his tobacco tin, Joe began to roll a cigarette.

"I'm doing what I always do," he said with a frown. "Trouble is, this is a tough little cookie. I've worked out most of it, and I think I know why, but I still don't know who and there are still one or two questions on how."

"I thought you had that solved," Sheila asked as Brenda came back towards them.

"Most of it, yes. It was a two-handed job. Hoad told me there was no way any crew member came into the Housies' area the night Ursula was murdered. That means it was one of the Housies. But the Housies did not have access to the control room, so it means one of the crew switched in the stock feeds allowing the Housies to move without being detected. You with me so far?"

Brenda rejoined them and passed a dish of fruit cocktail to Sheila. Tucking into her lemon tart, she invited, "go on, we're listening."

"There was no sign of any struggle, so we assume whoever it was, Ursula was expecting him, and that means it was a man."

"Not guaranteed, Joe," Brenda said. "Tanya sits on the other side of the fence, you know, and we don't know if Ursula could bat for both sides."

"She'd shown no such inclination all week," Joe pointed out, "but fair comment. Let's just say it's more likely to be a man." He completed the cigarette and tucked it into his shirt pocket for later consumption. "Now, how did the killer know it was safe to move? How did he – or she – know that the stock feeds were running?" He shook his head and dropped his tobacco tin in the pocket of his gilet. "I keep coming back to this same problem. How did the killer and the crew member communicate? Answer me that, and we'll probably find the killer, and once we have him –" He cast a defeatist eye on Sheila "– or her, we'll have the accomplice."

"Perhaps they didn't communicate," Sheila suggested. "Perhaps they worked out the timings beforehand."

Joe shook his head. "Leaves too much to chance. Suppose Bexley, the security guard was still awake?

Suppose the crew member secretly coming in, got caught out and didn't make it? The killer would move on a preset schedule, but he would then be caught on film. No, the accomplice had to let him know that he was good to go. They had to have some method of communicating, and what's more it had to be completely silent. Any noise, like a mobile phone ringing, or a pager alert would register on the sound pickups in the men's dorm."

"Or the women's dorm," Sheila said and smiled sweetly.

Chapter Seventeen

"However they did it, it can't have been with a mobile phone," Brenda said.

From the podium in the Victoria Hotel's function room, Joe surveyed the scene with satisfaction. Frankie Vaughan blared from the speakers, singing *Tower of Strength* and the members of the Sanford 3rd Age Club danced and jived like the reborn teenagers Joe often called them.

He, Sheila and Brenda were seated before his laptop from which he drove the disco and karaoke. Alongside him, on the floor, part hidden under the table he had commandeered, lay Ursula's laptop. He had promised himself a look at it the next time he took a smoke break.

"Why can't it have been a mobile?" he asked.

"Because none of the Housies were carrying one," Brenda said. "They went through our bags seven ways from Sunday, Joe. They were worse than the customs people at Leeds & Bradford Airport. They opened them, searched through them, and then put them through a scanner to look for hidden compartments."

"Did they search you?" Joe asked.

Brenda ran her hands down her body from waist to knee. "Pat down. Not a strip search." She laughed. "I'd expect a lot more than a search from any man stripping me."

Joe grunted at Sheila. "You were right. She's coming back to her old self."

"Have you two been talking about me?" Brenda demanded.

"Of course we've been talking about you," Joe replied. "Who would you expect us to talk about when your back's turned? Margaret Thatcher?"

Sheila laughed and took Brenda's hand. "We've been worried about you, dear. That's all. We're just glad to see you more like the Brenda we know and love."

"And while you've got all that money we wanna make sure we're mentioned in your will." Joe winked at her.

The victim of his badinage took it in good part, swallowed a healthy slug of Campari and soda, and abruptly changed the subject. "Leaving aside the communication difficulties, who do you think it is, Joe?"

"Ask me another." He frowned. "Scott Naughton is ex-army. He'd get over that wall no problem, and he has a chip on his shoulder the size of a hundredweight sack of spuds. Katy is young and frustrated…"

Brenda's sigh interrupted him. "I know that feeling so well."

Fading the Frankie Vaughan track, Joe called up the Rolling Stones *Nineteenth Nervous Breakdown* and left his audience to it.

"I was saying Katy is young and frustrated," he repeated. "She's eager to get on. Did her mother commit suicide? I don't know, but I know she's young enough and fit enough to get over the wall, which is more than can be said for Helen Catterick."

"Really?" Sheila asked. "You wouldn't have thought so earlier today." Joe raised his eyebrows and Sheila explained, "When we got back from shopping this afternoon, we met her in the lobby while we were waiting for the lift. She wouldn't wait and took the stairs two at a time."

Joe thought about it. "Climbing stairs and jumping over an eight foot wall are different propositions, you know. My money is on Scott Naughton, with Katy second favourite." He drained his glass. "I'll go to the bar. You know how the system works. When the Stones are through, just pick a track."

Joe made his way around the packed dance floor, smiling here, nodding there, to those members who acknowledged him. At the bar, he edged his way in alongside George Robson who was talking to Katy Flitt.

"Gimme half a lager, a Campari and soda, and a gin and it," he ordered, and nudged George in the back.

George twisted his neck to look over his shoulder. "Hey up, Joe. What do you want?"

"I want a word with Katy before you try to seduce her."

George laughed but his eyes beamed a fiery anger at Joe. "She's young enough to be my granddaughter."

"Never stopped you in the past," Joe commented. "Now come on, George, shove off. I need to speak to this girl. Go hit on Helen Catterick instead."

Grumbling to himself, George picked up a pint of bitter and wandered off.

"You don't seriously think he could pull me, do you?" Katy asked as Joe edged closer to her in the space vacated by George.

"Stranger things have happened on a STAC outing," Joe told her.

"STAC?" she asked.

"Short for the Sanford 3rd Age Club," Joe explained, and gestured around the room. "Almost everyone you see is a member. Except for you and your two pals."

Katy smiled thinly. "You don't mind, do you? Only one of your members, the old army officer, told Scott it would be all right."

Joe laughed. "It's no problem, honestly. Besides, I needed a quick word."

He was distracted by the barman delivering the drinks. He handed over a ten pound note, and collected his change.

"So what did you want to know?" Katy asked when she had his attention again.

"How's your mother?" Joe asked.

In the act of raising a glass of sparkling white wine to her mouth, she paused, frowned and put it down again. "That's an odd question."

"I'm an odd bod," Joe replied.

"Well, as far as I'm aware my mother is fine and healthy and still living in Welwyn Garden City. But then, I haven't seen or spoken to her for a few weeks. Do you know something I don't? Do you know my mother, even?"

Joe grinned. "No. But I do know you probably didn't kill Ursula."

"So that's what it was about?" Katy scowled. "All you had to do was ask. I could have told you. I'll tell you something else, too. I don't believe it was any of the crew. Have you thought about the security people? Rebecca and Ernie? It would be lot easier for them to do it from the inside rather than have one of us pole vaulting over the back wall."

"Oh, yes," Joe assured her. "But how well can the security wallahs handle the stock feeds?" He picked up his drinks. "Enjoy the evening, Katy."

Joe rejoined his companions on the stage as the Rolling Stones faded out.

"That's another suspect crossed off the…"

He trailed off as Michael Holliday rang from the speakers singing *The Runaway Train* and was greeted with howls of protest from the dance floor.

"What the hell are you playing at?" he cried, reaching for keyboard and stopping the music.

Sheila shrugged. "You told me to play anything, so I just put some numbers in."

"For god's sake, you should look at them first." Joe picked up his microphone. "Sorry about that folks. Numerical confusion on the computer. Tell you what, we have a great view over the River Dee here, and it's such a beautiful evening, so let's slow the tempo down with Danny Williams telling us all about *Moon River*."

The music began to play, couples began to sway to the gentle rhythms, and Joe fumed at the two women. "Much more from you two, and there'll be another murder in Chester. A double murder this time."

"By the time you're big enough, you'll be too old," Brenda warned him.

"Mind the store for a while longer, will you?" Joe said, his eyes scanning the room. "I want a word with Scott Naughton."

Fixing his target, he ambled through the slow moving dancers and joined the director at a table near the bar entrance where Naughton brooded over a glass of scotch.

"What do you want, Murray? Come to throw me out of your private party?"

"Nothing of the kind," Joe said. "I just told Katy, you're more than welcome, and as it happens, I need some information from you." He made a show of rolling a cigarette. "Tell me about the Housies. How are they chosen?"

Naughton clucked. "What is it with you? Why can't you just leave it to the law?"

"Because they don't know where they're going half the time. If you don't answer me, I'll get Frank Hoad to ask you, and you'll answer him or suffer for it."

Having rolled his cigarette Joe waited for Naughton to respond.

With a sigh, the director said, "They all send in an application along with a recent photograph. That's our first line filter. The one's we like the look of are invited for audition as near to their homes as we can arrange."

"I remember Brenda had to go to Leeds," Joe agreed. "Go on."

"From those auditions, we select our long list, and then audition them a second time. It's a sterner test. We put them through various situations and scenarios, and how they cope determines whether they'll make the short list. That short list comprises sixteen people. Eight Housies and eight reserves. If any of our first choice drop out for whatever reason, then we go to the reserve list and pull someone in. Dylan, for example was on the reserve list, but the lad, the original choice, Neil, er…" Naughton strained at his memory. "Sorry, can't recall his surname. Anyway, he was involved in a car accident about eight weeks ago. Laid up in hospital. He assured us he'd be fine, but his doctors wouldn't commit, and we didn't have time to take chances, so we contacted Dylan and drafted him in."

As Danny Williams finished and Sheila put on The

Moody Blues signing *Go Now*, Joe asked. "Does that happen often?"

Naughton nodded. "On almost every series. There is always someone who drops out. Usually their bottle goes, but we've had other issues in the past. One girl found out she was pregnant just after she'd been selected, and her boyfriend didn't want her coming on the show." The director laughed at the memory.

"So who votes on the auditions?" Joe wanted to know.

"There are teams working at every audition. But when it comes to the final selection, we use a team of five judges. Helen, Katy, me and two executives from the TV station." Naughton's stare turned suspicious once more. "What are you getting at, Murray?"

"What I'm getting at doesn't make sense," Joe confessed. "From all you're telling me, there is no way any Housey could, er, *wangle* his way onto the show."

"It would be almost impossible for him to do it, and if you're hinting that he was trying to get to Ursula, that, too, is impossible. The Housies know nothing about each other until they meet on the day they move in."

Joe stood. "Thanks. You've just blown me out of the water, again."

Leaving Naughton, he called back at the podium where he picked up Ursula Kenney's laptop. "I'm going outside for a smoke, and I'll give this the once over while I'm there. Keep the music going. Something lively. I won't be long."

He stepped out through the open doors onto the terrace, lit his cigarette, and sat at a nearby table, the laptop in front of him.

The view combined immediately and almost hypnotically with the memory of *Moon River* to carry him off for a few brief seconds to a teenage holiday on the Norfolk Broads, when he, George Robson and Owen Frickley had hired a motor cruiser for the week and plodded along the rivers Yare, Bure and Waveney. Memories of overnight stops at busy, riverbank pubs, the popular music of the early seventies blaring from George's portable radio

214

accompanying their East Anglian journey.

"Whatever happened to it, Joe?" he asked the night.

"They lock you up for talking to yourself, you know."

Joe looked up to find Helen Catterick stood in the doorway. "Hi Helen." He waved at the seat opposite, inviting her to sit with him. "I was thinking about a holiday back, oh musta been, seventy-two, seventy-three. Great times. Fun times. Hectic as hell, but wonderful. Where did it go? That zip, that zest?"

"Life takes it out of you, Joe. You're a businessman, and even back then your father must have been training you for the day when you would inherit his café."

"Probably," Joe agreed, and found himself thinking of Sarah Pringle and the Beachside Hotel in Filey. She, too, had had that air of 'business comes first' doom about her. "Not the same in your job though, is it?"

Helen wagged a disapproving finger at him. "It's much worse. Everyone hears how tough it is for actors to get their break, but you know, it's just as hard, perhaps harder for the production crew. I was getting on for forty before my break came along."

Joe scanned the river again, and a group of young men larking about on the far bank. He thought about the number 40. Forty years ago he would have joined them. Now he wanted to scold them.

Bringing his focus back to Helen as a method of forgetting them, he said, "I was talking to Katy at the bar. I didn't realise you people were staying here."

"We've been here for the last five or six weeks," she confessed, "and we have another week or so, while everything is dismantled at Gibraltar Hall. Then it's on to Norwich." The bright smile faded. "If the company decide to go ahead."

"There's some doubt?" Joe asked, and she nodded. "Ursula?"

"Yes," Helen replied. "I have to be in London tomorrow afternoon for a meeting. I'll be back on Tuesday morning, of course. Whatever the company decide regarding the series, the removal work at Gibraltar Hall must go on, and as producer, I have overall responsibility for our equipment." She crossed one elegant leg over the other knee. "You still suspect one of us, don't you?"

He grunted and relit his cigarette. "No. I suspect a member of your production crew. I'm not saying it's you, Scott or Katy." He tapped Ursula's computer. "I'm hoping this might tell me something. It belonged to Ursula."

"You think she knew her killer?"

Joe nodded and puffed smoke into the evening air. "She definitely knew her killer, but she also knew the someone in your team who helped the killer. I'm sure of it."

"She was a very devious woman, Joe. It's unlikely that she kept anything on the computer."

"It's a shot in the dark, true, but you never know." He puffed again on his cigarette. "So what will you do if I-Spy is cancelled?"

"Go back in the pool, and bid for work with all the other producers and directors." There was more than a hint of resignation about her words, and Joe thought again of Sarah Pringle. "It's a tough business, Joe, and even with my list of credits, it's not easy finding work. That's why I must be in London tomorrow. I'll do whatever I must to save the programme." She smiled indulgently. "I know you don't approve, Joe. You're from a different generation; one that experienced the golden age of TV. I remember those days, too, but nowadays, the executive attitude is take it or leave it, and most youngsters will take what we offer."

"Because they'll spend money whether they have it or not, and that's what the advertisers aim for."

"Very astute," Helen congratulated him. "Also probably accurate, although you won't hear anyone in TV admit it." She glanced at her watch. "It's almost half past ten. Time I was getting some sleep. I've a long journey in front of me tomorrow. Goodnight, Joe."

He watched her leave the terrace, then turned his attention to Ursula's computer, lifting the metal finish lid and switching it on.

It was slow to boot up, and when the desktop screen finally appeared, he checked the taskbar and found the battery depleted to 10%. He wondered briefly whether the adaptor from his disco laptop would work, but decided against it. Pushing music out through so many channels caused considerable drain on the batteries and if anything else went wrong, he could not rely upon the good folk of the Sanford 3rd Age Club to keep their collective temper.

There was little on the machine. A copy of Ursula's CV, one or two other, innocent documents relating to properties for sale in and around her home city of Liverpool, and a collection of photographs, mainly from her days in the theatre and on TV. None were of any use, and as far as he could see there was nothing to indicate or implicate members of the I-Spy production team.

He rolled another cigarette, lit it and stared up at the clear sky. There had to be something, somewhere to give him a clue.

"Joe." It was Brenda's voice. "Joe, are you coming back in, or what?"

"Yeah. Right with you." He reached for the computer's power button.

Brenda's eyes widened. "Well, look who it is."

Joe looked around. There was no one else to be seen on the terrace and anyway, Brenda was staring at a photograph on the laptop screen. Joe, too, studied it. The caption read, *Millennium Eve Amdram Group, Liverpool.*

"What? Who? Where?" he demanded.

"There." Brenda pointed.

Joe followed her finger. His eyes widened and his face split into a broad grin.

Gotcha!

***

Joe woke suddenly. His mouth tasted like sandpaper and he felt groggy and in need of the lavatory.

"Too much lager," he diagnosed accurately.

The moment he thought about it, his bladder reminded him that it was time to relieve some of the pressure.

Reaching across to the bedside table, he groped for the lamp. He was surprised at how dark the room was. Probably because it overlooked the river, he guessed. There were few street lamps this side of the hotel.

"Where is the damn lamp?" he cursed.

His fingers closed over something long and flat. Certainly not the brass base of the lamp. His mobile phone. He snatched it up and felt along the right hand edge for the button which would unlock the screen. The second he pressed it, light burst from the phone along with the photograph of the Lazy Luncheonette which he used as wallpaper. Now he could see the whole room.

"Almost as good as a torch," he muttered, reaching for the lamp and switching it on.

Rolling out of bed, shivering in the sudden chill, he made his way to the bathroom.

Something began to nag at him. What was it? It was something which should have occurred naturally to him, and it had happened only recently. Whatever it was, it could not fight its way through the lager-induced fog in his brain. So sharp and intuitive most of the time, whenever he had a little too much to drink, it began to wander.

Of course! The cold. He had felt it the moment he threw off the duvet. Did it mean that Marc Ulrich could legitimately have used a dressing gown?

Even as he thought of it, Joe dismissed the idea. Yes, he had felt the chill when he got up, but he wore only a pair of shorts to bed, Marc had worn pyjamas, and anyway, even though the initial loss of the duvet's insulation had caused him to feel cold, he was all right now. It wasn't really chilly. It was simply an effect of the temperature differential between lying under the duvet and the cooler room air. Like stepping out of the Lazy Luncheonette's kitchen and into the rear yard on a summer's afternoon.

Memories of Marc's overbearing, socially conscious mother assailed him. The perfect cover for using a dressing gown. *My mother insists on it.* No. Marc Ulrich was still in the frame.

Satisfied that he had the answer to his worry, he flushed the lavatory and made his way back to bed.

Dragging the duvet over himself, he killed the light, then groped for the phone again, to check the time. Once again, the room was illuminated by a surprising amount of light.

Just after 3:45. It had been almost one by the time he bid Sheila and Brenda goodnight. Right now, he'd had less than four hours' sleep. Pressing the button to lock the phone again, he left it on the bedside table, and rolled onto his back to go to sleep.

Waiting for his jackrabbit mind to switch off again, he thought about the mobile phone. Hadn't he read somewhere that in total darkness, the human eye could detect the light of a candle at 10 kilometres. Hardly surprising that the minimal light of a tiny LED screen could illuminate a hotel room. And it was one in the eye for those cameras. They could see nothing without giving out light of... their... own.

He rolled over, reached to the table, groped about until he found the mobile phone and hit the lock button again. While the main screen was active, he glanced around the room. He could see everything. Even the slim, black mains lead for his netbook snaking down from the table to the wall socket below. The human eye did not work well in near darkness, and he would not swear to it, but he thought he could detect the colour of his jeans and shirt, draped over the back of the chair beside the table.

He checked the time again. A few minutes to four. It was way too early. He knew he would not sleep again this night. He needed to be out at Gibraltar Hall, but it would be another four hours before the crew would be there to let him in. Brenda had identified one for him, and he wanted to be out there, working to pin down the other.

He didn't want to wait another four hours. He wanted to be there now!

Chapter Eighteen

Over breakfast Joe struggled to keep his eyes open. He had managed to catnap a few times before finally rising and showering at seven.

At that point, he returned to Dan Wellesley's website on the off-chance that it may have been a server error, but after receiving another 404 error, he went back to the notes he had made. Several times he thought he spotted something, but each time, it proved a false alarm.

Over and over again, he came back to the tale of how Victor Prentiss had 'wrecked' almost as many actresses as he had 'made'. Wellesley was careful; he named no names. Joe didn't know if Prentiss had any relatives (if so the site did not mention them) but that aside, many of the ruined women would probably still be alive and the potential for legal action by any of them would have been enough to make Wellesley tread carefully.

Joe had no doubt that Ursula Kenney was one of them, but at the same time Marlene Caldbeck had said Ursula was rubbish as an actress; always had been.

"It seems unlikely to me that Prentiss could have ruined Ursula's chances if, as Marlene claimed, she had no chance anyway," he said over chilly bacon and rubbery eggs.

"So you still come back to this idea that Ursula knew something about Prentiss' death and it was linked to someone on I-Spy?" Brenda asked. Unlike Joe, she had elected for cereal followed by buttered toast.

Sheila, grimacing at the tang of grapefruit, commented, "And you still think Prentiss' death may have been murder."

"I think it all ties in," Joe said with a yawn, "and even if I'm not sure who, I think I know how it was done. I'm going out to Gibraltar Hall to test my theory after breakfast."

"So you don't suspect Marc Ulrich anymore?" Sheila washed the grapefruit down with fresh orange juice, and shuddered again.

"On the contrary. Of all the Housies, he's the one in my sights. It was his dressing gown cord, and I can't understand why he was wearing the bloody thing in the first place. Also, he was the only one Ursula criticised who might have actually jumped her, although he denies it. Greg and Ben say they didn't, and Dylan openly admits he did. But she never criticised Dylan, did she?"

Swallowing the remains of a cup of tea, Joe rolled a cigarette and got to his feet. Rattling his knife against a glass, he called out, "Can I have your attention please?"

The hum and clatter of the dining room quelled and the Sanford 3rd Age Club members turned their eyes on the Chairman.

"I make no apologies for repeating this, but you must vacate your rooms by ten this morning. The hotel has a storage area here on the ground floor where you can leave your bags, and Keith will be here at three thirty this afternoon to pick us up. We're scheduled to leave at four."

"What about Brenda?" George Robson asked. "Is she being detained for questioning?

"Shut it, George," Brenda threatened, "or I'll tell the cops what you get up to when no one's looking."

A ripple of laughter ran round the room.

"You'll never know when I have one of them radio controlled cameras on you, Brenda," George riposted.

"All right, all right," Joe stepped in. "Enough of the funnies. Three thirty for a four o'clock departure, and you know what Keith is like in rush hour traffic. He's grumpier than me, so don't be late." He sat down again. "If I leave it with you, can you make sure my bag gets on the bus? There's only the one. I'll need my backpack and netbook."

Brenda and Sheila exchanged more smiles.

"Does he leave his wallet in his suitcase?" Brenda teased.

221

"No he does not," Joe grumbled. "Now, come on. I have enough to do today and I ain't had much sleep."

"The disco laptop is safely stored, Joe?" Sheila asked.

He nodded. "And like I said, I'll have the netbook with me." Swallowing the last of his tea, he got to his feet again. "I'm gonna grab a taxi and get off to Gibraltar Hall. I may need you both there later on, and if I don't, Hoad might, so keep your phones on."

He hurried from the dining room dialling a taxi as he did so. While he waited at the front entrance, he rang Hoad first.

"Frank, it's Joe. Listen, I'm on my way to Gibraltar Hall. I think I know how it was done. You'll need everyone there later today, but I know that Helen Catterick was leaving for London. Try to stop her. If not, you'd better get onto neighbouring forces and get them to intercept her."

"It's her?" Hoad asked urgently.

"I'm not sure. I'll know later on, but she'll need to be there."

"I'll get onto it, Joe," Hoad agreed, "and I'll see you out at the hall."

Joe killed the connection and then dialled Scott Naughton.

"Are your cameras still in place?" he asked.

"Some of them," Naughton admitted.

Joe's taxi turned into the hotel entrance. "Do you still have the feeds from the dorms and the landing?"

"Of course. We have all of it. We keep it for years."

"That's not what I meant," Joe said as he climbed into the cab. "Are the cameras still set up and able to record?"

"We have cameras in the dorms, but we're working on the landing."

"Tell them to hold at least one camera," Joe barked. "One second." He ordered the driver, "Gibraltar Hall, please. Quick as you can." Putting the mobile to his ear again, he said to Naughton, "I'll need your help to work with the cameras in both dorms, and I'll need to see some footage from during the week. Can you do that?"

"Any reason why I should?" the director asked.

Joe tutted and the driver said, "I can't help the rush hour traffic, mate."

Joe looked out at the packed, slow moving vehicles. "It's okay, pal. I'm not having a go at you. It's the muppet on the phone."

The driver laughed and Naughton protested, "Calling me a muppet isn't the best way of getting my co-operation."

"Then what is?" Joe asked. "I need you to do some recording in the dorms."

"And I asked why I should."

"The only possible reason you have for not doing so is because you murdered Ursula and if you refuse, I'll have Hoad arrest you. I'll be there in half an hour." Joe jabbed the disconnect button, glowered at his phone and tucked it in his shirt pocket.

Up front, the driver laughed. "I wouldn't like to meet you down a dark alley."

"Down dark alleys, I'm safe. Try taking the mick and you're in trouble."

***

Joe arrived at Gibraltar Hall just after nine thirty. He felt tired, more irritable than ever, and Naughton's obduracy served only to exacerbate his mood.

"I have enough to do as it is," the director complained, "without running round at your beck and call."

"You ever heard of a man named Dan Wellesley?" Joe asked.

"Yes," Naughton admitted. "He was a venture capitalist who used to put money into movie and TV projects. He was murdered sometime on Saturday night."

Joe's eyebrows rose. Naughton reached across to Helen's desk and picked up the *Daily Express* where the story of Wellesley's murder took front page headlines."

"You can read, too?" Joe dripped cynicism. "You could be in the frame for his killing."

Naughton shook his head. "I can prove where I was on

Saturday night. I was with Helen. So there's two suspects crossed off your list, Murray."

"You slept with her?"

Naughton almost exploded. "Of course not. What the hell do you take me for?"

"An arrogant sod who's so used to being in control that he can't handle it when others make demands of him. You know you didn't murder Wellesley, nor Ursula, but I don't know it. Or at least, I only know it intellectually. I couldn't prove you didn't do it. Now let's cut out the big 'I am' and see about proving your innocence."

The director sighed. "What is it you want?"

Joe took out his netbook, plugged the adaptor into a free mains socket, and switched it on. "Set up and run the sequence from both dorms at the time we suspect our killer climbed over the wall."

"Driscoll says she left at about half past midnight," the director said, "So if I run you from, say twelve thirty-five, will that be okay?"

Joe nodded.

It took Naughton a few moments to locate the specific feeds, and then the twin screens in the centre of the console began to run the footage.

"Speed it up," Joe ordered. "What I'm looking for could take some finding."

Naughton did as he was told, and the scenes moved quickly on.

"Nothing's happening," Naughton said. "They're all asleep."

"Patience," Joe advised. "We'll get there."

His eyes darted from screen to screen, watching the accelerated action. A body turning over here, a slight movement beneath a duvet there, until...

"There!" Joe pointed at monitor 2, showing the scene from the men's dormitory. "Stop and rewind, then play it at normal speed."

Naughton again carried out Joe's bidding.

As the video footage continued, nothing happened, until

suddenly there was a brief flare of light, so transient, it could have been missed.

"What is that?" Joe asked.

Naughton shrugged. "I told you before, it could be anything. A reflection on the camera lens, could be an anomaly on the camera iris. Anything."

"Can we copy that onto a memory stick and load it onto my netbook?" Joe asked.

"No problem. Less than five minutes."

Joe handed him the memory stick. "There's another, similar flash of light from the ladies' dorm. I need you to find and copy that too.

"So what is it?" Naughton asked. "What's so important about a tiny flicker of light on the video? It was probably a speck of dust in the air."

"Except that it wasn't," Joe said, and concentrated on the screens again. "Can I watch in the dorms?"

Naughton shook his head. "No monitor."

"Can you rig one up for me?"

The director let out an exasperated sigh. "We're trying to dismantle the equipment, Murray, not set more up."

Joe swivelled his chair round to face his antagonist. "Lemme ask a question. Ursula's death. Suspicion hangs around the crew and the Housies. Will that suspicion affect your career?"

Naughton gave Joe that condescending look again, as if chastising him for asking a stupid and obvious question. "Yes. Happy now? Content now you know I'll get the dirty end of the stick whether or not I'm involved?"

"I don't let my personal feelings get in the way," Joe told him, "but speaking personally, I think you need a good kick up the backside as a reality check. Putting that aside," he pressed on, picking up Naughton's look of thunder, "what harm will it do your prospects if we prove it wasn't you?"

"None at all," Naughton admitted. "In fact, it might do me some good."

"In that case, indulge me and get a monitor set up in the men's dorm. And bear in mind, I may need it shifting to the women's dorm later."

Huffing out his breath, Naughton snatched up the phone, dialled and barked orders into it. "I don't care what you think," he concluded. "I have an amateur cop here determined to hang me for killing the bimbo, and I need that monitor in the men's dorm, ten minutes ago." He slammed the receiver into its cradle and glowered again at Joe. "Satisfied?"

"Not yet. Only when I know that you understand what I want you to do." Joe dug into his pockets and took out his mobile. "You got one of these?"

"Who doesn't?"

"Write down your number and I'll send you a text. Store my number because you're going to be texting me several times."

His confusion and anger growing with every passing moment, Naughton did as he was instructed. Joe copied the number into his phone and sent an immediate text, and as he received it, Naughton again followed Joe's orders.

"Let me get this right in my head," Joe said eventually. "While I'm in the dorm, I can speak and you'll hear me. Is that right?"

"Yes."

"Good. Can you get back to me through Master Spy's microphone?"

Naughton leaned across the control console and flicked a couple of switches. "Yes."

"Good boy." Joe turned to the video feeds and ran them. When he reached that point where the flare of light in the men's dorm appeared, he paused it, and concentrated on Naughton again. "I'm going up to the men's dorm, and I'm going to try to recreate that flare. You understand? It may take a few attempts. I want you to record it all, and after each attempt, on my instructions, I want to you run it through the monitor your boys are setting up, so I can judge how close we are. If we don't get close, I'll do it again."

"You're going to try to capture a speck of dust in the room? You're out of your mind." Naughton declared.

Joe waved an irritated hand at the screen. "That flare has nothing to do with a speck of dust. Now, clue me up on something else. When I kill the lights and the monitor, I'll be in total darkness, won't I, and the camera will shift into night vision mode?"

Naughton nodded.

"When I give you the word," Joe said, "send me the text. And remember, Naughton, we may need to do this many times before we get it right. All right?"

The director heaved a sigh of resignation. "Whatever you want."

Leaving the control room, Joe made his way via the back stairs to the upper landing and into the men's dorm where two technicians were in the process of installing the monitor he had requested.

"You want it left on?" one of them asked.

Joe shook his head and as they left, he faced the camera. "You picking me up all right, Naughton?"

"Loud and clear."

"I'm about to kill the lights."

Joe made his way to what had been Greg's bunk, reached up and switched on the overhead lamp, then walked back to the door and killed the main lights. Returning to the bed, he lay down, turned away from the camera and switched off the light.

He was suddenly plunged into blackness so complete that it startled him. He could see absolutely nothing but the image of the doused lamp burned onto his retina. "Naughton. You still getting me?"

"Yes," the director's voice came over the Master Spy link. "And the cameras are in night-vision mode. I can see you."

"You're recording?" Joe asked.

"As per your orders, Führer."

"Cut the crap and send me the text."

There was a delay of many seconds before Joe's phone vibrated and the screen lit with an icon and short message telling him he had received the text. He opened the

227

message, read it, and the locked the phone.

He began to count in his head: one-one thousand , two-one thousand, three-one thousand… After five seconds, he said, "stop the recording and get ready to play it back through the monitor here."

"Wilco," Naughton replied, "but I'll tell you now, it doesn't look like you want it to look."

"Let me worry about that."

Joe activated his phone again, and by its light, reached up and switched on the overhead lamp. He rolled from the mattress, returned to the monitor and switched it on. "Okay, Naughton, let it roll," he said when the screen was up and running.

As Naughton had promised, he was clearly visible laid on the bed in night vision mode. He heard himself give instructions, and Naughton acknowledge them. The audio system even picked up the buzz of his phone when the text arrived, but when he activated the phone, the light was so bright that the camera tried switching to day mode and as a result blurred everything. The camera corrected itself within a second of Joe locking his phone.

Sat on the edge of what had been Ben's bunk, he drummed his fingers on his knees. Too much light. How had Greg muted it? More to the point, how did it tie in with Marc, whose bunk was next to Ben's on the opposite side of the room?

"All right, Naughton, we go again. This time I'll be on Marc's bunk."

Killing the monitor and the overhead lamp, he used his mobile to guide him to Marc's bed, lay down and they repeated the exercise. The results were similar, but this time, the light had come directly from Marc's side of the room, and bore even less resemblance to the original footage.

He tried again, this time clasping the phone lightly in his hand to dim the light, but the camera hardly picked it up. He did the same on Greg's bunk and the result was worse.

Sitting before the monitor after his sixth attempt, his brow furrowed. "How the hell did you do it?"

"What is he buggering about at?" Hoad demanded.

Naughton shrugged. "You tell me. He's been in there over half an hour now, trying to replicate this few seconds of footage, and he still hasn't done it."

They watched Joe as he rolled to face the camera, the phone buried in his hand before ordering Naughton to run the test again.

"What's so important about it?" Hoad wanted to know.

"He wouldn't tell me," Naughton replied. He reached across his console and kicked the recording in for the tenth time. "All he said was it would clear me."

The result was better this time, but still it did not match the original footage. When Naughton reported back, Joe said, "I'm coming back down. Do me a favour, will you. Dig out some daytime views of the dorm. I need to know whether anything is missing."

"Will do," Naughton agreed, and swung his seat to the adjacent monitors to seek out the relevant footage. "Do you often get nutters like this meddling with your investigations, Chief Inspector?"

"Don't know about nutters," Hoad responded. "This fella comes seriously recommended by his local police force. Not that he sees thing others can't, but he sees them that much quicker and puts some odd twists on them. Cornered a couple of killers in Filey earlier this year, got one of his chums off the hook before that. One of them from that club he runs. He has an eye for detail. Reckons it's what comes of serving lorry drivers for too many years."

Naughton grunted and having called up the footage Joe had asked for, paused it. "Running a truckstop gives you an eye for detail? My college education was a waste of public money, then."

"That's right," Joe said entering the room. "You professionals run on rails, I don't, and the reason I don't is because I've dealt with so many bull-headed truckers over the years. If one of my regulars comes in and he's wearing

229

different overalls, I know he's either changed jobs or his boss has sold out to a bigger company, so I find out which, because it might affect my turnover." He sat before the monitors. "Did you find what I asked for?"

Naughton waved at the console. "It's all yours."

He ran the footage and Joe immediately paused it.

There were many obvious differences between the current appearance of the dorms to when they were inhabited, most of them as a result of the Housies' personal effects scattered about both rooms. Aside from clothing hanging on doors, each had a little shelf space above the bed or, in Greg's case, on the far wall, at right angles to him and facing the camera. It was there that Joe concentrated his study.

The extraneous light source had caused the camera to lose focus for a brief moment, so that its true source point was difficult to pinpoint, but by studying it closely he realised that it had come not from the bed, but Greg's personal effects.

Switching his attention to the screen showing the room under full lighting, he studied those effects. A few paperbacks, with a small, framed photograph tucked between them, his shaving brush and razor, the head of which was tucked into a protective, plastic sheath, and a bar of soap on which rested a facecloth.

"Sad little collection," Joe muttered to himself.

"They were not allowed too many possessions," Naughton pointed out. "The whole purpose of the exercise was to cut them off from everything and everyone, or as near as was possible."

Joe scanned the screen again. Others had similar possessions on their shelves. Marc's shabby dressing gown hung beside his bed, but from his shelf hung a toilet bag and actually on the shelf were a few books and a photograph. Ben's was similar to Greg's and Dylan's looked like Marc's without the annoying robe hanging by the bed.

Joe checked the footage with the light on it. The only difference he could see was Greg's photograph, which was laid flat.

"What's with all the photographs?" Joe grumbled.

"Family mementos," Naughton replied. "You do have family?"

"Not so's you notice," Joe said. "My brother lives in Australia, my ex-wife moved to the Canary Islands and my nephew is my head cook."

"Those pictures reflect a person's true identity," Naughton argued. "Greg had a picture of his wife and children, Dylan one of his late mother, Marc…"

The light came on in Joe's head. "That's it," he shouted, cutting Naughton off. "A reflection."

Both men were completely nonplussed. "What?" Hoad demanded.

"Quick, where's the nearest shop?"

The chief inspector frowned. "I don't know. There's a supermarket down in Kelsall… I think. It's only a small one, but…"

"Can you run me down there?" Joe interrupted again. "And while we're gone, get young Azi to contact all the crew and Housies and get them out here."

"But…"

"Frank," Joe interrupted for the third time, "I know who did it and how, and probably why."

Chapter Nineteen

Joe came out of the supermarket and climbed back into Hoad's saloon car.

"I just spoke to Azi," the chief inspector reported. "He's managed to contact everyone, and they should be back at Gibraltar Hall for twelve."

"I asked our coach driver to collect Sheila, Brenda and me at the hall if necessary. He's moaning about it, but he'll be there. Did you manage to stop Helen Catterick this morning?"

Hoad nodded. "Close run thing. She was actually on the train when we got to the railway station. She's playing hell, too, so be prepared for a rough ride." Hoad fired the engine. "Still, if you're right, it shouldn't take that long," Hoad said.

"No, but you never know."

The chief inspector slid the car into gear and pulled off the supermarket car park. "I just hope you're sure of your facts, Joe."

"I have another few experiments to run when we get back to the hall, just to be sure, but this time I know I've got it right."

"Why call them all back? Why not just those you suspect?"

"Because I'm not sure which of the Housies it was. Not yet. I'll only know that when Naughton runs the tests for me again. Besides, having everyone there is a good way of putting the real culprits off their guard. That way, when they're accused, you can see it in their faces. Problem is, Frank, if you made your arrest this morning, you'd have put the killer on guard. It could have created more problems than it solved."

Rejoining the A54, turning towards the Hall, Hoad said, "What's this Terry Cummins tells me about you writing these cases up?"

Joe nodded. "Once it's all done, I write them up as booklets for my customers to read. I call them Joe Murray's Casebooks. They're on shelves in my café."

"Joe, if you name names before any trial, you could jeopardise the proceedings."

"I never name names, Frank," Joe assured him. "Never. The names are changed and so are the locations. That's made clear at the front of every book. Besides, I don't sell them… well, I do, but only as e-books."

"Are they popular?" Hoad asked, braking as they approached Gibraltar Hall Lane and the police barrier.

"Oh yes," Joe sneered. "I sell about one a year."

The chief inspector laughed. "Then why bother?"

"I told you, they give my customers something to read. See, you have to think of it from a business point of view. A trucker gets, say, half an hour for his break. He comes into my place, and while he has his meal, he starts reading one of my cases, but no way can he finish it in thirty minutes. If he's a local yokel, he comes back again and again and again until he's read it. If he's passing through, where do you think he'll stop for his dinner the next time he's in Sanford? The Lazy Luncheonette." Joe tapped the side of his nose as Hoad brought the car to a stop at the rear of the hall. "I may work with cabbage in the kitchen, but don't let that fool you into thinking I'm one."

Making their way into the hall, as Hoad had promised they found themselves confronted with an angry Helen Catterick.

"I'm supposed to be on my way to London, Chief Inspector," she grumbled. "You did say I could go. Now suddenly I find myself dragged back here under threat of arrest if I refuse. My employers are none too happy and neither am I."

"Circumstances have changed, madam," Hoad replied. "I need you here for the time being, and your employer will just have to wait or go ahead without you."

"The future of I-Spy depends on my being there," she complained.

"Then it's probably doomed," Hoad said and walked past her into the house.

Joe hurried along behind and headed straight for the control room where he once more dragooned Naughton into operating the recordings while he went back to the men's dorm.

This time he took four different recordings and with the last one, he was satisfied.

"Are you going to explain what the hell is going on, Joe?" Hoad demanded.

Joe eyed Naughton. "No. Not yet. I don't want any of you telegraphing any of this to the killer, but I now know who he is and how he and his accomplice maintained communication."

"If you're going to say he used a mobile phone, you're wrong," Naughton declared. "Mobiles were banned in the house, and the Housies handed them in before they ever went into the place."

"You think so?" Joe demanded with a grin.

"I know so."

"Then let me tell you something. At least three people smuggled mobiles into the house. And they all used them at different times during the week."

Both Hoad and Naughton gawped.

"That's not possible," the chief inspector said. "We searched everyone on the day of the killing."

"No, Frank," Joe disagreed. "You searched their personal effects. You never got around to searching them personally because you had no need. You already had the weapon – Marc's dressing gown cord – and at the time, you suspected nothing more than suicide. I repeat, there were three people in that house carrying and using mobile phones." Joe gathered his belongings. "There's one last thing I need from you, Naughton. A list of the Housies in the order they were accepted onto the programme."

Naughton frowned. "What? Why?"

Joe smiled. "Because I think it'll be the final clincher." While Naughton began to search through the computer database for the relevant information, Joe addressed the chief inspector. "I just need a little time to get everything together, Frank. If you wanna get everyone into the living room, I'll be there in a while."

***

By the time Joe made it to the lounge, everyone was already seated at the table and Naughton had reinstalled the three flatscreen TVs, which had been there all week. Sited on different walls they ensured everyone could see.

There was a delay while Joe set up his netbook and Naughton hooked it into the TV array so that everyone would know what he was talking about. At length, Joe took his seat between Sheila and Brenda at the head of the dining table, and broke the cap on a bottle of water.

"There were so many suspects in this case that it was hard to decide where to concentrate," he confessed, "but as usual it was the clever killer's attention to detail that gave him... or her... away. You see, I've investigated a lot of these cases, and what I find is that the killer pays attention to the tiniest details of the actual event and works hard to cover it up, but forgets to cover himself... or herself. If you add to that, details from the victim's past that the killer *can't* get at, then you slowly build up a case."

He called up his notes and studied the computer screen for a few moments.

"Okay, let's take the victim first. According to my friend Brenda, Ursula was on some strong painkillers. Dihydrocodeine Tartrate. Powerful stuff. A slow release opiate analgesic, which can leave you dopy for hours on end. I know. I've taken them. And yet, according to the pathology report, she wasn't taking anything of the kind. She swallowed a couple of paracetamol every night. Headaches? Period pains? Or was she just putting on a show? I dunno, but these are ordinary, boring painkillers you can buy over the counter at any pharmacy."

"So what are you driving at, Joe?" Hoad asked. Having been briefed much earlier by Joe on this aspect of the investigation, he knew what Joe was doing, and his question was designed purely as a prompt.

"Paracetamol would not make her sleepy, and yet when she went to the Romping Room on Thursday night, she was staggering around like she'd drunk half a bottle of vodka. So it's exactly as I told you a couple of days ago. Someone slipped her a mickey."

"Slipped her a mickey?" asked Sergeant Rahman.

"You wouldn't understand, son," Joe replied. "Mickey Finn was a familiar expression from the movies when I was a boy. It means she was doped. In this case we know it was Zimovane. But there's more. It wasn't only Ursula who got it. Everyone did."

A hubbub of chatter ran round the small audience.

"How?" Tanya demanded.

"Really simple when I thought about it." Joe looked into Brenda's eyes. "It was in the pie Brenda cooked on Thursday evening."

She glowered at him. "I've known you since we were children, Joe Murray, and if you're accusing me of doping every other contestant…"

"No, Brenda," Joe interrupted. "I'm not accusing you. I'm saying it was in the meal you cooked, but I know you didn't put it there. Someone else did."

"Who? How? And how do you know?"

"How do I know? Because every one of you slept through the night on Thursday. If we watch the videos from all the other nights, we find people were getting up, sitting up chatting, even sloping off to the Romping Room to do what comes naturally. But not on Thursday. From lights out to reveille, you all slept like good little girls and boys with clean consciences. Someone needed to make sure you slept all night. And that same someone put the Zimovane in the meal and also lured Ursula to her death in the Romping

Room."

"You can't possibly know this," Naughton complained, "unless you saw something on the videos. Saw the culprit put the stuff into Brenda's cooking."

"I can infer it," Joe told him. "On Friday morning, the morning they found Ursula, everyone was hanging round the living room waiting on Frank and his boys talking to them. And everyone had a raging thirst. They were drinking water, soft drinks, tea, like it was the new rock and roll. Know what one of the side effects of Zimovane is? Thirst."

"So you're saying someone put this in the pie I baked," Brenda said. "Who?"

"You," Joe declared. In order to head off her inevitable outburst, he hurried on. "You did it in all innocence, Brenda. Let me explain." He addressed the whole room again. "As Brenda said, she and I have been friends since we were school kids. Now, I've been in catering all my life. There is no meal that I don't know how to produce. I've trained any number of cooks, too, including my nephew, Lee. But I never taught Brenda or Sheila how to prepare anything. Both had been married for many years. Both learned from their mothers and fathers. Brenda, when she's preparing a meal, has some habits that I disapprove of. One of them is to put a light dusting of flour on top of her pies. To me it's wasteful, not tasteful." He smiled at his rhyme. "It may be very pretty, but it doesn't suit a workman's café in the North of England. However, it doesn't matter how much I complain over it, when Lee's off and she's baking she still does it. And she did it on Thursday night when she prepared the meat and potato pie for dinner. And *that* is where the Zimovane came from. It was mixed into the flour. A large quantity of it, I've no doubt, but spread between the Housies it probably wouldn't be even noticed, never mind threatened anyone's life."

"Two things," Naughton pointed out. "If it was in the flour, how come it only made its way into the dusting Brenda put on top of the finished pie? It would have been baked into the crust."

237

"Not necessarily," Joe declared. "Think about it. What would a temperature of 220º do to a drug like that? Would it neutralise it? Would it burn it away altogether? Maybe the pie would even catch fire. I don't know, and since none of our, er, suspects is a pharmacist, I'll bet they don't know either. But it wasn't an issue. Brenda needed so much flour for the crust that she used it directly from a bag. But she used a shaker when she spread it on the finished product, and *that* is the flour that contained the Zimovane."

"If that's what happened, then he or she would have been picked up on the cameras putting the drug into the shaker," Brenda said.

"True, but as it happens there are several glitches on the recordings from the kitchen. Scott and Katy pointed it out to me. The camera had been acting up all week. They changed it three or four times and it still wouldn't play ball. According to Scott, they believed the heat from the kitchen was affecting the wiring leading to the camera. I have a different theory. Suppose those glitches were deliberate, designed to puzzle the tech staff. When the culprit dropped that drug into Brenda's flour shaker the camera would be cut, a stock feed would run, and the technical staff would think no more of it. Just another glitch. But in reality, the camera had been made to play the fool all week simply to mask the one action that would ensure that everyone in the house was asleep on Thursday night."

"Hang on, Joe," Brenda protested again. "How could he know in advance that I'd put flour on top of the crust. We didn't know each other before this week, and none of them even knew what I would do for dinner."

"No, but Master Spy did. Not only that, but Master Spy also knew about your stupid habit of dusting the top of the pie. You told him that. And he – or she, I never could work out which – knew when you first applied to come on the show because you put it all on your application letter form. You had to so they could arrange for the correct ingredients and cookware."

Hoad shot a glance at Helen, and she nodded

confirmation. "Remember, Chief Inspector, this is a TV show. Much though it may appear live and spontaneous, we need as much information from the Housies in advance as we can get, including any particular method of cooking." She smiled weakly. "Fire regulations. We have to be prepared."

Naughton still shook his head. "Even if I accept all this, how come it didn't put Ursula to sleep along with the rest of them?"

"I expect better of a man like you, Naughton," Joe told him. "You being so clever and all. Zimovane is a tranquiliser, not an anaesthetic. Everyone would get a good night's sleep out of it, Ursula, too. The Zimovane would see to that. But Ursula had something else on her mind. A meeting in the Romping Room. A meeting with her killer, although she didn't know at the time that he would kill her. So it may have made her feel sleepy, woozy, but it wouldn't put her to sleep. We've seen her on the videos, haven't we? On her way to the Romping Room, she's weaving like she's stoned out of her mind. That was the Zimovane at work. We also know she was in there for a good half hour, maybe longer, before she died. She probably got bored and nodded off while she was waiting for the killer. That only made his job easier."

Helen leapt on Joe's words. "He? His job? Twice you've hinted that it was a man." He spun his head round to fix his eye on Scott Naughton.

"That's right," Joe said. "Her killer was a man."

"Don't look at me like that, Helen," Naughton said wearily. "Murray may or may not be right, but it wasn't me."

The attention of the entire room came back to Joe.

"He's telling the truth. It wasn't him. In fact, it wasn't any of the crew. It was one of the Housies."

The announcement was greeted by awed silence. Anne broke it by laughing wildly, and it was quickly followed by Dylan's sneering opinion.

"How do you propose we got out, Mr Detective, while

239

the cameras were watching us?"

"We know how that was worked, son." Joe deliberately belittled him with the added sobriquet. "See, while the Chief Inspector and I were working on this, we assumed all along that it was a member of the production crew. We never, for one minute, figured on teamwork, and we should have done." He smiled grimly. "What's I-Spy about if not teamwork?"

"Are you telling me there was more than one person involved?" Naughton was as surprised as everyone else.

Joe nodded. "I even kept Frank in the dark earlier today. I only realised it myself at four o'clock this morning, and I've spent most of the last few hours working it out. In fact, even though I realised yesterday that there were two people involved, I only learned the whole truth about twenty minutes ago. One of the production crew was working hand in glove with one of the Housies."

"Impossible," Helen declared. "How could they communicate? Unless you're suggesting it was Master Spy."

"You know, Helen, you put your finger on the one flaw in my theory. The one bug I couldn't get over. There was no way they could communicate, and if they couldn't communicate, how could the crewman tell the Housey the stock feeds were running and it was safe to leave the dorm, how could the Housey know that Ursula was asleep? Just take a look at this."

Joe hit the keyboard of his netbook and the screen came alive with footage of him in the men's dorm. Without warning, a light flashed on and went off again inside a second.

"That," he said, "is the light of a mobile phone receiving a message. Most mobiles are the same. You put them into sleep mode but when a message comes through, the screen flashes and when you read the message, the entire thing lights up."

"That is impossible," Helen said. "No one had a mobile phone. It's against the rules."

Joe shook his head. "I had this debate with Naughton earlier." He gazed at the Housies. "Three of you were carrying mobile phones which you'd smuggled in. But only one of you was the killer." He hit the keyboard again. "Here's the original footage I based my experiment on."

They watched in silence as the light hovered briefly above Greg's bed. When Joe stopped it, all eyes turned to Greg.

"Now wait a minute," he protested. "I killed no one."

"Do you deny you had a mobile phone?" Joe demanded.

"I... er..." His face sank. "No. No, I don't deny it. All right, I know I wasn't supposed to have one, but you don't know what it's like to be separated from your wife and family for a week. I missed them. I wanted to keep in touch with them. It was only the occasional text, just to let her know I was thinking about her."

Joe nodded. "You had a picture of them on your shelf, didn't you?"

"Yes. Is that so surprising? I wasn't the only one." He pointed at Anne. "I know for a fact she was carrying a phone because I heard her talking to her husband when she was alone in the Romping Room. And she hated Ursula. Ask your friend, Brenda. She'll confirm it."

"I don't deny it," Anne shouted, "but I didn't kill her."

"I already know Anne had a mobile," Joe said, "and the video caught her using it the same way it caught you." Summoning his anger, he glared at Greg. "But the photograph of your wife and children was laid flat on the shelf on the night Ursula was killed. Because you knew it would reflect the light of your phone back to the camera. Didn't you?"

"What? No. I swear I didn't do it."

"Then explain the photograph?" Joe pressed.

"I can't. It should have been stood up. I didn't even notice it was laid flat." Sweat broke on Greg's forehead. "I put that photograph up so that it was facing the camera on the far wall. That way, my wife would see it every time they showed the inside of the men's dorm and she'd know I was

241

thinking about her. I was tired on Thursday night. Really sleepy. I just never noticed it was laid flat. If I had, I'd have stood it up." His face worked and worried and pleaded with them. "You have to believe me. I'm innocent. And you –" he pointed a shaking finger at Joe. "You're making a big mistake."

Joe smiled. "No I'm not," he said as Azi positioned himself behind Greg. "I believe you."

Chapter Twenty

Pandemonium ensued for a moment. Even Hoad and Azi joined in the chorus of complaints. Joe waited for quiet.

"The photograph really was laid flat to prevent it reflecting any light," he said. "But Greg didn't do it." Joe swung his attention round the room and fixed it on the killer. "Did he, Dylan?"

In contrast to Greg, Dylan was his customary, easy-going self. "What is this? You gonna accuse each of us in turn? Why not Marc? It was his dressing gown cord she hung herself with."

"I'm told the proper word is hanged, not hung," Joe riposted. "See, I told you all, I've spent almost the whole morning trying to recreate that bit of video, and I couldn't. It didn't matter whose bed I tried it from, the light was either too much or too little. But then I checked footage from the dorm when it was fully lit, and that's when it hit me. The reflection didn't come from Greg's photograph. It couldn't. The photograph was laid flat. Instead it came from this." He reached down to his bag on the floor, and came back up with a newly bought razor, the head tucked into a shiny plastic safety sheath. He tossed it on the table. "That's the same razor as Greg uses. A Gillette Fusion, four-blade wet razor. I bought it an hour ago at a supermarket in Kelsall, about a mile from here." He picked up the object and turned it over in his hands. "When I put that on Greg's shelf and tried the experiment again, I managed to duplicate the scene. But again, I had to try it from every bed, and the only one it worked from was yours, Dylan."

The young man laughed again. "You're talking outta your pants, man. So you got me using a mobile phone. What of it. I ain't the only one."

"True," Joe agreed. "But you're the only one using it just before Ursula's death. And why? Because that's when your accomplice texted you to say the stock feeds were about to run and you had to check on your buddies in the dorm, make sure they were all asleep."

The young man shook his head. "Garbage," he laughed, but the amusement sounded forced and unreal.

"We'll see," Joe promised. "I've been doing a lot of research over the last few days into the death of a man named Victor Prentiss. He was a nasty piece of work, Victor. A movie producer, but one who used unusual methods of casting his films. It involved movie wannabes getting into bed with him. If they didn't, they couldn't expect much help from him. One of those wannabes was Ursula Kenney. She was interviewed soon after his death, but cleared of any involvement. What we do know is that Prentiss was seen with two women on or around the night of his death. No one really knew what happened and the official verdict was death by autoerotic asphyxiation. I don't think it was. I think it was murder. I think the two women he was with that night grew tired of his constant abuse and decided to strangle him with his own belt. Since he had a penchant for scarfing, it was easy enough to pull off... no pun intended."

"You'd never prove it, Joe," Hoad pointed out.

"I know. But four people knew the truth. The two women who murdered him, Ursula Kenney and Dan Wellesley. We know what happened to Ursula, and Dan had his head caved in before I could get to him. Why? Because they both threatened to expose the truth about Prentiss' death, and someone on I-Spy needed to shut them up."

"That lets me out," Dylan declared. "I never heard of this Victor Pratt."

"Not quite, Dylan," Joe said. "And by the way, his name was Prentiss. No, you didn't know him. You were only a kid when he was killed. But your mother did."

Dylan's laughing face, soured and darkened. "You leave

my mother out of this."

"Touched a nerve, did I?" Joe smiled easily. "You should learn to chill out, boy. It does wonders for your stress levels." He addressed the room again. "Victor Prentiss is the reason your mother committed suicide while you were a child, and you know it."

Fury built in Dylan's eyes. "You talk about my mother like that, and you don't even know her." His voice was a hiss suddenly exploding into a roar. "I'll kill you."

He leapt from his seat, but Rahman clamped an arm around him and wrestled him back down into the chair.

"Thanks, Azi," Joe said. Checking his notes, he went on, "Let's think about Ursula, for a minute, huh? Everyone here agrees she was a complete bitch. Those who knew her – Marlene – said she was a crap actress. Victor Prentiss knew her years ago, and he probably thought she was crap, too, because he never did anything to advance her career. But he enjoyed her. Eventually, she gave up on stardom and became an estate agent. So there she is sailing gleefully through life selling houses when I-Spy hits the screens and she sees names she recognises on the credits. Not only that, she sees a face she knows. Marlene Caldbeck, who back when she appeared with Ursula was known as Margaret Billingham."

"I told the plod, I had nothing to do with her death."

"You're very much alike, you and Ursula," Joe said. "Neither of you ever learned how to shut up long enough to let others speak. We know you didn't kill her. Dylan did that." Before Dylan could protest his innocence again, Joe went on. "But did you help in the background, Marlene?"

"I told you…"

"No, you didn't help," Joe interrupted. "You were only guilty of covering up your association with her because it would have barred you from presenting I-Spy, which in turn would have cost you money. So let's get back to Ursula. She sees these names and faces and all the old anger comes back. They're successful, she's selling houses. She wants what they have. Fortunately, she knows something about one of them. Something linked to the death of Victor Prentiss. She knows he was murdered. So she writes in with her demands. 'Get me on I-Spy, or I go to the cops with what I know.' She doesn't need to win it. She only needs to appear so she can show everyone what a great talent she has. But she's miscalculated. The person she's recognised is prepared to go to extreme lengths to shut her up. Permanently. And later, when Dan Wellesley gets in touch, after he's spoken to me, he, too, put himself in the firing line… isn't that right, Helen?"

Her face drained of colour. For a moment Joe thought she was about to confess, but she retained control of herself and in a voice choked with indignation, said, "I beg your pardon?"

"Right at the beginning, Scott was telling us about you tearing a strip off Marlene at some final meeting, because she'd hinted that she may have known one of the contestants. As it happens she did, but you knew her, too, Helen. You were the one who foolishly opened your mouth about that night with Victor Prentiss."

"Wrong," Helen declared. "I was never an actress."

Joe smiled. "Who said we were looking for an actress?"

"You did. Just now."

Joe shook his head. "I said we were looking for two movie *wannabes*. That could mean actors, writers, directors, camera people… and producers. You told me that the competition is just as fierce for crew as it is for performers, and back then, even though you're fiftyish now, you were still a wannabe, still looking for the big break. In fact, you told me that, too."

Helen shrugged. "I'm telling you, I did not know Ursula Kenney. I had never met her."

"Then how do you explain this." Joe hit his computer key and a photograph appeared; the same image, Brenda had been so intent upon the previous night. A casual shot, it showed a much younger Ursula in the foreground, smiling falsely into the camera, and amongst the several people in the background, also many years younger but clearly recognisable, was Helen. "Ursula tagged this photograph with the caption, '*Millennium Eve Amdram Group, Liverpool*'. You knew her because you were working with her. What happened? Did you get drunk on Millennium Eve, start whinging about men, and how you'd screwed one for a contract but he died while you were playing your games? Or did you get really drunk and tell her that you'd murdered Prentiss? And how did Dan Wellesley know? Was he there the night Prentiss was murdered?"

Helen gaped.

Joe pressed home his advantage. "Let me ask about that permanent irritation on your right leg, huh? A childhood accident you said when you showed me the scar. We all have accidents like that when we're kids. Trouble is, flat scars don't grow as you do. They stay the same size. It's about three or four inches long. For that scar to have been caused in your childhood, it would have sliced out a huge proportion of your infant leg, and would probably have been an emergency. It wouldn't have been a 'minor incident' as you described it. That is an adult scar, and it was caused when you cut your leg on a stray branch as you were covering the body of Victor Prentiss in Hogshead Wood."

Silence fell. It was Sheila who broke it.

"I'm sorry, Joe, but there's so much of this that I don't understand."

"You'd have to check Dan Wellesley's website to get a clear picture, and you can't do that now because someone wiped the website out the morning he was killed. Fortunately, I'd already had a good look, and I'd made notes as well as downloading a number of photographs." Joe checked his netbook and called up the relevant documents. "Wellesley was a venture capitalist. He sank money into viable propositions, and he financed a number of Prentiss' projects. In return, he got invited to some pretty wild parties with Prentiss. There were plenty of pictures on his website of actresses and other women from the movies who Prentiss had coerced into bed. Amongst them were two women I recognised." Joe hit the keyboard again and a picture of a much younger Helen appeared. "Helen Catterick aged about, I dunno, thirty, I guess." He hit the keys again and another picture appeared. "No names, no pack drill. That was Wellesley's policy and I had trouble remembering where I'd seen this picture before. But when I saw her, she was a little older. She was your mother, Dylan. You showed her photograph to the camera earlier in the week. She was one of the two women who were with Prentiss the night he died. One of the two women who rang Dan Wellesley to tell him what had happened. Helen, you and Dylan's mother bought Wellesley's silence with the threat of exposing him if he opened his mouth, and he bought your silence with the same threat. Then, when Ursula died, he remembered and decided to see if he could make any more out of it. What did he want on Saturday night? Your knickers off one last time?"

Helen folded her arms and said nothing.

"Joe," Hoad said with great restraint, "would you like to explain just what was going on?"

"Sure. No problem." Joe called up his notes on the netbook. "Ursula was from Liverpool. My guess is when it was announced that I-Spy was coming to Chester, she wrote or emailed Helen with her threats and Helen arranged it. I saw the original list of Housies and Ursula's name was first on it. At the bottom of the list was a kid named Neil someone or other, but his name had been crossed off and Dylan was drafted in at the last minute. When I asked Naughton about that, he said Neil had been involved in a car accident. I don't know what really happened but I guess Helen got in touch with Dylan and told him that Ursula was about to drag his beloved mother's name through the mud over the Prentiss business. So Dylan came on the show with one of two options. Either lay Ursula and shut her up, or kill her to shut her up. His mother didn't hesitate to throttle Prentiss, and Dylan loved his mother, so he would be ready to do anything to save her reputation."

Dylan leapt to his feet again. "Don't you talk about my mother like that."

Rahman restrained him again.

"I'm not judging your mother, Dylan." Joe said. "I'm stating facts. Between them, Helen and Dylan came up with a plan, and he hit it off with Ursula right away. Why not? He's young, fit, good looking. He played Ursula like a reluctant fish all week, and on Thursday he put the proposition to her. Shut up about Victor Prentiss. Ursula refused. Remember what Marc said when he came outside on Thursday? He'd heard Dylan and Ursula talking in an excited manner. Everyone drew the wrong conclusion. They thought the couple were getting it on. I think they were arguing. So Plan A went into action. At some time on Thursday, Helen slipped the Zimovane to Dylan through one of the hatches. Probably in the Romping Room. It was probably already in powder form. Several people went near those shakers in the kitchen that day, including Greg and Dylan, both claiming to be looking for the sugar. But why would Dylan need to look for it? He'd cooked a meal the night before and he used two teaspoons of plain flour in that goulash, so he knew which contained the flour. And that's how the Zimovane got into the flour shaker."

Brenda glowered at Dylan. "I ought to horsewhip you."

"He'd probably enjoy it," Greg said, and the room broke down again in a melee of threat, counter-threat, accusation and recrimination.

When order was restored, Joe went on.

"If you check the video of Brenda's dinner, Dylan eats less of it than anyone else and pleaded a tricky tummy. Nonsense. He was making sure he didn't get too much of the Zimovane. Somewhere on Thursday evening, he slipped a note to Ursula. 'Meet me in the Romping Room at midnight and we'll have some fun to make up for this afternoon.' Ursula goes along, but Dylan keeps her waiting for so long that she falls asleep. Meanwhile, Helen has slipped a couple of Zimovane in Bexley's tea. She knew Driscoll was always concerned about her kids, and she put that information to good use. She rang Driscoll, told her there was a problem with her kids, stood outside waiting for the woman to leave, then hopped over the wall to check on Bexley. He's asleep, she comes in and texts Dylan to tell him to check on the other Housies and get ready. Then she runs the stock feeds, texts him a second time to go. He goes along to the Romping Room and strangles Ursula with one of her own stockings. Then he puts the stocking back on her, which is why you couldn't find it, Frank, and he hangs her with the cord from Marc's dressing gown, which he probably took earlier in the day. There's no log of a stock feed running, but the video shows one running at about half past midday, and you'll find that Dylan was in the dorm at that time."

"This is nuts," Dylan protested.

"Absolutely crazy," Helen agreed. "How do you propose a woman of my age could get over that rear wall?"

"One of my members did it," Joe pointed out, "and he's ten years older than you. And you, yourself, told me you keep yourself fit."

Helen fell silent again, her arms folded across her chest.

"The rest is simple," Joe said. "Dylan hands her the mobile through the Romping Room hatch, then goes back to bed. She goes to the control room, restarts the live feeds, then leaves the way she came. You're presented with a suicide and a crowd of Housies who all appear to be ill, but who are in fact suffering the after effects of the Zimovane."

Joe stared pointedly at the two accused. "But it doesn't end there. They think they're in the clear when Dylan overhears me talking about Victor Prentiss and one of his contacts. Helen knows who he is and she's not surprised when she gets a call from him later that day. Check the call log for the production office, Frank. My guess is you'll find an incoming call from his number. If not, check with Helen's agent. He may have called her and asked Helen to bell him back. She goes out there Saturday night, meekly following Wellesley's orders, but when she gets there instead of giving him what he wants, she gives him a clout on the head with that bronze statuette."

Closing down his netbook, Joe stared expectantly at

Helen.

There was a long silence. Eventually, Helen drew in a deep breath and glared naked malevolence at Joe.

"You want me to tell you how much I regret what happened?" she asked. "You'll wait until hell freezes over. Ursula Kenney was a blackmailer, plain and simple. She was prepared to ruin my reputation in order to project her slutty image. Dan Wellesley was no better. He wanted what he wanted at any price. And you know the annoying thing, Murray? You're wrong about Victor Prentiss' death; it really was his own doing. Him and his silly games."

"In that case you should have gone to the police and told them what happened." Hoad said.

"And ruined my own career before it even started?" Helen shook her head. "I think not."

"And I won't have mother's name dragged through the mud," Dylan growled. "Not by you, not by Wellesley, not by anyone."

Joe shook his head sadly, "You don't get it, do you? You're both as bad as Prentiss, Ursula and Wellesley."

Helen glared pure hatred at him. "I don't regret a single action this week. Not one."

Chapter Twenty-One

With the bus cruising along the M62, down the hill past the junction with the M1, the first signs of Sanford could be seen, five miles distant.

Perched on the jump seat on the opposite side of the aisle from Keith, his mobile phone pressed to his ear, Joe concluded the call with a yawn. "Thanks, Frank. I'll keep an eye on the papers for the trial." He closed the phone, yawned again and, half turning to face his two companions, said, "I'll be glad to get home. I need some serious shuteye."

Ignoring his fatigue, Brenda asked, "What did Hoad have to say?"

"Helen and Dylan have given statements and admitted it all. Helen insists that Prentiss' death was accidental and his own fault."

Sheila looked up from her paperback. "I'm not sure who I feel most sorry for: Ursula, or Helen and Dylan."

"Helen and Dylan," Brenda said, echoing Joe's yawn.

The man himself shook his head. "None of them. Helen and Dylan took the law into their own hands and they had no right to do that, no matter what the provocation. And do you know what the real shame about it is?" he asked as Sheila opened her mouth to challenge him.

Sheila bit back her original words. "What?" she asked.

"Victor Prentiss was a grade one user and abuser of women. You know me; I've never been politically correct, and I don't hold with those feminists who try to make everything political, but Victor Prentiss was an out and out disgrace. He abused his position for the favours of young women who were desperate to get ahead in the movies, and that, for me, is appalling. If he really did go too far and throttle himself, then it's exactly what he deserved, and if Helen and Dylan's mother had come forward at the time, I'm sure no blame would have attached itself to them."

"And Ursula would never have had a hold over Helen," Sheila concluded.

There was a brief silence and they looked through the windows as Keith pulled into the nearside lane at the mile marker for the Sanford exit.

"What do you think they'll get, Joe?" Brenda asked.

"Life," Sheila declared. "It's mandatory for murder, and in both instances, it was murder."

"Helen may be able to plead spur of the moment in Dan Wellesley's case, but I doubt that it'll work. She knew what he wanted when he rang, and she knew she had only two options. Give in or kill him off." Joe shook his head sadly. "Premeditation on both counts. They'll both get life."

"I can't understand Dylan's motivation," Brenda said. "He may have been angry at Ursula's threat to drag his mother's name through the mud, but many people get angry without resorting to murder. Perhaps it wasn't planned after all."

Joe grunted. "Nice to have you back, Brenda. Living in your usual dream world. Helen and Dylan cooked this thing up between them before I-Spy ever got under way. Frank is looking into Dylan's background to see what's known about him. We don't know how thickly Helen laid it on when she first contacted Dylan, but assuming he doesn't have a predisposition for murder, the idea of his mother being exposed as a harlot, a woman willing to use her body to get where she wanted, must have driven him insane with anger."

The drone of the engine changed, slowing down as Keith braked for the exit. The evening sun picked out the sharp angles of the buildings on the Sanford Retail Park.

Joe yawned again. "Good to be home, but I feel like I've had no rest at all."

"It's been a busy weekend for all of us, Joe," Sheila

agreed, "but especially you. Flitting between Chester and Gibraltar Hall, and Mollington, you've hardly stopped."

"And I've been on the go since just turned four this morning," he complained. He stretched and reached up for the PA mike above Sheila's head. Checking it was working, he switched it off again. "You know," he said to his two companions, "I think I may just take tomorrow off."

Sheila and Brenda gaped.

"You?"

"Taking a day off?"

Joe grinned. "Only joking."

THE END

Thanks for reading this Sanford Third Age Collection title.

Why not read the next? **STAC #3: A Halloween Homicide**

Fantastic Books
Great Authors

darkstroke is
an imprint of
Crooked Cat Books

- •Gripping Thrillers
- •Cosy Mysteries
- •Romantic Chick-Lit
- •Fascinating Historicals
- •Exciting Fantasy
- •Young Adult and Children's
  Adventures
- •Non-Fiction

Discover us online
www.darkstroke.com

Find us on instagram:
www.instagram.com/darkstrokebooks

Printed in Great Britain
by Amazon